Dating
&
DISMEMBERMENT

Dating

&

DISMEMBERMENT

A.L.BRODY

Preview of *Weddings & Witchcraft* copyright © 2024 by Jason Pinter

Entangled Publishing, LLC
644 Shrewsbury Commons Ave., STE 181
Shrewsbury, PA 17361
rights@entangledpublishing.com

Amara is an imprint of Entangled Publishing, LLC.

Visit our website at www.entangledpublishing.com.

Cover illustration and design by Nicole Goux
Interior design by Britt Marczak

Paperback ISBN 978-1-64937-761-6
Ebook ISBN 978-1-64937-762-3

Manufactured in the United States of America

First Edition October 2024

10 9 8 7 6 5 4 3 2 1

AMARA
an imprint of Entangled Publishing LLC

*For everyone else who always believed
the monsters were the good guys all along*

Dating & Dismemberment is meant to entertain and make you laugh while maybe even giving you a case of the feels. With that being said, please review the list of possibly questionable content below to ensure your reading enjoyment. Be wary of:

- Bad things happening to people named Kyle
- Decapitation (but in a fun way)
- Long-distance hurtling of irritating camp counselors into large bodies of water
- Drinking water of highly questionable purity
- Overbearing mothers
- Absent fathers
- Monsters dealing with repressed trauma due to aforementioned overbearing mothers and absent fathers
- The wielding of deadly weapons that are both attached and unattached to their wielder
- Summer camp bullies
- Bad decisions
- Being single and not knowing what you want to do with your life while all your friends seem to have their sh*t together...but at least monsters don't have to deal with gender reveal videos on social media
- Banter (with risk of death)
- Dismemberment (I mean, you read the title of the book, presumably—you have to know you're getting at least a little of that)

If you may be triggered by anything on this list,
or if your name is Kyle, please proceed with caution.

CHAPTER 1

Darla Drake, aka the Duchess of Death, aka the Creature of Clear Creek, and one of the most feared monsters on the planet, stood over her soon-to-be victim, a cruel camp counselor named Kyle Browning, and prepared to turn him into either a Lego set or paste, depending on what kind of mood she was in.

Darla raised her weapon of choice, the infamous bronze scourge that had been passed down to her from her mother, and right as she was about to render justice unto this unfortunate soul, Darla stopped.

She stood there, arm raised, scourge rattling in the wind, as Kyle covered his eyes as though playing a baby game where if he couldn't see her, she didn't exist.

But Darla did exist. And yet, her hand stayed.

Come on, she thought. *This is* not *the time to have an existential crisis.*

This crisis came at a particularly inopportune and frankly embarrassing moment for Darla. Kyle was not walking away from his injuries, which, to be fair, were largely self-inflicted, having tripped on a tree root while attempting to flee, which bent his ankle in a way that defied human anatomy, his toes now able to touch his shin and his dignity evaporating somewhere into the night sky.

And while Kyle moaned, his girlfriend, a counselor named Melanie Wootens, having apparently followed them, screamed as she saw the Duchess of Death preparing to filet her lousy lover. Melanie turned and ran away, screaming like her hair was on fire. Or, far more traumatizing, been subjected to a terrible dye job.

And Darla just watched. And shrugged.

Instead of ending Kyle's suffering and sentencing Melanie to a lifetime of therapy, Darla stood there, unmoving, staring blankly at Kyle. For the first time in her thirty-two years, the last twenty of which she'd spent hunting the very worst counselors at Camp Clear Creek, Darla couldn't finish the job. One word pinged through her skull, topped with its infamous bone crown that had terrified thousands of teens and sold millions of Halloween costumes: *Why?*

Darla had never asked herself that question during a hunt. Hunts were simple: find the prey. Scout the prey. Know the prey. Then turn their lives—if not their body cavities—inside out. Up until this moment, Darla's hunt of Kyle Browning had gone rather swimmingly.

Kyle, along with two other counselors named Randy Horvath and Lewis Cawthorn, had been given the moniker of the Terrible Trio based on how they would gang up on and terrorize young campers at Clear Creek. Randy and Kyle had returned this summer, while Lewis had been fired. Darla had made it her mission this summer to hunt down Randy and Kyle and let them know they wouldn't escape with a mere slap on the wrist. And possibly not even escape with their wrists at all. Lewis, well...there was always the counselor reunion, and she could only pray he was dimwitted enough to stick his neck out for her to lop it off.

Kyle had been asleep in his cabin when Darla struck. She had been watching Kyle for a week, biding her time, waiting for the perfect moment. She knew everything about him. How he slammed Melanie into cabin walls when nobody was looking. How he bullied and intimidated the younger campers, then threatened to leave them in the woods alone if they reported him. Seeing her bronze scourge around Kyle's thick, abusive neck—then Randy's, then Lewis's—would make Darla's summer. It was time for Kyle Browning to meet his painful destiny. It was time for him to face the wrath of the Duchess of Death and feel the sting of her legendary scourge.

Darla's scourge had belonged to her mother, Dolores Drake, the original Duchess of Death, who had hunted in Clear Creek for decades before passing the baton—or medieval torture weapon, to be precise—to her beloved daughter. The scourge consisted of nine leather tails attached to a thick, wooden grip, each tail studded by heavy bronze ball bearings. The Drake scourge was legendary, iconic. And with the proper windup, angle, and wind resistance, Darla's scourge could cut through stone.

Dolores had taught her daughter everything: how to hunt, how to scare, and how to traverse (but not how to do laundry, that was one of Dolores's few weaknesses, and good lord did their cave smell after a week's worth of hunts without changing her tunic). Traversal was a method of fast travel, allowing Darla to cover incredible distances in no time at all, her feet barely touching the ground while remaining as quiet as a blade of grass bending in the wind. Prey could run and run and run, thinking they were getting away, only for Darla to magically appear in front of them. Often, the last thing her prey saw was the moonlight glinting off the tips of Darla's bone crown as she swung her scourge.

So, when the day of Kyle's hunt came, Darla waited until the darkest hour of night to traverse to the Clear Creek campgrounds from the cavern where she and Dolores lived, gliding through the dark woods like a blur, scourge strapped to her black leather belt, only the faint humming and bending of grass below her dark green tunic giving away her presence.

When Darla arrived at Kyle's cabin, she rattled the windows and creaked the floorboards, performing classic monster foreplay to let Kyle know he wasn't alone. Then she snuck into the cabin and knocked a lamp off a shelf, turned over a heavy dresser, and finally cut the power (why the camp buildings all kept their breakers easily accessible, Darla would never know).

And once Kyle came bounding out of the cabin, eyes wide in fear, Darla knew she had him. It was time to take down the Terrible Trio one by one.

And now all that planning. All that anticipating. Gone, in one feeling of *meh*.

"Get back here, you bleached blonde bitch!" Kyle shouted at Melanie, mustering whatever strength he had left to insult his poor, beleaguered girlfriend.

What does Melanie see in this waste of tissue? Darla wondered. She supposed Kyle was blandly handsome for a human. Sharp cheekbones, blue eyes, and cavernous dimples. And he'd look even more handsome with Darla's boot stomped through his cranium. Yet, for some reason, she hesitated.

Questioning herself.

Is this all there is? Chasing down and maiming pimply douchebags forever?

Darla concentrated. She could feel thousands of small vibrations in the earth and had become an expert at identifying each one. Which rumblings were animals, which were fallen branches...and which were human. Darla's nine-chambered heart pumped just twelve times per minute, and isolated Melanie's movements in less than one heartbeat. She could sense the girl running through the forest, could feel every footstep, the noise of her feet crunching leaves and twigs, the sound echoing beneath her loud as cannon shots. And even though Melanie was moving fast—maybe she ran track?— Darla's traversal ability could have her waiting next to an oak to greet the girl with any number of sharp objects. But Melanie did not deserve Darla's ire. This pusillanimous young dipshit, however, deserved it and then some.

Under normal circumstances, Darla would have used her scourge to bludgeon Kyle into little pieces of arrogant pulp. Or, if she was feeling feisty, maybe even rip off Kyle's injured leg and use his own limb to finish him off.

A year ago, hell, a *week* ago, pieces of Kyle would have ended up all over the camp, to be found by his fellow counselors. But now, as Darla stood over her victim, Melanie running through the woods, her screams at a pitch that could shatter half the cabin windows in Camp Clear Creek, Darla felt like her will to do dastardly deeds had simply evaporated. She didn't want to chase Melanie down to scare her. She wanted to chase her down and tell her that she shouldn't lower herself to dating this popped collar troglodyte whose entire purpose in life seemed to be preparing himself to become paste on Darla's boot.

Then Darla heard a scraping noise. She looked down. It was Kyle. He was crawling along the ground and whimpering like his favorite tennis court was occupied.

"Help...me..." Kyle whispered. Darla watched the boy crawl. Kyle reached out for Darla, grasping at the thick, dark blue fabric wrapped around her leg from the knee down, winding its way around her heel and beneath her foot. She wore no shoes. Darla respected Kyle's tenacity, if nothing else about him. "I'm sorry, Duchess. Please. Just let me go."

Kyle was a jerk. Darla had seen him manhandle Melanie. Watched through the trees as he pushed young campers' faces in the mud, or held their heads beneath the surface of Clear Creek Lake while other counselors weren't looking, a sadistic smile on his face that said he enjoyed tormenting those less powerful than he was. Darla usually took such pleasure in *ending* guys like Kyle. Some people—okay, *everyone*—called her a monster. But really, she was just de-weeding the human population.

She could end it quickly. One swing of her scourge could cut Kyle's head clean off. But that urge, that desire, that necessity had left her. Instead, she looked down at Kyle and said, "Unlike you, this is the first time I haven't been able to perform."

Kyle did not smile or laugh.

"Oh, come on," Darla said. "That was funny. I'm just trying to lighten the mood."

Kyle's lips peeled back, baring his perfect white teeth in a forced, awkward smile, clearly trying to placate Darla in the hopes of getting on her good side and prolonging his potentially very short lifespan.

"Okay. Stop that. It's creepy," Darla said. Kyle closed his mouth. "Listen, Kyle. I'm going to make you an offer. An offer I've never given to anyone in my life. So don't be stupid. Or stupider."

Kyle looked up at Darla, terror in his pallid face, probably assuming her offer would be that he got to choose which of his limbs she removed first.

"I'm going to let you go," Darla said. Kyle looked confused. He probably looked confused quite often. "But if you manage to crawl back to camp without being eaten by animals or insects, you have to stop being such a colossal prick. You touch Melanie again, you so much as look at a camper unless it's to teach them how to do the backstroke or tie a square knot, and I'm coming back for you. I will take you apart piece by piece. And I'll do it *slowly*. You know who I am. You know what I've done. So you know I'm telling the truth."

Kyle strained his neck to see her. His chin was covered in mud and grass. The color had drained from his face.

"So, what do you say, Kyle? Do we have a deal?"

Kyle nodded, but didn't blink, his eyes fixed on her scourge.

"Good," Darla said. "Now run along back to camp. Or crawl along, since I don't think legs are supposed to bend the way yours is."

Kyle moaned as he rolled onto his side. He then slipped his hand inside his pants pocket, groaning at the exertion, and came out with his cell phone. Darla was impressed. He was going to call 911. Kyle had to know he wasn't getting far on that leg. The young man might be a dick, but he clearly wanted to live.

Then, instead of dialing 911 and putting the phone to his ear, Kyle held the phone out in front of him and turned the camera app on.

"What are you doing?" Darla asked, incredulous.

"Shh," Kyle croaked. "I'm making a Reel."

"Oh, for fuck's sake."

Darla sighed, strapped her scourge to her belt, and began her traversal back through the Clear Creek woods. Her head swam as she dodged the trees and bushes, trying to understand why she left Kyle not in excruciating pain, but making content for his social media feed. For the first time in her life, Darla Drake, the Duchess of Death, the Creature of Clear Creek, one of the most feared monsters alive, had left a victim before she was finished with him.

Now she just needed to understand why in the name of Cthulhu's butthole she'd done it.

CHAPTER 2

Darla traversed around the swampy water of Maker's Marsh, trying to come to grips with what she'd just done. She had let two people live. Four, if she counted the entire Terrible Trio, plus Melanie. Though there was a strong chance Kyle would be eaten by either mosquitos or a giant snake before his digital manifesto finished uploading, and given Melanie's hysteria and lack of general awareness, she may have impaled herself on a tree branch on her way back to camp.

This wasn't like Darla. In the twenty years since she'd taken over full time as the Duchess of Death, Darla Drake had never let any prey walk (or crawl) away before she was done with them. If you saw the legendary Duchess in person, you would only live as long as she let you. She took pride in the fact that the only proof of her existence was a few grainy cell phone videos, the legacy she'd built in Clear Creek, and lots (and lots) of fan fiction. She'd even read some of it, appalled by the deviant (yet oddly sexy) acts of carnage people had dreamed up for her to take part in. And though Darla's body was capable of quite a number of things human bodies were not, it was not *quite* as flexible as some of the Darla Drake fanfic authors believed it to be.

The vast majority of her victims were d-bags like Kyle, and the rest were people who protected the d-bags like Kyle. As a matter of fact, the more Darla thought about it, she was pretty sure about 80 percent of the guys she'd hunted were named Kyle. Was it a rule that all Kyles were assholes? Come to think of it, Trevors were pretty shitty too. And Blakes. Kyles, Trevors, and Blakes. If she only killed Kyles, Trevors, and Blakes, Darla was pretty sure the world would be a better place.

Jacques. She was willing to bet half the jerks in Paris were named Jacques. She'd have to ask the Seine Sea Urchin the next time he was in town for a Monster Mash.

As a young monster, Darla found the hunt absolutely exhilarating. Darla's first kill was a thick-necked brute—probably named Kyle—who'd pushed a female counselor down the stairs for rebuffing his advances. Darla had traversed to "Kyle's" cabin late that night—hitting a few trees and thorny bushes along the way before realizing that she could not traverse *through* objects. When she arrived, dirty and irritated, she rattled the windows outside of "Kyle's" bunk. When his eyes fluttered open, she slammed the front door. Then, as his fright level increased, she turned the circuit breakers off. When he got up to inspect, she hurled a tree branch through the window. And when "Kyle" finally ran outside to escape whatever monster was inside his cabin, he found a *real* monster, Darla Drake, Duchess of Death, waiting for him.

Darla had then taken "Kyle's" head (who would have guessed that a severed head could *still* look like an asshole) and placed it inside the kitchen's walk-in freezer, next to the ground beef the alleged camp chefs used to make Sloppy Joes. The ensuing screams had delighted Darla, and she'd traversed back through the woods that day, slower this time, making sure to avoid all manner of flora and fauna, with a smile as wide as the openings she would routinely carve into counselors' necks.

But those joyful days felt like a lifetime ago. Now, Darla just wanted to get home. Away from Kyle. Away from Camp Clear Creek. Away from everything.

The woods were blue-black in the early morning dusk, pale moonlight glistening off the murky green water of Maker's Marsh. Just as Darla and the Drake family had hunted in the territory of Clear Creek for years, Darla's best friend, Gretl Sneed, aka the Gullet Gobbler, had always found happiness in other pursuits (cute monsters), other interests (sexy monsters), and other joys (making out with cute, sexy monsters).

For Darla, her joy, perhaps her only joy, had come in the hunt. And now, she had lost even that.

Darla felt a chill as she traversed through the muck, feeling the vibrations of all manner of creatures just below the surface. Maker's Marsh was filled with fish and snakes and frogs, many of which were poisonous, which came in handy in keeping counselors and other unwanted guests from following Darla home. Every now and then some naïve amphibious creature would leap out from the depths and sink its teeth into her flesh, unaware that their poison did as much to harm Darla Drake as a falling leaf.

Just like most monsters, Darla had healing capabilities that would make Wolverine jealous. She could recover from just about any manner of wound; the more grievous the injury, the more irritated it made her. This healing factor served her well, especially when she was younger and hadn't yet learned that even though humans were pretty slow and mostly dumb, if they swung a sharp weapon at the right angle, she'd spend the rest of the night letting her spleen reform.

At the far end of the swamp, through a copse of oak and juniper trees, Darla approached a large, moss-covered boulder that was tucked neatly and seamlessly into the hillside. She dug her long fingers into the narrow crevasse in the wall, got a good grip, and heaved the enormous rock to the side. She then stepped into the darkness and gently let the boulder slide back into place.

The cave was pitch black, but Darla could see everything. Her night vision bathed the world in a greenish-yellow tint, and picked up all manner of liquids, secretions, and fluids. If her prey was wounded, their blood glowed a hot pink in the dark. They might as well send up a road flare then run around naked singing show tunes. Her night vision had improved as she grew, and had proven invaluable over the years, making it easy to track down teenagers in the darkest of night. Or to simply find the cave bathroom without snagging her bone crown on a stalactite.

The walls and floor of the cave were slick, water dripping down the rock onto the floor to form shallow puddles. The entrance tunnel was narrow, only a few feet across and barely high enough for Darla to walk through without crouching. She remembered being led through these tunnels when she was a little monster, bumping into sharp walls, smashing her shins against rock outcroppings, stepping on all manner of insects and small animals as her night vision developed. She grew up in this cave and would die in this cave—if she could actually die, that was. But nobody had discovered Darla Drake's frailty yet.

And with any luck, they never would.

The tunnel began to widen and brighten, moonlight trickling in from holes in the hillside. Darla's eyes refocused, no longer needing her night vision. The tunnel led into a larger antechamber, with several rooms and tunnels branching out from the main hub. One path led to an old mining tunnel, which Darla had sealed off with another massive boulder. The mine itself had been closed for decades, but the boulder prevented any trespassers, tourists, or monster hunters from accidentally stumbling upon Darla Drake's lair. The last thing she needed was a group of foolish tourists accidentally stumbling into her bedroom (even if Darla made sure they didn't make it out alive, she would forever have to live with the shame of a human having seen her while indecent).

She went to the natural spring at the cavern center and splashed cold water on her face. Just enough light filtered through the rocks to allow Darla to look upon her natural reflection in the shallow pool without the filter of her night vision.

Branches of bone protruded up from Darla's skull, encircling her head from ear to ear like a beautiful yet macabre tiara. It was that bone crown that had been genetically passed down from her father, Darwinus Drake, aka the Sand Shark, and which had garnered Darla the nickname of Duchess of Death.

Darla's orange eyes were set within deep, dark circles, like natural eyeshadow, which ran from mid-forehead to just above her razor-sharp cheekbones. Her arms and fingers were slightly longer than a human's, and while standing up straight, Darla could touch her knees without bending over. This came in handy when needing to subdue a victim who happened to be athletic or intuitive enough to make Darla work for it, or if she needed to reach a particularly high apple on a tree. Darla Drake was both majestic and frightening. Her innate beauty would not make her look out of place sitting atop a gilded throne; her innate monstrosity would not make her look out of place sitting atop a pile of bones.

As she gazed at her visage, Darla delicately touched the tips of her bone crown. Still as sharp as ever. When she was a girl, she marveled as the bone slowly grew out from her head, willing it to come in faster, for her to grow up quicker to be more like her father. She'd grown up with tremendous pride in being a Drake, in following in her parents' fearsome footsteps. Yet while she took pride in her abilities and pride in her heritage, she also took pride in the fact that she had escaped their exceptionally long shadow and managed to forge her own fearsome reputation in Clear Creek. As a girl, she wanted to be her parents' daughter. As a young monster, she realized she just wanted to be herself.

But that pride had vanished. Something was missing. The hunt was no longer enough. Doing unspeakable things to unsavory people no longer fulfilled Darla the way it used to. Darla Drake was only thirty-two years old, but when she looked at her reflection, even though she knew she would live forever, and thirty-two out of infinity was less than zero percent of her life, she saw a monster who seemed far older than she actually was.

"Darla? Is that you?"

Darla sighed. She picked up a rock and tossed it into the water, her reflection shattering among the ripples.

"Who else would it be?"

"You can never be too careful. And it's not like I could do

anything about it if it wasn't you. Now come here."

Darla hung her scourge from an iron nail and followed the voice. The rooms off the cavern's antechamber were all dark—save one. A lone room where a healthy yellow glow emanated from the entryway. Darla walked to that room and stepped inside.

Candles lined the walls, tucked into the rocks' natural crevasses. Against one wall sat an old wooden dresser. Despite its age, the wood was well-maintained. Darla dusted it every day, oiled it frequently, and made sure the rocks above were always dry and free of spider webs and insect nests and mold. She had to keep the room clean. It held the most precious thing in her life.

A red cloth lined the top of the dresser. In the center of the cloth sat a severed head.

The head's hair was white and frizzy. Its face was wrinkled with age, its violet eyes set deep within the flesh of its sockets. Atop its head was a bone crown, the skin around it dry and weathered. The head smiled when it saw Darla enter the room.

"Hi, Mom," Darla said.

"Hey, hon, do you mind?" the head said, gesturing upward with its eyes. "It's itching like crazy up there. The humidity in this cave gives me rashes. Would you mind?"

"Sure thing." Darla took a bottle of moisturizer from the dresser drawer, squirted a dollop into her palm, and gently rubbed it over the scalp of Dolores Drake, the original Duchess of Death, and Darla's mother. Or at least what was left of her.

"Ahhhh," her mother said. "That's been bothering me all day. Thanks, sweetheart."

Darla put the moisturizer back, then pulled a rickety chair over so she could talk to her mother at eye level.

"How was your day, hon? Is that Kyle boy regretting the day he was born? I swear, they all seem to be named Kyle. There were no Kyles in my day. Lots of Georges. Not a lot of young men named George these days."

Darla shrugged. "It went all right."

"Come on, honey, you have to give me more than that. Did you maim him? Bisect him? Leave his entrails for the crows? Have you started planning the hunt for the others? I need details. I'm here all day with nothing to do but stare at the wall. The least you can do is let me live vicariously through you. Where did you deposit his pieces?"

"Only one piece," Darla said.

"Oh," Dolores said. "Impaled on a tree? Skewered with a fishing pole?"

"Not quite. Kyle is…alive."

"What do you mean, alive?" Dolores said. "You told me you were hunting him tonight."

"I was," Darla said. "And then I let him go."

Dolores blinked. "I'm sorry. My ears must have been cut off too. Because I thought I heard you say you let him go."

"Nope, your ears are still there and, apparently, they're still working. Because that's what I said."

"Darla, why on earth would you do that?" Dolores said. "We don't let our prey live, Darla. We are Drakes. We have been the Scourges of Clear Creek for over eight decades. We have a *reputation* to protect."

"Well, I guess my reputation just took a hit."

"What about the other two boys in that Terrible Trio? Randy and Lewis? You had deliciously diabolical plans for them, didn't you?"

"I did," she said. "Now I don't."

"Darla Drake, if I had hands, I would smack some sense into you."

"Well, it's lucky for me, then, that you don't."

"Tell me what's going on, Darla. I need to understand."

Darla rubbed the hard skin between the triangles of the bone crown, trying to will the thoughts and reasoning behind her spontaneous, life-changing decision to come to her.

"I just didn't have it in me today to finish the hunt," she said. "Sometimes it feels like that's all I do. Stalk a bunch of teenage brats and kill them in creative and outlandish ways. Which, to be fair, has generally been a whole lot of fun. When I'm done I come back here and tell you about it and we have dinner and I moisturize you and go to bed. Rinse and repeat."

"I don't see the problem."

"Maybe I just want something else. Something more."

"Something else? Darla. We're *monsters*. Hunting is what we were *born* to do. We scare. We stalk. We hunt. And if we're lucky, we get some shut-eye and maybe eat a decent meal or two in between. That's what I did until my...incident. And that's what your father and I raised you to do."

"Don't talk about Dad like he's some example for me to look up to," Darla said. "If I had known he was going to leave us, I wouldn't have been so nice to him all those years."

"He loved you," Dolores said.

"Until he didn't."

"Your father was a good hunter," Dolores said with a trace of sadness, "even if he wasn't a good monster to me. And it is the biggest regret of my life that he didn't want to stay and see you become the strong, terrifying woman you are today."

"A bigger regret to you than..." Darla gestured to Dolores's head.

"It's not even a comparison," Dolores said. "But even after Darwinus left, you always seemed to find fulfillment in the hunt. What happened?"

"I don't know what to say, Mom. The hunt has always fulfilled me. But today it didn't."

"Is there something wrong? Are you getting enough protein? You can't only eat the prepackaged crap you steal from the camp. There's no nutritional value in any of it."

"Don't worry, I get plenty of protein from woodland creatures."

"Are you getting enough fiber, then? Are you regular?"

"Am I *what*?"

"Never mind," Dolores sighed. "It's the pockets. Ever since you sewed pockets onto your tunic, you've been different."

"They're helpful!" Darla shouted. "Besides, what the hell do pockets have to do with anything?"

"Monsters do not need *pockets*," Dolores said. "I understand hunting changes with the times, but some things were better the way they were. Such as pocketless tunics."

"Everyone needs pockets," Darla said.

"And what exactly do you *put* in those pockets?" Dolores asked. "Certainly not the head of Kyle Browning."

"I could put anything I want in them. Maybe I'll put cheese in them."

"Why on earth would you put cheese in your pockets?"

"It's just a hypothetical, mom."

"I think that's a brilliant idea," her mother scoffed. "Run through the forest with stinky cheese-laden pockets. Maybe throw some melted chocolate into your tunic while you're at it, make them nice and gooey."

"Maybe I will."

"Fantastic. Why don't you just get a megaphone and yell, 'Hi, I'm Darla Drake and I'm coming to get you!'"

"I could think of a way better catchphrase than 'I'm coming to get you'. But it doesn't matter. Because I'm done hunting."

"I don't know what's gotten into you, Darla," Dolores said with a dramatic sigh. "Do you have any idea how much worry you're causing your poor mother?"

"Worry? You're a head, Mom. What do you have to worry about other than maybe sneezing while I'm not here and not having anyone to wipe your nose?"

"Your sarcasm does not impress me," Dolores said.

"How about the fact that I still have my limbs?" Darla said, then regretted it. "Sorry. Low blow. But I guess everything is a low...nevermind."

"Do you know that the only thing that gives me solace each and every day is knowing you're out there swinging your scourge and living up to the Drake family name?" Dolores said. "After everything that was taken from me, if I don't have that small consolation, then I have nothing."

"That's not true. You have your books. And if you recall, I offered to hook up a TV for you. There's a satellite dish a few miles away and I'm pretty sure I could find a way to splice a signal into your room."

"Don't do me any favors. Obviously, you have too much on your mind to think about how your impetuous decision affects me."

Dolores's head sneezed. A dribble of saliva caught on her lower lip.

"You need to dust this table," Dolores said. "Or have you decided that basic housekeeping doesn't bring you fulfillment anymore either?"

Darla sighed and wiped the errant spit from her mother's face. Then she dusted around and underneath Dolores's head before placing it back on the cloth.

"Things would be a lot simpler if you'd just found my body," Dolores said. "Our healing powers are strong. You could reattach me. Unless you're too busy *not* hunting."

"How many times do I have to tell you, Mom?" Darla said, frustrated. "After Franklin Shine decapitated you, he and the other counselors took your body and buried it somewhere in Clear Creek."

"It was his own fault," Dolores said.

"Didn't you tell me you hunted him because he was making out with a girl?"

"He most certainly was. And you know very well what we did to people who looked like they were about to engage in premarital sex back in my day."

"How could I forget. Back when all you monsters had some weird puritanical streak going."

"Premarital sex or recreational drug use may have been poor excuses to commit murder, but it's just how things were done back in my day."

"So Franklin fought back. And now you're in two parts."

"That other part has to be somewhere in Clear Creek," Dolores said. "Franklin Shine was a kid. He couldn't drive. And there's no way he could have carried my body all that far."

"You can say that again," Dolores said.

"I'll have you know that my body may have been dense, but I took damn good care of it. I looked better at seventy-five than I did at twenty-five."

"Unfortunately, Clear Creek is a big place," Dolores said. "Your body could be anywhere."

"Clear Creek isn't *that* big."

"It's, like, thirty square miles, Mom. I could dig for the next twenty years and never find it."

"Well, if you're not hunting, then it's not like you have anything better to do."

"You're just lucky Franklin Shine didn't find your frailty and use it against you instead of that shovel. If he did, we wouldn't even be having this conversation."

"Don't joke about frailties," Dolores said. "I don't know what mine is. You don't know what yours is. If any of these humans discovered ours, they could kill us for good."

"I know, Mom," Darla said. "I take our frailties very seriously. That's also why I keep you in here. If someone found out the original Duchess of Death was still alive, they might try to find a way to finish you for good."

"I understand your reasoning," Dolores said. "Though I do miss seeing the sun rise over Maker's Marsh and hearing the actual screams of camp counselors rather than just living vicariously through you."

Every monster had a frailty, or a weakness. An object or artifact that was tied to them on an emotional or physical level, whose properties, if weaponized, were the only way a human could kill a monster for good. Some frailties were a weapon itself—an axe the monster's father used to chop wood or femurs, fire made using kindling from the tree they were born under, holy water (this usually only worked against demons or Clergymonsters), a sharpened bedpost from the monster's childhood room. Some were articles of clothing or pieces of jewelry—a family heirloom, a favorite sweater. Each frailty, if used properly, was the only way to dispatch a monster for good. Most monsters didn't know what their frailties were until it was too late. Which meant they couldn't protect themselves from them—or plan for them.

"Thankfully, in here, nobody else is looking for you *or* your frailty," Darla said. "Monsters are the only ones who know you're still alive and…well…I was going to say kicking, but, you know."

"I could be kicking if you worked harder to find the rest of me."

"You're lucky all the other monsters who know you're still here are friends with our family," Darla said, "because I could tell Gretl to sick her Gobbler on you."

"All these jokes at my expense," Dolores said. "And I can't do anything about it. Besides, Gretl is like my second daughter. And that Gobbler of hers would actually come in handy helping to dig holes."

"Listen, Mom. I've dug more holes in Clear Creek than a gravedigger in Haddonfield, but Clear Creek is a big place. And because your body can't move without your head, I can't sense its vibrations under the earth. Trust me, I would love to find the rest of you, I just have no idea where the rest of you is."

"Maybe you're just not looking hard enough."

"Maybe you shouldn't have been careless enough to get decapitated by a kid."

"Everyone has a bad day," Dolores said. "Didn't you get your hand cut off once?"

"Yeah. Some Kyle got lucky with a machete. But I reattached my hand and tied him to a boat propeller to teach him a lesson. I didn't let some pimply humans take it and bury it god knows where."

"One day," Dolores said, "and as your mother I hope that day never comes, but one day you might find yourself in a situation just like I did. How was I supposed to know a shovel could be that sharp?"

"The whole purpose of a shovel is to dig through clumps of heavy things, Mom."

"Someday, you might have a child of your own. And I hope for your sake that child is just a little more helpful so that you don't have to spend all of eternity staring at a wall counting drops of water and reading the same four books over and over again."

"It's not my fault we don't have a credit card to buy more for your e-reader. I'm going to hook up that TV just so I don't have to hear you complain about being bored anymore."

"Screw the TV. Find my body!"

"You shouldn't have lost it in the first place!"

"If you ever have monsters of your own," Dolores said, "I hope they are just as ungrateful as you can be sometimes."

"Um, yeah. I don't think that's in the cards."

"What isn't?"

"Having kids," Darla said.

Dolores gasped. "My only daughter is taking a knife and stabbing me right here," she said, her voice pained. "You can't see it because I don't currently have one, but I would be pointing at my heart right now."

"Well, then, you don't have to worry about me ever stabbing you in it."

"Do you really not want to meet someone? To have a family?"

"I never said I didn't *want* it. I just said I didn't think it was in the cards. I refuse to settle for any monster, and let's just say I've seen better dating options underneath rotted logs than in the monster community."

"You need to have an open mind and an open heart, Darla."

"I do," Darla said. "I just don't want to take any chances with it."

"What do you mean, take any chances?"

"I just...I saw what happened to you when Dad left. What happened to our family. I'd never want to go through that, or subject any hypothetical little monsters to that kind of pain. I guess you never really know what's in a monster's heart. Or hearts. So I don't know if I'd be willing to trust anyone with mine."

"Not all monsters are bad," her mother said. "Your father was..." Dolores trailed off. "You could *try* to meet someone."

"Why would I try? Are there *really* any decent monsters out there?"

"I liked that William Wendell you used to see," Dolores said. "He used to say the nicest things about my hair."

"Maybe you should date him," Darla said.

"*Feh*. He wasn't such a bad monsterfriend. I've seen far worse, trust me. I dated worse, before your father, of course. What was William's weapon of choice again?"

"A weed whacker," Darla said, exasperated.

"Ah, right. William Wendell, the Weed Whacker of Barkerville. He was a good-hearted monster. And you broke up with him. Probably broke that good heart into pieces."

"He wasn't right for me, Mom. I'm sure some other monster will fall in love with him and have a whole litter of weed-whacking babies."

"Maybe you just didn't give William a chance."

"Either way, it's over. Last I checked, there are no monster dating apps. And I will not travel the earth just to meet some crusty warlock who only owns one towel and doesn't know the difference between 'your' and 'you're.'" Darla paused. Her mother's head was silent, looking down at the table. "You miss him. Don't you. Dad. Even after all this time."

"I do," she said. "I'll never lie to you."

"Even though he left you so long ago. Left us so long ago."

Dolores raised her eyes to meet her daughter's. She offered a weak smile. "Love doesn't play by rules. You have no control over it. I couldn't control falling in love with your father. And I can't control the fact that part of me still loves him after all this time, as much as the rest of me hates him for abandoning us."

"Well, I'm pretty sure I know which part of you still loves him," Darla said. "Not a lot to choose from."

"Har-har."

"Well, I despise Dad for what he did to you, and it's a good thing he's never come back here because I would find his frailty and use it," Darla said.

"Don't talk about frailties in such a joking manner," Dolores said.

"Don't worry. I know how serious they are. But at least if Dad was still around, I'd have a little help looking for your body. Just one more reason to be a little pissed that he clawed his way out through the rock wall without so much as a note or a goodbye."

"You're going to live a very, very long time," Dolores said. "Holding on to all that hatred for your father will only poison yourself. He's not around to feel it."

"Yeah, well, I'm not ready to let it go just yet."

"Maybe one day."

"Maybe." Darla turned to leave. "Night, Mom."

"At least set my book up for me before you run off."

Darla took a tall stool from the corner of the room and

set it up in front of Dolores's dresser. From one of the dresser drawers, she took an e-reader and propped it up on the stool against a rock. Thankfully, these things had a ton of battery life; there were fewer things that made Darla feel sillier than sneaking into a cabin while the campers were at soccer practice to charge her mom's book. Darla opened the settings and made sure the text font was large enough that Dolores could read it from her perch. She then took out an unsharpened pencil and put it into her mother's mouth. Dolores began to read, turning the pages by poking the device's screen.

"Batt*ewy* i*th* almo*tht* dead," Dolores said, holding the pencil between her teeth.

Darla sighed. Of course it was.

"Pollywog group has an overnight camping trip," Darla said. "I'll sneak into their cabin and charge it after they leave."

"*Fanks*." Dolores poked the screen again and continued to read.

Darla left her mother's room and went back into the cave's antechamber. All three of her stomachs growled like she hadn't eaten in days, which, other than some tree bark covered in moss, she hadn't. Darla slid a boulder away from the wall to reveal a makeshift pantry. There wasn't much. Mainly non-perishables. Meat and milk and produce didn't last long in a cave without refrigeration, and while two-month-old warm meat could be surprisingly tasty, other cave critters would always find it and devour it first. Most of their food came from campers' unattended backpacks or the camp's canteen. Occasionally, she'd traverse over to the highway and scare off a delivery car or gig driver, though, given her luck, they'd be delivering salads. And who the hell paid fifteen dollars *plus* delivery fees *plus* tip for ingredients they could get off the forest floor? Occasionally, she'd get lucky and intercept nachos or a pizza. Right now, though, pickings were slim. Darla took a Pop-Tart from a box and looked at the date. Two years old. She shrugged and removed the foil wrapping. Then she heard a small *ping*. Her mother had spit the pencil out of her mouth.

"Can I at least sit with you?" Dolores shouted.

Darla put the Pop-Tart down on the old wooden communal table in the center of the cavern and went back into her mother's room. Gently, she lifted Dolores's head and brought it to the table, placing it down at the opposite end.

"A little light?" Dolores said. "My night vision isn't as sharp as it used to be."

Darla lit several candles and placed them around the table, careful not to put them too close to Dolores. She had no idea if her mother's hair would grow back if it caught on fire and she didn't want to tempt fate, lest Dolores have one more thing to be annoyed about. Darla ate her Pop-Tart in silence, then wolfed down some stale kettle corn and a warm cherry soda. Dolores watched quietly, a look of concern on her face that felt like a cold knife against Darla's heart.

The cave was nearly silent. All Darla could hear was the steady *drip, drip, drip* of water droplets falling into puddles on the cave floor, the peaceful skittering of various animals and insects. There was a tranquility to the quiet. She couldn't remember the last time she'd come back from a hunt and just... listened. Maybe she needed to do more of that. A break from the hunt would do her good. Give her mind a chance to focus.

When she was finished, she brought Dolores's head back into the bedroom and placed it on the table.

"Night, Mom."

"Night, hon. Sleep well. I hope you wake up in the morning

and forget all about this foolishness and go rend Kyle into a thousand itsy bitsy Kyle pieces."

Darla merely smiled and put the pencil back between her mother's lips.

Darla blew out the candles on the table and went into a room on the other side of the cave. A small wooden table sat against the wall. A pile of books lay scattered across its top. Mostly fantasy and romance, a few mysteries, and a classic or two. Just like the snacks, she'd "borrowed" these books from the backpacks and bedsides of campers and counselors over the years. And just like those snacks, she'd "forgotten" to return them.

For a long time, they were the only books Darla and Dolores had access to. Then Darla saw a counselor using some fancy new thing called an e-reader, and took it upon herself to liberate it from his backpack. One week later, she saw the same camper using a brand new one. That was one thing Darla had learned after years hunting in Camp Clear Creek: parents would overnight their kids a moon rocket if they asked them to.

She picked up a book called *Swords and Soulmates*. The cover showed an image of two warriors, a man and a woman, each wielding gleaming weapons and wearing what must have been a thousand pounds of steel armor. They looked ready to slay whatever manner of man or beast might attack them, but they were also glancing at each other with slight smiles, as if to say that the moment they finished slaying whatever horrific baddie that had been sent to skewer their livers with a spear, they would then find a medieval hotel room, hopefully one not too sticky with spilled grog, shed their armor, and wield a different sort of weaponry.

Darla brought the book to the dining room table, propped

her feet up, and read for a few hours. The fighting scenes were exciting, the shagging scenes were more tepid than cave water runoff, and finally she felt her eyelids growing heavy. She placed the book down and went into the room that she'd slept in for the last thirty-two years.

Darla's mattress was a pile of twigs atop a slab of rock, her pillow a sanded-down log with a small groove where her neck fit perfectly. She lay down and closed her eyes, remembering the days when she was small and her legs barely reached halfway down the rock slab. She'd dreamed about being a hunter just like her mother, scaring the bejesus out of Clear Creek, and building the legacy of the Drake name for decades.

But tonight, she just couldn't do it anymore. She still couldn't believe she'd let Kyle walk—or crawl—away. Yet somehow, she knew she had to do it, that sometimes you had to do what felt wrong to get to what felt right. You couldn't change your life if you kept doing the same thing over and over again. Hopefully, this break would clear Darla's head. Show her the way forward. Let her know what she was meant to do and who she was meant to be.

No more hunts. No more Kyles. No more blood.

Darla Drake, Duchess of Death, the Creature of Clear Creek, was done with it. Tomorrow was a new day.

Though, deep down, she still hoped that Kyle may have been devoured by a slow-digesting python.

CHAPTER 3

ONE YEAR LATER

Darla sat at the edge of a swamp while the pregnant monster next to her ate frogs. Well, she wasn't quite sure if what Gretl Sneed, aka the Gullet Gobbler, did could be considered eating. Every few minutes, Gretl would emit a sound from her stomach that sounded like the love child of a trombone blast and a carbonated belch. Then she'd open her mouth, and the living tongue inside her esophagus known as the Gobbler (which looked like a small, homuncular, cranky, bald child) would shoot forth, snatch a frog in its tiny hands, and pull it back inside of Gretl's mouth. The whole process took about 2.3 seconds. The frog was in her stomach before it knew what had hit—or grabbed—it.

"Needs salt," Gretl said, wiping her mouth.

"I've always meant to ask, what do frogs taste like?" Darla asked.

Gretl cocked her head, thought for a moment, then replied, "Kind of like chicken."

"I should have guessed that."

"It's really good to see you, Dar," Gretl said. "I was going to say it's been too long, but I totally know it's my fault. I promise to be a better friend once this baby comes."

"I'm not sure you want to promise that," Darla said. "I don't think having a baby monster gives you *more* free time."

"No," Gretl said. "Probably not. And based on how much activity is going on in there, it could be at least two, maybe three little monsters."

"You're going to have your hands full."

"Seriously. I know a million monsters who all have four or more hands and they don't know how lucky they are. What I wouldn't give for another appendage or two or three to make changing diapers a bit easier, but nope, just these two."

Darla Drake and Gretl Sneed had been best friends for twenty years. Gretl was the daughter of Angela Sneed, aka the Masticator, and Fred Woosnum, aka Farmer Psycho. Angela had grown up in Normantown, which was adjacent to Clear Creek, which was home to the legendary Maker's Marsh.

Gretl's mother had hunted in Normantown for decades, and, by virtue of proximity, had befriended Dolores Drake. The Drakes and the Sneeds had grown up together—Darla and Gretl learned to hunt together, slayed their first victims together, teased each other about made-up frailties (Darla told Gretl that her frailty was probably bottled human farts and Gretl told Darla that her frailty was probably a booger-filled tissue from a smelly human named Kyle). Darla always imagined that she and Gretl would continue along the same path, slaying and hunting and hunting and slaying for years and years until it was time for Darla to finally lay down her scourge and for Gretl to, well, stop spearing people through the neck with her Gobbler.

They would have their whole lives to live, side by side, traveling along the same path, friends until the end of time.

And then, two years ago, Gretl went and fell in love with Tyrone Binks, aka Hatchetman, and was now sitting next to Darla, her stomach the size of a small hippo, pregnant with their first hatchetbaby. Gretl absently caressed her abdomen as they sat and talked. She was in her nineteenth month of pregnancy, with no end in sight. Her stomach ebbed and swelled, making it difficult to gauge just how big the baby was, but Darla knew that baby monsters could grow *fast*. Some little monsters were hunting by their first birthday.

"I swear, I can't wait to not be pregnant anymore," Gretl said. "My mom said she was pregnant with me for just three and a half months and I was thirty-seven pounds, six ounces when I came out. And I was on the small side. But, you know, different monsters and different mating combinations equals different gestational periods and blah, blah, blah. For all I know, by the time this baby shoots out of me, it will be the size of the boulder at the entrance to your cave."

"God, I hope not, for your body's sake," Darla said.

"Tell me about it. It could take all week for my monster parts to repair themselves, and you know even then I've heard they might never look the same."

"I'm in pain just thinking about it. So do you and Tyrone have a name picked out?"

Gretl nodded. "I like Wilmer if it's a boy and Shatterspine if it's a girl. Tyrone is iffy on Shatterspine, but said if it's a boy he wants to name it after his father, Saberface. But we also have a few backups in case we see her and something else just fits."

"Those names are lovely," Darla said. "I'm really happy for you, Gret."

"Thanks, Dar," Gretl said, laying her head on her friend's shoulder. "I can't believe in just a few...however long it's going to be...I'm going to be responsible for a little monster."

"Seriously. I still remember you getting blitzed at Monster Mashes when we were kids and trying to eat rocks with your Gobbler."

Gretl laughed. As she did, the Gobbler poked its head out of her mouth and shook its head disapprovingly before retreating.

"Do you remember the first time we came out here?" Gretl asked.

Darla laughed. "You kidding? It was after our first hunt. I disemboweled a counselor who'd just tried to assault his girlfriend. Strung his guts around his bunk like Christmas lights."

"You had a piece of small intestine hanging from your pocket," Gretl said with a laugh. "I really didn't want to tell you. I wanted to see how long it would take you to notice. I could totally see you going on hunts with random entrails hanging off you for all eternity."

"Yeah, you were real slick. You laughed so hard a finger came out your nose."

"I remember that!" Gretl said with a laugh. "I still don't even know whose finger it was!"

"Things were a lot simpler back then," Darla said.

"Tell me about it," Gretl said, patting her stomach. The creature inside her abdomen let loose a growl so loud Darla could sense all the fish swimming away. "Baby's hungry." She opened her mouth and the Gobbler shot out and snagged an unlucky frog.

"Did you always want this?" Darla asked.

"What? Frogs?"

"No, stupid. That. Your kid. Your husband."

"Ah-ah-ah, we're not technically married yet. Tyrone has only completed four of the five Hell Tasks my mother laid out for him. So, we're still engaged until he brings her a toe from SlothMan."

"Tyrone seems like a pretty stand-up monster. He'll finish all five Hell Tasks."

"Yeah, he is. And he will," she said with a far-off, dreamy look in her three eyes. "I think somewhere deep down I did always want this. A family. I used to think about how much I loved going hunting with my parents as a little monster. How they taught me to scare humans to get them running, all the best angles to take on a chase, how to use my environment, how to make it all theatrical to help grow my own legend when the time came. I guess I loved the idea of doing all of that with my own little monster."

"I hope your kid doesn't growl like that when it finally comes out," Darla said. "It'll scare all your victims away."

"I know, right? So, I think I did want all of this. But I also wanted to wait for the right monster to come along. You have no idea some of the d-bags I dated before Tyrone." Gretl leaned in close. "Can I tell you a secret?"

"Please do."

"I hooked up with Mantula."

"You did *not*."

Gretl nodded in both embarrassment and amusement. "I met him at a Monster Mash in the abandoned quarry in TohoTown. I invited you to it, if you remember."

Darla sighed. "I remember. I wanted to go, but my mom had *just* been decapitated and she gave me such a hard time about leaving her alone when I wasn't out hunting. You know, 'You spend all this time maiming and killing and you can't take a few minutes for your poor old mother's head?'"

"Ugh, the guilt," Gretl said, rolling her eyes. "My mom already wants to pick out the baby's hunting outfit. We don't even know what size it'll be or how many limbs it'll have."

"That should be a decision between you and Tyrone. Period." Darla paused. "So, tell me more about this dalliance with Mantula."

Gretl giggled. "We drank a lot. I mean a *lot*. He said he was thinking about relocating. Let's just say we 'relocated' somewhere outside the quarry that night."

"That's gross," Darla said. Then, curious, she added, "So how was he?"

"Shockingly good? Let's just say he knows how to use all eight limbs."

"Excuse me, I need to go barf."

Gretl laughed. "It didn't go further than that. He's a player. One of those guys who makes you think he's all about settling down and starting a family but then a week after you go out with him, he's laying egg sacks in half the monster chicks on the Eastern Seaboard."

"Having a beau with eight limbs would come in handy when it came time to raise a litter of little monsters."

"Literally handy. Suppose Mantula did have one thing going for him." Gretl put her hand on Darla's shoulder. "Don't worry. You'll meet your Mantula."

"I'd rather meet a rusty chainsaw with my face than meet my Mantula. And I've been hit in the face with a rusty chainsaw, and I'd still go with the chainsaw."

"Well, you're definitely not going to meet anyone with that attitude. You just have to be open to it."

"I am open to it."

"You're open like a barn door that's nailed shut and on fire," Gretl said.

"Yeah, well, you try to change every monster you meet," Darla said.

"Oh, now that's not true."

"Remember Griffin?"

"Ugh. Stop."

"His whole thing was divebombing hapless boats at sea. Didn't you ask him, like, two weeks into your quote, unquote *relationship* if he'd consider staying on land for you?"

"Was it really too much to ask him to stay closer to shore and just, I don't know, divebomb kayaks or boogie boards?"

They both laughed. Gretl nudged Darla.

"I didn't try to change you."

"No. You didn't."

"And I didn't have to change Tyrone. He was already perfect."

"Lucky for him."

"He was the first monster I didn't have to convince to stay," she said. "Who really wanted to be with me. At first, I thought that was a red flag. Like, why isn't he playing hard to get? Why don't I have to fight and work to convince him to want to be with me? I always thought dating someone meant you had to bludgeon them into submission. Literally. I had to whomp the Regenerator with a tire iron and tie him to a railroad track just to get him to agree to a second date. Thankfully the dent in his head healed, but the second I let him go, he ran off and I never saw him again."

"You should have hit him harder," Darla said.

Gretl laughed. "Or at least tested to see whether he

regenerated *everywhere*."

The girls broke out in loud, hearty laughter. It made Darla think about the days when she and Gretl were young monsters, their whole lives and scores of maimings ahead of them. They would become legends. Have movies and songs and books written about them. Kids would dress like them on Halloween, and campers and counselors would sit around campfires scaring kids with tales of Gretl the Gullet Gobbler and Darla Drake, Creature of Clear Creek.

But none of that seemed to matter anymore. Gretl was starting a family with the love of her life and Darla was... nowhere. The hunt used to give her all the fulfillment she needed. But now it wasn't enough. She needed to figure out how she was going to spend the rest of her endless life. And it could not involve her morosely roaming the woods of Clear Creek, wailing about her misfortune for all eternity. (Wanda the Wailer of Wales already cornered that market.)

"Hey, sweetie, you okay?" Gretl said.

"I don't know," Darla said. "I thought taking this time off would get my head straight. Like things would magically fall into place, but they haven't."

"Dar. Duchess. Scourgey-poo."

"Please don't call me that. One idiot kid wanders by and records you saying that with his cell phone and posts it online and my career is over. Nobody fears a Scourgey-poo."

"Seems like your career might be over anyway, right?"

"I don't know. Too soon to say. I haven't made any permanent decisions. I'm just on a hunting sabbatical right now."

"Listen. Dar. *Nothing* just *falls* into place. You have to work for it. *Look* for it. If I'd sat around waiting for the monster of my dreams to just fall into my lap, I would have ended up with some D-grade blob who smelled like moss and couldn't hunt a sloth. If you want to figure out what's missing from your life, you have to look for it. You're not going to find anything sitting at home. So, sharpen up that bone crown and oil your scourge and get out of your cave."

"I like my cave. My cave is comfortable. I don't have to answer to anyone."

"Except your mom's severed head."

"Yes. Except for my mom's severed head. But, you know, if I throw a blanket over her, it kind of muffles the sound."

Gretl laughed. "Speaking of getting out of your cave, there's a Monster Mash coming up in a few weeks. *Please* tell me you're going."

"Please tell me you're *not* going," Darla said. "You're really going to lug that growing abdomen in your abdomen to a *party*?"

"Are you kidding? I have no idea how long I'm going to be carrying this thing around. It could be months. And then, once it's here, you think I'm going to be able to go out and have *fun*? Not if all sixteen of my nipples are raw and bleeding, no thank you. This could be my last chance to get out for a long time. If you think I'm going to miss it, you're insane."

"What if Mantula is there?"

Gretl offered a sly smile. "Then he'll get to see what he missed out on."

"What if he meets Tyrone?"

"I mean, perfect?" Gretl said enthusiastically. "Maybe they'll even fight. Tyrone could tear off one of his legs and… ooh, I'm shivering just thinking about how cool it would be to see my monster battle one of my exes over my affection. Could you imagine your paramour beating Mantula senseless to protect your honor?"

"Only Mantula wasn't your ex, he was a one-night stand, and you're madly in love with Tyrone, so it's not a battle for your affection at all since he's already won."

"You are *such* a buzzkill," Gretl said. "Whatever. I'll be at the Mash. And you'd better be, otherwise I'm throwing you over my shoulder cave-monster style and dragging you to the quarry and pouring enough punch into your mouth to make your crown melt."

"You really need to work on your salesmanship," Darla said. "Fine. I'll think about it."

"Okay. I'll accept that answer. *For now*. But, Dar?"

"Yes, Gretl?"

"Find whatever it is you're looking for. And do it fast. Because I want you back out here doing what you're meant to do."

"And what is that, exactly?"

"Making crusty teenagers pee themselves before having their limbs ripped off."

Darla smiled and put her hand on Gretl's arm. "You always know how to cheer me up."

CHAPTER 4

Darla woke up with a crick in her neck. She slid off the bed and eyed her pillow with disdain. The cavern was still dark. It was the middle of the night, but she couldn't sleep. Not that this development came as a surprise. Since she'd ceased the hunt, she hadn't been able to sleep. Whatever was wrong with her, it wasn't the hunt that was causing it. It was something else.

She thought about what Gretl had said. She *had* expected the answer to fall into her lap. She assumed she would wake up the day after giving up the hunt and the piece of the missing puzzle would drop into her lap.

She'd tried to change the way she lived. This meant, among other things, no more sleeping on twigs and logs. She'd replaced the twigs with sheets and a duvet—both taken from the Clear Creek lost and found—and a pillow she'd swiped from a counselor who fortified his morning coffee with several shots of bourbon. Previously, Darla would have gladly used her scourge to separate the irresponsible counselor's torso from his legs. But he'd lucked out; now, his punishment was relegated to Darla stealing his goose down pillow while he was out drinking on the dock. He didn't realize how lucky he was that the Duchess of Death didn't come for him.

She'd tried eating different. Less processed foods stolen from the camp canteen. Drinking less runoff cave water. But it was all superficial. The real problem wasn't what she slept on or what was digested by one of her three stomachs. If she didn't fix what was going on beneath her bone crown, she didn't think she'd ever sleep again.

Darla stood up and stretched. She did not feel rested or relaxed. She couldn't believe that humans slept with pillows and sheets. How would they be able to see if weevils were crawling up their toes while they slept?

"Darla? You up?"

"Yeah, Mom, one second."

Her muscles felt soft, unused. She touched her bone crown. Even the tips felt less pointy. Darla had always sworn that she wouldn't become her mother. But if she didn't figure this out, she'd basically just be a head attached to a meat sack. She might as well just lop off her own cranium and plant it on the table next to Dolores.

She went into her mother's room. Two months into her... whateveryoucallit...Darla had grown tired of her mother's incessant complaints and stolen a smart TV from the camp lounge. She'd then spent two weeks gathering enough cable to hook the TV up to the nearby generator through a small hole in the cave wall, all in an attempt to stop the unending stream of questions about *what do you plan to do with your future?*

The TV's screen had cracked after hitting a few branches during Darla's traversal back, but when Dolores had the gall to complain, Darla reminded her that severed heads couldn't be choosers.

Unfortunately, getting Wi-Fi into the cave was beyond Darla's expertise, which meant the TV only got three channels: sports, Hallmark movies, and one that showed nothing but cooking shows. And while the monotony did wear on Darla, there was tremendous entertainment value in watching someone without arms learn how to make a soufflé.

When Darla poked her head into the bedroom, Dolores looked at her with disdain.

"These are prescription sunglasses."

Darla sighed. A few weeks ago, her mother had complained about the glare from the TV screen, so Darla had stolen a pair of sunglasses from the camp nurse's bedside.

"I'm getting tired of being the burglar of Clear Creek," Darla said. "That was the only pair of glasses I could find that wasn't kid-sized."

"No, it was the only pair you bothered to *look* for," Dolores said. "If I'd asked you to get me a pair of sunglasses before your...*vacation*...you would have maimed half the camp just to find them. These are also far too big. They keep slipping down off my nose."

"Are there any problems of yours that *aren't* my fault?"

"You know, part of me was looking forward to having you around more," Dolores said. "But you're just a giant grump."

"I may be a giant grump, but you're a grump stump."

Dolores sighed. "I just don't see the point of taking time off if you're not any happier than you were before."

"It takes time," Darla said. She tried to convince herself that this was true, that she was just so used to the grind of the hunt that going cold turkey like she did meant her body and mind would need to adjust to the new situation.

"At least you could take up a hobby. Something to occupy your time."

"What's a hobby?" Darla asked.

"Something that interests you. Knitting. Scrapbooking. CrossFit."

"That all sounds awful."

"Better than you sitting around the cave moping all day."

"I do not *mope*."

"Wait, hold on, I think I see a mopey monster in my room," Dolores said. "If I had hands, I would have pointed at you."

"I think it might be time for me to get a cave of my own," Darla replied.

"So you'd just leave me here all alone, a head with nothing and nobody? This is the thanks I get?"

"I think the less there is of you," Darla said, "the bigger the guilt trip."

"So, find the rest of me and maybe we can rectify that."

Darla headed toward the cave entrance. She needed to get out. She needed air. Her own head was a mess without being scolded by someone else's head.

"I'll be back," Darla said.

"Where are you going? Hunting? Please be hunting."

She hauled the boulder away from the entrance and stepped into the night, sliding the rock back into place without responding to her mother.

The dark woods were a balm. They calmed her. Darla walked over to the bank of Clear Creek Lake and sat down on a rotting log. The waters were still. She could sense fish swimming beneath the surface. Every movement sent a pulse through the air, like a reverse radar. Every step was a signal, every breath loud as a cannon. She used to laugh when her victims would do silly things like hide inside closets or underneath beds. They might as well have set off fireworks.

She could feel the animals all around her. Feel something as gentle as a leaf falling onto the surface of the water. The world around her may have seemed still as a glass of water to anyone else, but to Darla Drake, it was a never-ending carnival of movement.

Then, her head snapped to attention. There was something out there. Something bigger. Not an animal. She knew the vibrations of every animal in the Clear Creek region. She could feel an undulating in the distance. A rumbling among the trees. Something headed in the direction of Camp Clear Creek. It was large. What kind of animal that size could make that kind of vibration in the trees?

Then, a few minutes later, she felt more vibrations. On the ground. Lots of them. She recognized these sensations.

People.

People were running. And not just one or two. Dozens.

But why? Why would so many people be running around Camp Clear Creek in the middle of the night?

Darla stood up. She smelled the air, searching for smoke. A fire at the camp could explain the crazed activity at such a strange hour. But she smelled nothing, not even a campfire. Whatever was causing this panic was external. Something had come *into* the camp. But who?

Or what?

Darla had to know.

She went back inside the cave and looked at her scourge hanging on the wall. She hadn't touched it in a year. She ran her fingers over the whip, caressed the bronze studs at the end.

"Hey, old friend," Darla said. "Sorry it's been so long."

Then she removed the scourge from its hook and strapped it to her belt. She wasn't hunting tonight. But something told her she might need it.

Camp Clear Creek was three and a half miles from her cave. Darla traversed the distance in less than seven minutes. She glided through the trees, winding around bushes and rocks, ducking under branches and low-flying birds. It had been twelve months since she'd been to Camp Clear Creek, but she remembered the route like it was yesterday.

She stopped a quarter mile from the campgrounds and hid behind the orange fence that divided the soccer field from the basketball courts. The rumblings grew louder on the other side. There was so much commotion, Darla's entire body seemed to vibrate, a tuning fork in a blender. Then she heard the screams. Not one scream. Or two. The whole camp seemed to be screaming all at once. Darla could differentiate at least twenty-six different voices, all at different pitches and volumes, genders, and ages.

What in the blue Brundlefly was going on? Darla stood up and prepared to climb over the rock wall when something flew by overhead. It was moving fast. It wasn't a tree. Or a log. Trees didn't flail about. Or scream like a Banshee (Darla had met several Banshees and they did not scream the way it was commonly assumed).

Whatever had flown overhead wasn't a some*thing*. It was a some*one*.

The someone landed twenty feet away from Darla with a *thud*. She traversed behind a tree ten feet away from the... projectile. The launchee was a guy, seventeen or eighteen, with blond hair and a polo shirt whose collar had, miraculously, remained popped despite its owner's air travel.

Darla traversed behind a tree just a few feet from the guy's prone body. He was still alive, having miraculously landed in a rather large pile of pine needles. He got to his feet, moaning and shaking his head like it was a bell that had been hit with a sledgehammer. That's when Darla saw what was on the guy's shirt.

His shirt was soaked. But not with blood. Something else. Something thick. A gel or slime of some sort. The viscous substance dripped off him, almost like he'd been coated in saliva.

"Where did it go?" he muttered. "Where did it go?"

He whipped his head around, looking for something. He was confused. Scared.

Then Darla heard a *thwup* sound from somewhere far away, and a tentacle shot out of the gloom, wrapped itself around the guy, and yanked him back into the darkness with a faint *ayeeee*!

What. The hell. Was that?

Darla had to know what was going on. Where did that tentacle come from? And what was it attached to? She traversed in the direction the young man was pulled. There was a stench in the air, something mildewy, and it grew stronger as Darla approached the central campgrounds.

Then another body flew by her, this one smacking against a tree with a loud *CRUNCH*. When it fell to the ground, Darla could see a slimy imprint on the tree where the body had hit.

More screams. Darla had to know what was causing this mayhem but couldn't risk being seen. She looked up. The main office building loomed ahead. It was twenty feet high and offered a perfect vantage point of the central campgrounds. Darla surveyed the scene. Saw a clear path. Then she moved.

She traversed over to a pine tree, swung herself up to a high branch, then used the branch to swing herself onto one of the office's windowsills. From there she clambered to the roof in less than five seconds. She lay down flat and inched her way forward until she had a clear view of just what in the world was going on at Camp Clear Creek.

And when she saw what was happening, Darla gasped.

Who—or what—the fuck was that guy?

CHAPTER 5

Something stood in the center of the campground. It wore a long black jacket that went down to its knees, with long sleeves that hid its hands. A hood shrouded its head and face. It seemed to be surveying the havoc it had wreaked with a sense of amusement. It was tall, maybe six foot six or seven, and in the shape of a man, and was no doubt the catalyst for the campground chaos. One word went through Darla's mind as she watched: *Monster.*

But why would another monster be in Clear Creek?

People were strewn about the grounds like discarded matches. They all seemed to be alive and in various states of terror, dishevelment, and bewilderment. Several had cell phones out and were recording the *thing* wearing the long black coat. Darla thought back to her last hunt, of Kyle Browning, and wondered why it was some people's instinct not to run, but to commemorate. Who cared how many imprints your video got if your eyeballs had been plucked out with chopsticks?

Then a burly guy wearing a too-tight Camp Clear Creek t-shirt came out of one of the cabins. He gripped a shovel and took a baseball stance. He shouted, "Die, asshole!" and ran toward the creature, bellowing some sort of high-pitched pathetic war cry. Darla just hoped the young man had health insurance.

The creature spun toward his attacker, and, before Darla could blink, a thick, purple tentacle shot out from the creature's sleeve and wrapped itself around the burly guy's waist. The guy shrieked and beat at the tentacle with the shovel handle. The tentacle then retracted into the creature's sleeve, pulling the guy toward him as the young man frantically tried to escape. Then, once the burly guy was up close and personal with the monster, their faces mere inches apart, Darla heard the creature whisper something. Something that sounded like, *I hope you can fly. Or float.* The guy's eyes widened in terror and he shrieked. And then the creature flung the guy high into the air, way out into the distance toward the water, the shriek growing quieter and quieter until he landed with a splash in the middle of Romero Pond.

Another counselor dropped a log and ran. Nobody else dared challenge whatever had just turned their friend into the world's heaviest slingshot. Then the *thing* turned around. And for the first time, Darla saw its face.

The creature's skin was grayish blue, with curly, pitch-black hair that fell just over its piercing yellow eyes, the color of glittering citrine. Its nose was long and thin, with a wide, almost aquiline tip. Other than its skin tone and eyes, the creature's facial features looked very human. And she hated herself for even thinking it, but the creature was...kind of hot?

Suddenly, Darla's foot skidded from underneath her, and a

shingle came loose and slid off the roof and clattered upon the ground. The creature immediately looked up, searching for the source of the noise. Darla ducked down, her heart thudding in her chest. She waited for what felt like hours before peeking back over the roof.

The creature was still there. It was staring at her with a confused look on its face. Like it knew who she was but was also surprised to see her. How could that be?

Then the creature's thin lips spread into a smile. Or a smirk, to be more precise. The monster clearly knew who Darla was. And it was amused, if not surprised, by her presence.

Then the creature shot a tentacled arm out and wrapped it around a tree branch twenty feet in the air. It looked back at Darla and gave what she swore looked like a slight bow. The creature then swung swiftly away into the woods, its movements graceful, its movements...fast. *Really* fast. Maybe even as fast as her traversal.

Darla surveyed the scene. Groaning bodies were strewn across the campgrounds. Burly shovel guy was slowly swimming back to shore. And Darla Drake, Duchess of Death, sat on the rooftop in shock wondering who in the hell this octopus creature was, why he seemed to recognize her, and, more importantly, why he'd come to Clear Creek.

CHAPTER 6

Darla watched from afar as the sun came up and Clear Creek regrouped. Two ambulances came, but only one person was loaded in, and she was kicking and screaming at that, seemingly more annoyed than injured. The creature had caused an enormous ruckus, but, to the best of Darla's knowledge, hadn't even maimed anyone. The attack seemed more about terror. Chaos. Announcing his presence with tentacled fanfare. But the fact that this *thing* had descended upon Clear Creek irked Darla. Shady Pines had been the territory of the Drake family for decades. Another monster's presence was intrusive, insulting, and absolutely *could not stand*.

Darla needed to know who this monster was, and to make sure he left Clear Creek to never return. Whether he did so in one piece was entirely up to him.

There was a code among monsters. Everyone stuck to their own territory. Cratos the human Crab terrorized the shores of Lake Michigan, while Lobstra bisected fishermen along the Gulf of Maine. The Giantess hurled boulders from atop the Appalachian Mountains. Mantula was a humanoid spider with a man's body and eight limbs that devoured anyone who wandered into its path in the midlands of South Carolina (and also gave Gretl quite a roll in the hay). Barnaby the Butcher cleaved his way through the finest eateries in Paris, while Gretl the Gullet Gobbler ransacked Maker's Marsh. Every monster had a place. They did not venture outside of their territories. Hunting grounds were sacred.

The Drake family had always hunted in Clear Creek. Dolores maimed many a counselor here before losing her head. And then Darla took over the family business, modernized her mother's methods, proving she was just as fearsome, if not more so, than her forebearers. Darla had been laser-focused, perhaps to a fault, as Gretl had often told her. Darla was so obsessed with the hunt and furthering the Drake family legacy that she left little room in her life for anything else. And once she got this…ennui…out of her system, Darla had no doubt she would be back bigger and badder than ever. On her terms. On her timeline.

But this creature. This *stupid* creature could ruin all of that. Darla didn't know who he was or why he'd come to Clear Creek. But she knew just sure as her aim with a spear gun that she was going to find those answers, and then make this literal slimeball sorry he ever stepped a tentacle in Clear Creek.

Darla waited on the roof until after the police had left and EMTs had pulled the camper from Romero Pond and checked his vitals while he shivered and whispered, "Tentacles… tentacles…" over and over. Once the hysteria had died down, the counselors managed to get all campers back into their cabins. A few counselors stayed out to drink, smoke, or fool around near the pond. Something about being scared made them lose their inhibitions, and Darla approved. She didn't much care about extracurricular activities, unlike her mother's generation, who hunted with a near-puritanical fervor reserved for the clergy and certain Floridian politicians.

Back in the old days, some monsters used to rend teenagers limb from limb for the unfathomable and unforgivable sin of being drunk and/or horny (and, heaven forbid, sometimes both at the same time).

There were no exceptions. You procreated, you got loaded, you got high, you died in unrelentingly brutal fashion. Two consenting young adults could take a rowboat out into the middle of a placid, shimmering lake, drink cheap red wine straight from the bottle, disturbing nobody but the fish, and start to get it on. And then, just as things started to escalate from PG to PG-13, some prude "traditional" monster would leap up from the depths, capsize the boat, and drag the poor, libidinous youngsters down to a watery grave.

That wasn't Darla. She didn't care if kids got off—as long as it was consensual—or had a drink or smoke as long as they didn't put anyone in harm's way. Modern-day monsters had a new set of rules. Only the assholes who broke them would see her bad side. And you did *not* want to see Darla Drake's bad side.

You touched someone who didn't want it? Drank before teaching swim class to the four-year-old Seahorse group? Tried to be the Big Man at Camp by holding a plastic bag over some kid's head? Well, then you'd meet the business end of Darla Drake's scourge. And if you were lucky, you'd die of shock before she *really* got started.

But when Darla took her, what else could she call it,

sabbatical, it did *not* mean some bootleg monster could wander in and cause some tentacled fracas in Clear Creek. This was *Darla's* place for pandemonium. And she couldn't let an interloper remain here without putting him in his place. She had to find this octopus guy. And either he'd see the error of his ways and leave or meet the business end of Darla's scourge and be buried here in several graves.

Once the camp had gone quiet, it was time for Darla to find the creature. She found the tree the monster had swung away on and squinted, her night vision coming into focus. She was looking for a clue. A hint. A trail.

There. She saw it. A faint purplish glow on one of the high branches. A sheen of slime, right where the creature's tentacle had latched onto the wood. He'd left a trail for her. Amateur.

Darla traversed over to the tree and leapt to an adjacent branch. Right there, on the branch, she could see a purple smudge, clear as daylight. She ran her finger over it. Slick and thick and even a little pungent. She scrunched up her nose. Not only was this *thing* on her turf, he stank worse than a terrified counselor the morning after Sloppy Joe Saturday.

She was pretty sure the creature had swung away in a northwest direction. Darla scanned the trees until she saw another purple smudge on a branch about ten yards away. She leapt down and traversed to the tree. Looked around. Found another purple smudge. Traversed. Found another. And another. He was definitely heading northwest. To where, she didn't know. The forest surrounding Clear Creek was over a thousand acres, with all sorts of caves and hollows to hide. Assuming this monster was still even in Clear Creek, and hadn't just barged in for a tentacle-and-run before moving onto his next hunting ground.

Darla followed the stinky purple smudges for four miles through the dark forest. Then, after traversing to the bottom of a large oak, she stopped. Looked around. Surveyed the woods around her. She slowed her heart to help her concentrate. She couldn't see any more smudges. The creature's trail had gone cold.

She looked around. Tried not to panic. Had she been out of the hunt that long? What use would she be if she couldn't even track a monster who left a glowing purple slime trail?

She closed her eyes. Listened. Leaves rustled from dozens of trees. Cicadas chirped all around her. And between all of that she heard the sound of...water.

Running water.

She traversed northwest and found a stream fifty yards away. Looking back, it was entirely possibly he'd swung into the stream, then gone on foot. Darla unhooked the scourge from her belt and followed the stream. Her breathing quickened. Her heart began to race. She didn't want to risk traversing. Moving at that speed could force her to miss something. A clue. A hiding spot. She had to be smart. She had to be...was that a waterfall?

Sheets of water cascaded down from a rock outcropping about fifteen feet high. She couldn't see past the water. She looked around. No purple smudges. No trail. She didn't know how high he could jump, and it was very possible he'd leapt onto the outcropping and continued on. She wouldn't know until she checked.

Darla approached the cascade. She could feel the scourge in her hand, and tightened her grip. The water sprayed against her cloak, soaking her legs, but she didn't feel a chill. She swung her scourge through the water in case something was hiding behind it, but the weapon came away with water rather than blood or flesh.

Darla sniffed the air. She couldn't see anything beyond the water, but she could have sworn she recognized the familiar pungent odor.

And then quicker than she could blink, a tentacle shot through the cascading sheets, wrapped itself around Darla's neck, yanked her off her feet, and dragged her through the waterfall.

CHAPTER 7

Before Darla had a chance to do or say anything, she found herself face-to-face with the creature she'd watched terrorize Clear Creek. He had one tentacle wrapped around Darla's neck and the other around her torso, pinning her arms to her body. She was a foot off the ground, her feet dangling, but his grip around her was loose enough not to choke her. She still held the scourge but couldn't gain enough leverage to use it for anything other than a light dusting.

The monster was, as she suspected, human, or at least humanoid. He stood around six and a half feet tall, with broad shoulders and a thick chest. He wore black pants and a black and red striped T-shirt. His chest and shoulders resembled that of a human, but the arms extended past the biceps into the very tentacles that restrained Darla. He had short black hair and a stone-gray face with yellow eyes and a pointed, almost regal nose. His facial skin looked smooth—either he was clean-shaven, or he did not grow facial hair.

She noticed the long, black overcoat he'd worn the other night hanging from a pointed rock on the wall. A small campfire was set up against the far wall, with an iron post hanging between two branches over an extinguished flame. Wherever this monster had come from, it was clearly planning to stay a while.

"Let...me...go," Darla rasped, struggling against the tentacles' grip.

The monster looked Darla up and down. Its eyes stopped at the scourge in her hand.

"What are you planning on doing with that?" he said.

"Depends," Darla said. "Right now, I'm thinking about hanging your head on the wall next to your coat."

The monster chortled. Its voice was deep and seemed to echo, like it was coming from deep within a cave. It released the tentacle from around her neck. Darla took a long breath as its arm tentacle shrunk back into its shirtsleeve. It was clearly an extendable appendage, and actually ended in some sort of hand. Its five "fingers" were all the same length, with no fingernails, and a rough-looking texture on the palm that must have made it easier to swing, grip things, and restrain people. Or monsters.

"You're barely in a position to step on my foot," the monster said, "let alone decapitate me."

"Loosen your grip and we'll find out."

The monster smiled. "I've heard about you. Darla Drake. Creature of Clear Creek. Duchess of Death." He ran a finger—if you could call it that—over her bone crown. Darla shuddered in revulsion.

"Well, I'm glad," she said. "Because I haven't heard a thing about you."

The monster's smile vanished.

"If I let you go," he said, "will you agree to a détente?"

"A détente? Are you French?"

The monster sighed. "Some of us have spent our lives outside of campgrounds," he said. "Now, do we have a détente or not?"

Darla looked him over. If he wanted to hurt her, he could have already. She could whip the scourge around and try to lop off his head the moment her arm was freed, but something about his willingness to talk told her he didn't want violence. She didn't either, necessarily. She wanted answers. And she wouldn't get them by making his neck even with his shoulders.

"We do," she said.

"All right, then."

He retracted the tentacle gripping her torso. Darla dropped to the ground. The monster watched Darla's hands, as if waiting to see if she meant what she said, or if she would try to lop off a limb or two. She could feel her heart thumping in her chest. In all her years hunting, she'd never felt truly threatened. As a girl, her mother had told her about her invincibility, how her body could repair itself from all manner of wounds. She could still feel pain, of course, but once you learned to accept the pain and realize that it could never kill you, you could do anything. Yes, standing there opposite this monster, this monster who'd gotten the drop on her, Darla felt exposed. Vulnerable.

Yet, he hadn't made a move since putting her down.

"Jarko Murkvale," the monster said. He extended a five-fingered tentacle. Darla looked at it long enough that he retracted the appendage. "Okay, then. Guess you weren't raised with any manners."

"Why are you here, Jerkvale?" Darla asked, absently rubbing her neck. The flesh had been sore for a moment where the tentacle had grabbed her, but it had dissipated as soon as he let go.

Jarko cringed. "Jerkvale? What are you, twelve? I hope your scourge is sharper than your wit."

"Go fuck yourself."

"Better," he said. He pointed to her bone crown. "Hey, are those things real? They look real, but I've heard of monsters getting all sorts of weird plastic surgery to make themselves look scarier."

"I'll let you find out for yourself when I embed them in your neck," Darla said. "Now why are you here?"

"On this earth? Well, that's a long story. I'll start at the begin—"

"No, smart-ass. Why are you in Clear Creek?"

He sniffed and said, "Why does it matter to you?"

"Because, jackass, Clear Creek is *my* territory. You're encroaching."

"To answer your second part, no, I'm not. To answer your first part, Clear Creek is *not* your territory. Or at least not anymore."

Darla felt heat rise up her neck into her cheeks. The scourge was practically itching at her side. Jarko seemed to sense what she was thinking.

"You don't want to go there," he said, gesturing to the weapon. He craned his neck.

"What are you looking at?" Darla said.

"Nothing. I've just never seen a monster with pockets on their tunic before."

"They're useful," Darla said defensively.

"I mean, sure. Every monster needs a place to keep their car keys, loose change, breath mints."

"I have tons of uses for them."

"Like?"

"Like...cheese."

"Cheese. You keep...cheese...in your pockets."

"No, but I could. Or maybe I keep the severed limbs of my victims."

"No way. You'd need way bigger pockets. Or a purse. Maybe you should get rid of the pockets and carry around a purse."

"The Duchess of Death does *not* carry around a purse," Darla said.

"Just trying to make your life easier," Jarko said.

"I need you to explain to me," she said, fingertip brushing her scourge, "why Clear Creek isn't my territory anymore."

Jarko laughed. "Seriously? I mean, just check your MFU."

"My what?"

"MFU? Monster Finder Utility?"

"I'm still not understanding."

"You're kidding, right?" Jarko said. Darla shook her head. "That's impossible. You're famous. Your mother was famous before you. The Drakes are a Clear Creek institution. There's no way you didn't get an MFU. The United Monster Authority gives all registered monsters an MFU. I got one. Hell, even Mantula got one, and he sleeps nine months out of the year. Nobody from the UMA gave you one?"

"No. They didn't."

"Is there someone else they might have given it to? Do you live with anyone else?"

Mom, Darla thought, but didn't say. Instead, she just replied, "I don't have one."

"Weird. You and your mother are both registered with the UMA. They keep track of all registered monsters and update territories daily. You should have been given an MFU. You would have known all of this. Including the fact that you are no longer the registered monster for Clear Creek."

Jarko went over to the campsite and opened up a burlap sack. He took something out and brought it over to Darla.

"This," he said, "is an MFU."

The device was square, like an oversized cell phone. The screen was smudged and had a large crack running from one corner to the other. Jarko tapped the device. A red lock screen appeared.

Identification Please

Jarko placed one tentacle finger on the screen. After a moment, the screen turned green and read, **Welcome Back Jarko Murkvale**.

The lock screen disappeared and a map came up. In the center was a small, purple icon that looked like a mutated octopus.

"That's me," Jarko said.

"I figured."

Darla recognized the topography of the map instantly. The woods. The lake. The camp. It showed that they were on the outskirts of Clear Creek.

"Great. You have GPS. Congrats."

Jarko rolled his yellow eyes. "You've really never seen one of these."

"Shut up and tell me what it does and why it has anything to do with you being where you shouldn't."

"I'm getting to that," Jarko said. He tapped the screen and a menu appeared with two options:

Find a Monster
Find a Territory

He tapped **Find a Territory**. A search bar appeared at the top of the screen, along with filter options. Jarko tapped the filter icon, then selected **Show Open Territories**.

A list appeared on the screen, sorted by distance. There were half a dozen open territories. But at the top of the list, to her shock and anger, was Clear Creek.

"That's...that's impossible," Darla said.

"Nope. You haven't been seen at Camp Clear Creek in a year," Jarko said. "If a territory goes unhunted for over six months, the MFU declares it a dark territory and it becomes open. Meaning any monster can lay claim to it. You would know all of this from your MFU."

"I must have misplaced it," Darla said.

"Misplaced your MFU," Jarko said with a sneer. "Listen. *Duchess*. You gave up your claim to Clear Creek when you went...wherever you went. Clear Creek is mine now. You have as much right to it as I do to Haddonfield or Springwood."

"Who says I gave up my claim?" Darla said.

"Look. Right here," he said.

Jarko tapped the Clear Creek territory and a text bubble popped up. It read:

Clear Creek
Location of Camp Clear Creek
Established 1937
Hunters:
Dolores Drake: 1937-2001
Darla Drake: 2001-2023
Current Status: Unoccupied (Pending)

"What does that mean, pending?" Darla said.

"It means I've already put in a claim. Once it goes through, Clear Creek will officially be mine. And then *you'll* be the trespasser."

Darla grabbed the device out of Jarko's hand and flung it against the rock wall. It bounced off and fell to the floor with a clang.

Jarko uttered an irritated sigh. He went over and picked it up and brushed it off.

"Apple wishes it could make products that could take a beating like the MFU," he said, putting the device back in his rucksack. "Trust me, mine has been through a lot more than a hissy fit from a retired monster."

"I'm not *retired*," Darla said. "I was just taking a break."

"We don't take breaks," Jarko said. "We're monsters. Or at least I am."

In less time than it took Jarko to blink, Darla grabbed the scourge from her side and swung it at his head. His yellow eyes went wide and he ducked, the whip sailing a centimeter over where his head had just been. Several black hairs fluttered to the floor, shorn from his scalp.

Without hesitating, Jarko shot out a tentacled arm and grabbed Darla's weapon hand.

"Don't," he said firmly. Jarko's grip was tight. But Darla was ready.

She dropped the scourge from one hand and caught it deftly with the other, then swung it across Jarko's tentacle. The monster cried out and released his grip on Darla. She quickly leapt back, putting distance between them. Jarko rubbed his arm. Darla could see a streak of green where she'd whipped him.

"That hurts!" he said. "What the hell?"

"You're lucky you still have your...whatever that thing is attached to your shoulder," she said. "I have to ask. Why?"

"Why what?" Jarko said, cringing as he cradled his arm.

"Why here? Of all places? I have to think there are a thousand unclaimed territories."

"You'd be thinking wrong," Jarko said. "In case you haven't noticed, monsters tend to live a long, long time. We don't die of old age, and unless you have the misfortune of your frailty being discovered, we're impossible to kill. Not a whole lot of turnover. Which means good hunting territories like Clear Creek don't become available all that often."

"But you had to have a hunting territory before this, right? I mean, you're hardly a young monster."

Jarko said nothing.

"I take that as a yes. So why leave? Why come here in the first place?"

"That is absolutely none of your business," Jarko said.

"Fine. I don't really care one way or another. Now I'm going to ask. Nicely. Leave Clear Creek. Go somewhere else. Find an actual open territory. Because this one is taken."

"Sorry," Jarko said. "I'm staying."

"Then you and I are going to have words."

"More words than these?" Jarko said. He looked at the non-existent watch on his tentacled arm. "Listen, Duchess, this has been fun. Well, not really. But either way, I'm tired. I have a busy night ahead of me tomorrow. It's time for Clear Creek to get a load of a *real* monster."

"Clear Creek *has* a real monster."

"Oh yeah? Then where has she been?"

"I'll give you a day," Darla said. "If you're still here the next morning, I won't have any more words for you. But my scourge will."

Jarko went over to the campfire and lay down, resting his

head on the rucksack. "I'm terrified. Truly. Go home, *Duchess*. You don't belong here anymore."

The way he said the word *Duchess* made her want to free his tentacles from the rest of his body.

"One day," Darla said. Then she strapped the scourge back to her belt and stepped through the waterfall. She could hear Jarko yawn and then pretend to snore behind her. But when she looked back at him to give one last death glare, to let him know she was a woman of her word, she could see one of Jarko's yellow eyes open. It was fixed on her. Jarko might have talked a big game, but he knew the stories. Knew Darla's reputation. He knew he had to keep an eye on her because if he didn't, her scourge might be the last thing he ever saw.

CHAPTER 8

Darla hurled the boulder away from the entrance to the cavern, then shunted it back, lopsided, muttering every four-letter word she knew as she straightened it out. She couldn't get Jarko out of her mind. His arrogance. The feeling of that slimy tentacle around her neck. The feeling of pride when she wounded him. The frustration that he didn't seem to care much about her warnings.

Darla had killed many people during her time as the Creature of Clear Creek. But she'd never killed a fellow monster. She never had a reason to consider it. There were definitely days she wanted to wring her mother's neck—back when she *had* a neck—but she no more wanted to actually kill her than she did lop off her own head.

But Jarko. Something about seeing his body impaled on a tree branch made her smile. Maybe she would zip him up in a sleeping bag and slam him against a tree a few dozen times, or toss an oxygen tank into that big, stupid mouth and shoot it. She had to find a way to get Jarko out of Clear Creek. And it didn't matter to her if it was in one piece, or many.

But first, she had a bone to pick with Dolores.

Darla hung her scourge on the wall and stomped through the cavern.

"Mom?" she called out. "Mom, you up?"

"In here, Dar!" her mother replied. "Where else would I be?"

Darla entered her mother's room. She had an e-reader propped up in front of her. When Darla walked in, her mother's tongue shot out and tapped the screen. The next page of her book loaded.

"That's gross," Darla said.

"Better than holding a pencil in my mouth for hours on end," Dolores said. "Just gets a little smudgy. Speaking of which, would you mind cleaning the screen off?"

"In a minute," Darla said. "First, I need to ask you something."

"All right," Dolores said. "This sounds serious."

"It is. Mom, do we have an MFU?"

"A what?"

"Monster Finder Utility. It's a device about the size of...you know what, never mind. You'd know."

"We do not have a Meefoo, or whatever you call it. What we have in here is what we have. Nothing more. Nothing less."

"Okay. I believe you. But did anyone ever come here?"

"Well, you come here every day."

"Not me. Someone from the United Monster Authority. Apparently, it's an organization that tracks all monster activity. Ours included. All registered monsters are supposed to get one of these MFUs."

Dolores looked around the room, as though expecting the answer to be written on the ceiling.

"Mom…" Darla said. "What are you not telling me?"

"It's nothing," Dolores said.

"Nothing? Mom, did someone from the UMA come here?"

"UMA? Doesn't ring a bell."

"Mom, did *anyone* come here? While I was out hunting?"

Dolores refused to meet her eyes.

"Mom…"

"I thought they were Jehovah's Witnesses!" Dolores finally said. "I told them to get the hell away from our cave."

"Jehovah's Witnesses? They don't try to recruit monsters, Mom. And how the hell would they even know where we are?"

"Well, I'm *so sorry*," Dolores said in a snippy manner that did not sound sorry in the least. "I was trying to protect our home from outsiders. And anyone other than me and you—and Darwinus, before he left us—is an outsider."

"What about Gretl?"

"Okay, Gretl isn't an outsider. But she came over for dinner one time and wouldn't stop staring at my neck stump and she hasn't come back since."

"I don't know if I'd eat with you if I didn't have to."

"I will not apologize for trying to keep us safe."

"You just said sorry and now you're saying you won't apologize."

"The sorry was insincere."

"I figured that."

"Why are you asking all these questions?" Dolores said.

Darla pulled up a seat across from her mother and folded her arms across the back. She ran her hands over her bone crown, the familiar points and ripples comforting her. When she decided to stop the hunt, she'd felt unmoored, a boat lolling in the harbor waiting for a light to show her the way. But now, with Jarko here, it felt like she was being pushed out to sea. And there was no lighthouse to be found.

"Someone came to Clear Creek. To hunt," Darla said.

"Someone came here to hunt? To Clear Creek? Who or what on earth would do that?"

Darla looked up. "Another monster."

Dolores's eyes widened. "Another...what do you mean, another monster? This is *Drake* territory and has been for nearly a century. Who is this summer camp usurper with a death wish?"

"His name is Jarko Murkvale. He's staked a claim in Clear Creek. Says we—I—don't have jurisdiction here anymore after my sabbatical."

"Well, that's crap, sabbatical or not," Dolores said. "Just tell him the Drake family has been carving teenagers up like jack-o'-lanterns since long before he was born. And after my unfortunate accident, my daughter has been carrying on our family legacy as the Creature of Clear Creek until she..."

Dolores trailed off.

"Finish your sentence," Darla said.

Dolores eyed her daughter and said, "Until you decided to shirk your duties. I'm guessing your *sabbatical* is the reason this bootleg monster came here."

"It is," Darla said. She explained to her mother about the MFU, how due to the lack of monster activity in Clear Creek it had been relisted as an unclaimed hunting territory. And that opening had allowed Jarko Murkvale to step in and claim it as his own.

"Well, all you need to do is find this Dungvale and explain

to him that sabbatical or no sabbatical, Clear Creek belongs to the Drakes. I'm sure he'll understand and go find somewhere else to ply his trade."

"I already tried telling him that," Darla said. "He won't listen."

"You tried that?" Dolores said. "You met this monster?"

"I followed him to his cavern beneath a waterfall. We had a very polite, respectable chat. After he wrapped a tentacle around my neck and I whipped him with my scourge, that is."

"You let him keep the tentacle?"

"I did."

Dolores made a *hmph* noise. "So I lose my body, but he gets to keep his. He's lucky you didn't carve him to bits."

"I don't need to go cutting off any limbs just yet."

"I think you're sweet on him."

"Stop it, Mom."

"So is this monster cute?"

"Ew, mom."

"Oh come on," Dolores said. I'm your mother. Of course I'm going to ask. So? Is he?"

"Is he *what*?"

"Cute! Is Jarko Murkvale cute?"

"You're really asking me that question. After telling me he's lucky I didn't carve him to bits."

"It is my job to be curious about any monsters you come into contact with. You haven't talked about any monsters in any sort of romantic way since you broke up with William Wendell. And that was a long time ago. In fact, this is the first non-Gretl monster I've heard you mention in years."

"I only mentioned him because he's in our territory and he shouldn't be."

"Still, he got a rise out of you. I just miss that spark in your eyes when you spend time around someone you care about. It's almost like…your bone crown becomes extra pointy."

"I really don't want to talk about William Wendell," Darla said. "It's been over for a very, *very* long time."

"I know it has. But he was such a good monster. And a terrific hunter. The way he used that weed whacker to cut off—"

"You don't have to remind me of his weapon of choice," Darla said. She still thought about it—about him—sometimes. Though they hunted in different territories, she used to tag along on William's hunts from time to time, trying to be a supportive girlfriend, encouraging him to let loose, to let his fearsome flag fly.

She would hide as William stalked his prey, the sound of the whacker striking fear into the hearts of residents of Barkerville. She remembered the way her heart swelled as people ran away from the long reach of William's infamous weed whacker, and how he would mow them down without mercy. But she also remembered how emotional William could be, how needy he could be, how when he got sad or upset, thousands of pores would simultaneously open up all over his body, as though he'd turned into a monster sprinkler. When Darla broke off their relationship, William's pores opened like literal floodgates as he cried. Gallons upon gallons of water puddled in the street around him, like William himself was melting. And while she felt sorry for William, she also felt pity, and pity was not a foundation to build a relationship (nor was a literal puddle of tears).

Every now and then she thought about going back to Barkerville. Seeing how William's life had progressed since her, seeing if he still missed her or if he'd just moved on and found someone else (though even if he had, he or she wouldn't be half the monster Darla was).

Part of her wanted to know if she was still capable of getting that intense tingling in her bone crown, like electricity tickling her skull when she was with someone she cared about. Most likely, William would be married with a litter of little monsters by now, happily settled down with some gorgeous young creature with nine perfect boobs and none of the emotional baggage Darla carried with her. They weren't right for each other. But sometimes companionship wasn't about the perfect fit, and sometimes a loose fit felt better than none at all.

"You need to move on," Dolores said. "I'm not trying to plan a wedding between you and Jerkvale. It's just…now there's another monster living and hunting here, *at* Clear Creek? Maybe this is a sign. An omen. Speaking of which, I'm pretty sure if you are interested in this monster, we could find an actual omen and possess him…"

"I'm as interested in Jarko Murkvale as I am in being impaled by a rusty fireplace poker," Darla said, her voice steely and resolute.

"I took one of those right in the liver," Dolores said. "Came down the chimney, had no idea they were already armed. They thought they killed me. Stupid teens. I decapitated three of them with one swing of my scourge."

"I guess what goes around comes around."

"I'm just saying you've never had much of a life outside of the hunt," Dolores said, sympathy in her eyes. Bright orange eyes, just like Darla. "Even when you were with William, there was a part of you that wasn't. I think you know what I mean."

Darla couldn't deny that. "I have Gretl," she said.

"Please don't get me wrong, hon. I love Gretl. She's like the little daughter who has a tiny little man living in her mouth that I never had. But you told me you don't get to see her as often since she met Hatchetman. And now they have a little monster on the way."

"I don't get to see her as often as I'd like. But I get to see her enough for me. Even if I'd *like* companionship, I don't *need* companionship."

"Gretl obviously found a purpose other than the hunt. There are plenty of monster moms who find time to raise kids *and* maim on a regular basis. You *can* have both, sweetie, if that's what you want."

"I'm not sure that's what I want."

"Maybe you do," Dolores said, arching her eyebrows, "but you just don't know it yet."

"Look at you," Darla said. "Lost ninety percent of your body weight and gained ninety percent more wisdom."

"Well, if this Jerko is really just a usurper and nothing more, then he has no right to Clear Creek. We Drakes built a legacy in this town. I hunted in this territory for fifty years. The only person who has a right to turn humans into Swiss cheese here is my daughter."

"So, what do you suggest I do?" Darla said.

"Simple. Find this sorry excuse for a monster and show him who the *real* Duchess of Death is. Sharpen your scourge and your wits and whip his sorry ass over to Clear Creek Lake."

Darla smiled. She'd never hunted a monster before. This was going to be fun.

Chapter 9

She waited atop the waterfall for three days. Still. Patient. *Maddeningly* patient.

She ate nothing. Didn't make a sound. Crouched in wait, not wanting to miss her moment. She knew Jarko was still in there because every now and then she would see a faint glow of orange and yellow through the water, and she knew he was starting a fire for either food or warmth. She was jealous. Especially on the second night when it rained. She would have given anything to be sitting by that fire, warming her hands over the flames, a fresh muskrat or even a strawberry Pop-Tart cooking over it. Provided Jarko wasn't there. Well, maybe if he was there, but in itsy bitsy pieces. That would have been perfect.

But to her disappointment, he never left the cave. He was patient. She'd give him that. Newbie monsters would hunt too often. They wanted to go out every day and raise hell, like they were trying to reach some invisible dismemberment quota. But hunt too often and you'd scare your prey away—sometimes permanently. Too many attacks over a short amount of time and people would just stay home, lock their doors, or, worst-case scenario, leave. The trick was to go on a hunt and then... wait. Waiting lulled the people in your territory into a false sense of security. Humans had short memories, and monsters had long lives.

What was that old saying? Shear a sheep once and you get to keep its skin. No, that wasn't it. You can shear a sheep many times, but only wear its skin as a hat once. No. Darla couldn't remember the saying. That's what she got for being homeschooled by a monster.

Perhaps she was hoping Jarko would come out to hunt over and over again, driving the Clear Creek community away, then get discouraged and leave for good without Darla having to intervene. But it seemed that while Jarko Murkvale was a lot of things—irritating, conceited, intrusive, dumb, shallow, tall, dark—he was not a moron. Sadly.

She wondered where he'd hunted before he came to Clear Creek. And, more importantly, why he'd left. Most monsters stayed in the same place their whole lives. They became synonymous with one area. Boogeymen weren't quite as scary if it felt like they were just road tripping. There had to be a very, very good reason for Jarko to have left...wherever he'd been. Darla felt torn. She wanted to know what had happened—but also didn't give a damn. She didn't want to ask him. Didn't want to give him the satisfaction of knowing she was curious about his past. Maybe there was a piece of lore hidden somewhere that would explain things, a parchment or a scroll or writing on a wall somewhere. Some way for her to get information on his past without getting it from *him*.

Finally, after seventy-two hours waiting (a *long* time to hold off on a bathroom break, as she didn't want to miss him), Jarko Murkvale stepped through the waterfall and into the stream beyond. Just the sight of him made Darla's black blood boil. And Darla's blood literally did boil. If she got angry enough—if prey was lucky enough to get in a shot, or Dolores wouldn't stop complaining about her lack of in-cave entertainment— Darla's blood would actually boil inside her, releasing tendrils of smoke into the air from her nostrils. At that moment, Darla saw a steady stream of gray mist curling into the night sky and realized she was angrier than she'd ever been in her entire life. Angrier even than the day her father left, because that was at least tinged with sadness and remorse. This, though, was pure, unfiltered *rage*.

Jarko was wearing his long, black overcoat, tentacled hands barely visible inside the cuffs, along with heavy boots that left large, deep depressions in the ground. His yellow eyes gleamed in the night. She had to assume he had night vision as well, which meant she had to be extra careful. This mission wasn't just about confronting Jarko. It was about sending a message.

He looked up into the sky. And didn't move. Darla was getting impatient. What the hell was he waiting for? Darla tried to see what he was looking at. A hang glider he could knock out of the sky? A bird he could grab and eat as a pre-hunt snack?

Then she realized he wasn't looking at anything in particular. He was just staring at the stars, as if mesmerized by them. The sky was beautiful, thousands of twinkling white dots like gems on a bed of velvet. Darla had rarely taken the time to notice such things. Always traversing. Always preoccupied by the hunt. Clear Creek was quite beautiful. She'd lived here her whole life and was just starting to realize that she'd taken it for granted. Jarko, though, had come here and instantly noticed it and embraced it.

Three days she'd waited for him to make a move. Three days she'd spent irritated and wet and hungry and chafing. But for some reason, looking at the sky, Jarko in the stream below her, Darla's annoyance had melted away.

Until one tentacled arm shot out from its sleeve, latched onto a nearby tree, and Jarko swung away, heading in the direction of Clear Creek. Darla's eyes narrowed.

The hunt was on.

CHAPTER 10

She traversed through the woods, Jarko in her sights as he swung from tree branch to tree branch like some sort of mutant octopus-monkey. If said monkey wore a rather fashionable black overcoat and left a faint trail of slime wherever it swung. Darla lessened her speed so as to stay behind the monster. She didn't know if Jarko had extrasensory hearing, and she didn't want to take a chance. He'd already surprised her once. She could chalk that up to sloppiness and underestimating him. A second time and she would start to lose self-respect.

His swinging was smooth and even. He only latched onto strong, thick branches or tree trunks. Sometimes birds would squawk and fly away as he disturbed their nests, squirrels jumping off the branches for dear life like they were fleeing a sinking ship. He acted like he owned the woods, and it made Darla hate him even more.

He was headed exactly where Darla thought he would go—

the Clear Creek campgrounds. Yet while she knew *where* he was going, she didn't know his methods. Every monster had different methods for their hunt. Some liked to leave mysterious objects or markings to raise the fear level. Some liked to drop into a crowded space and wreak havoc. Some liked to hide and then jump out at unsuspecting passersby. Some used knives or other sharp weapons, some used their appendages, some used whatever was handy (the Slicer was so fast that she could reportedly deal out five hundred paper cuts a minute using nothing but the ripped-out page from a book).

Darla liked the slow and steady approach. Surrounding her prey with strange noises and sounds. Raising the fear level bit by bit until it reached a boil, at which point she would show herself. She would always give her prey the chance to run, then traverse after them and do what she wanted. Sometimes, like with that doofus Kyle, they'd mangle themselves and save Darla the trouble of chasing them down. She was very curious to see what method Jarko Murkvale used on his hunt.

It took seven minutes for him to swing to the outskirts of Camp Clear Creek. Not too shabby. On a good day, Darla could do it in a shade over six. Jarko swung to the top of a high pine tree, wrapping one tentacle around a branch, leaning at a diagonal toward the ground. He was mostly shielded by the branches, hidden from view of anyone below.

Darla stayed low about twenty yards away. He didn't move. Neither did she. Immediately, she knew what kind of methods Jarko liked. And they were not subtle.

About twenty-five counselors were gathered around a roaring fire, apart from the cluster of cabins where the campers slept. She breathed a sigh of relief. Jarko wasn't going for the campers. She still didn't know if he was the kind of monster, like some, who tore everyone and anyone apart. Or if, like she, he focused his hunt on those who harmed others. She couldn't say for certain it was the latter, but it did seem to not be the former. The campers were easy prey. Helpless in their cabins and bunkbeds. But Jarko was ignoring them. One point for stinky octopus-man.

Some were drinking. Some were smoking. Some were making out or giving each other flirty eyes like they were about to start.

She recognized some of the counselors, back again from last year. They looked a year older. A little taller. Some of the boys with wisps of hair above their upper lip. The girls with new ear piercings, a newfound confidence. Many of the counselors were new. They looked unsure, hesitant. Looking for direction from their older counterparts.

She saw Randy Horvath and her eyes narrowed. Last summer, Randy, Kyle Browning, Lewis Cawthorn had taken several campers out overnight and left them in the woods without food, water, or any sort of directions. Thankfully, they'd returned the next day with just bites, scratches, and a severely twisted ankle.

But then the following week, Randy, Kyle Browning, and Lewis Cawthorn took three junior counselors out on a boat, then capsized it. One of the counselors hit her head on an oar hook and would have drowned if not for the camp medic seeing it happen. Following that, they'd been given the moniker of the Terrible Trio. Randy and Kyle blamed both events on Lewis, who was unfortunately fired before Darla had the chance to hunt him. And Kyle Browning, well, Darla tried to put the vision of her allowing Kyle to escape from her mind.

While Randy Horvath deserved a fate far worse than

maiming, his parents were both prominent bankers whose charitable donations to Clear Creek had helped keep the camp afloat. They made an ultimatum: if Randy was fired, or even disciplined, they would not only cease all donations, but sue to gain ownership of Clear Creek and turn the whole thing into a parking lot.

So Lewis had taken full blame, but Darla knew the truth. Randy and Kyle had not only been allowed to skate, but they were invited back. *With* a pay bump. Randy felt he was untouchable. It was up to Darla to show him how wrong he was. Randy Horvath was lucky he'd escaped the sting of Darla Drake's scourge. Unfortunately for Randy, his luck had run out.

Then she saw Jarko crouch down. His tentacled arms began to slowly extend. He looked like an animal—well, a human/octopus animal hybrid—about to pounce.

And then he did.

Jarko leapt high into the air, for a moment, his large form blotting out the pale white moon. He was graceful. Even elegant. Darla watched as he rose higher still, then fell downward straight from the sky like a meteor, landing directly into the roaring campfire, spattering sparks and wood everywhere.

Counselors fell backward in shock. Several screamed. Then Jarko slowly lifted his head, the black hood falling down to reveal his face, which bore a wolfish, almost charming half smile.

She had to give him credit. Jarko had style.

The counselors around the campfire froze in terror. The screams halted as if someone had pressed the pause button. Two long tentacles slithered out from Jarko's jacket sleeves. He slowly spun around, surveying the counselors. Then his smile disappeared and he said, "Let's play."

He swung his tentacles in a swooping, circular motion, knocking over half a dozen counselors and making others run into the woods, screaming like they were being followed by ravenous wolves. Then he spun faster and faster, like a human-tentacle food processor, whipping people to and fro.

Darla saw Randy Horvath pick up a flaming log from the pile, run up to Jarko, and smash him over the head with it.

The monster turned around, not even stunned, and said, "Hello, counselor."

Randy Horvath's lower jaw trembled. The log fell to the ground. Jarko wrapped a tentacle around Randy's waist and yanked the young man close to him, close enough to see his yellow eyes up close.

"Who...who are you?" Randy sputtered.

Jarko smiled. Prepared to speak. And that was when Darla made her move.

She leapt down from her tree and traversed into the middle of the campfire in milliseconds. Before Jarko could respond, she whipped her scourge into Jarko's arm, causing him to howl in pain and drop Randy Horvath.

He looked at Darla with a mixture of surprise, annoyance, and hate. She looked at him and offered the same half smirk that he had. Then she looked at Randy and said, "He's a nobody. I am Darla Drake. Duchess of Death. And I am the forever Creature of Clear Creek."

Darla traversed over to the tree line and whipped her scourge through the trunk of a pine tree, cutting it clean through. The tree toppled over and landed with a crash. The rest of the counselors ran screaming into the woods. Randy Horvath got to his feet, shaking his head.

"You..." he said, staring at Darla, eyes wide. "We thought

you were dead."

Darla let loose a full-throated laugh and began to spin her scourge. "Evil never dies," she said, then raised her scourge, ready to cleave Randy right in two. Thankfully, Randy got the hint and booked it into the night, the rest of the stragglers joining him. She could hear people shouting, "The Duchess of Death! Holy crap, she's back! Run!"

Darla smiled and felt a tear come to her eye.

Then Darla turned to face Jarko, again nursing his arm.

"What in the muskrat munching fuck are you doing?" Jarko said. "This is *not* your territory anymore, Duchess!"

"Those kids sure seemed to think it is."

"I don't give a goddamn *what* those kids think. You relinquished your rights to Clear Creek. This territory is *mine*."

"Not while I'm still alive," Darla said.

"Well, then," Jarko replied, "maybe we'll have to do something about that."

A tentacle shot from Jarko's wrist. Darla barely had time to sidestep it before it splintered a tree trunk behind her. She raised her arm to whip Jarko with her scourge, but the other tentacle swung low, sweeping Darla's feet out from under her.

She crashed to the ground, and for a moment saw nothing. Where had he gone?

Then she heard a faint *whoosh* and rolled to her right just as Jarko's heavy boots landed right where her head had been. Darla didn't hesitate, whipping her scourge and wrapping it around the monster's legs, and then yanking with all her strength.

Jarko lurched sideways and fell to the ground, dirt and grass spewing into the air as the breath was knocked from his lungs. He shot out a tentacle and wrapped it around Darla's neck. Darla released the scourge from his legs and whipped it hard, cinching it tight around Jarko's neck.

They lay there, side by side, each holding the other's neck. Then, to her surprise, Jarko laughed. It was a faint, coughing laugh, but still a laugh.

"Nobody is going to win this," he said. "You can't kill me. And I don't want to kill you."

"That right?" Darla said. "And why not?"

Jarko released his grip from Darla's neck. The tentacle retracted back into his sleeve.

"I came here to hunt," Jarko said. His voice was more solemn than Darla expected. "Not to kill you. Or even fight you. If anything, I respect you."

The words took Darla by surprise. Nothing about Jarko's actions had indicated respect.

"Now, please," he said, pointing to the whip wrapped around his neck. "Let's talk like civilized monsters."

Darla considered it for a moment. Then she pulled the scourge back, its whip leaving a deep purple gash in Jarko's neck which immediately began to heal.

He rubbed the wound and shook his head. "You're something, you know that?"

"You wanted to talk," Darla said. "Let's talk."

Jarko looked around. "Maybe not in the middle of the campgrounds where we just fought in front of a few dozen counselors and where in just a few minutes a whole bunch of law enforcement types will be here with guns. I just don't feel like dealing with the agita of bullet holes right now. I haven't even had coffee yet."

Darla thought for a moment. "Okay. I know a place. Just try to keep up. One thing, though."

"What's that?"

"I haven't decided whether or not I'm going to kill you."

"Fair enough," Jarko said with a smile. "All right, Duchess. Where are we go—?"

But Darla had already traversed into the woods. Jarko watched her for a moment, and then swung away into the night.

CHAPTER 11

Darla arrived at the swamp and took a seat on a fallen tree overlooking the murky greenish-blue water. Jarko swung in and landed atop a log opposite her mere moments later. He was fast.

"You can't traverse," Darla said.

Jarko shook his head and held out his arms, the tentacles retracting inside the sleeves of his black jacket.

"Nope. Only way I get around is these things," he said, gesturing to his hands, "and these," he raised his legs.

"What if you need to cross an, I don't know, desert. Or field. And you have nothing to swing from."

"Then it just takes a while," he said. "Thankfully, I'm caught up on my cardio. Speaking of which, traversing looks exhausting. Is it?"

"It's not tiring. It's more like...I can feel my body heating up. Like it's an engine running. If I use it for short bursts—a half mile, a mile—it's no biggie. Longer than that and it stings.

But that's it. No big deal."

Jarko nodded. "What's the longest distance you've ever covered with it?" he asked.

Darla thought for a moment. "A few years back, a counselor named Richie Witmer pushed a kid off the dock who couldn't swim, then left him. I hunted him that night. Turned out the dipshit had a motorcycle and managed to get to it while I was still enjoying the hunt. Led me maybe eight or so miles before I caught up to him. Let's just say his liver was found several counties over."

Jarko laughed. "You got a little vindictive streak in you, Duchess."

"Enough with the Duchess," Darla said. "I hate small talk. Remember, I didn't agree not to kill you."

"You didn't agree not to *try* to kill me," Jarko said.

"Intestine, intes*teen*," Darla said. "You need to leave Clear Creek. Tonight."

Jarko sighed and leaned back against a branch. It creaked under his weight.

"We've been over this. I'm not going anywhere. So, you can *try* to kill me, or you can cockblock my hunt every day for the rest of both of our lives. But I promise you, you'll get bored of it long before I will."

"Why are you being so stubborn?" Darla said.

"Me?" Jarko said. "You gave up on Clear Creek. You gave up on the hunt. You don't have the high ground here, Duchess."

Darla stood up and paced around her log. She ran her fingers over her bone crown. When she was little and needed to think, she would always slide her fingertips over the points, pressing down gently so she could feel them digging into her skin. The sensation would focus her. She found more answers from respecting and admiring the uniqueness of her own body than just about anywhere else in the world. Darla was one of a kind. It may have taken a while for her to understand that, but that realization meant everything.

"I need to know," Darla said, turning back to face Jarko. "Why did you come here?"

"Because Clear Creek was an available territory. And a good one at that. Campgrounds means you'll never run out of people. Like fish in a pond. This place just keeps restocking."

"I still don't understand why you needed to come," Darla said. "You must have hunted in a different territory before you came to Clear Creek. You're, what, eighty? Ninety?"

"Ninety? Wow, I really need to try a new moisturizing cream," Jarko deadpanned. "I'm thirty-eight."

"You are not. Let me cut you in half and count the number of rings."

"Trust me, Duchess. I have no reason to lie to you. Ever."

"Fine, then tell me the truth. Where were you before Clear Creek?"

Jarko's eyes narrowed. He looked down at the water. Kicked a rock, which flew into the air and narrowly missed hitting a bird perched in a nearby spruce.

"I don't want to talk about it," he said.

"You told me you have no reason to lie to me."

"I'm not lying. I just don't want to talk about it."

"Why not?"

"Seriously? You think saying 'why not' after I said I don't want to talk about it is going to suddenly make me talk about it?"

"Withholding information is the same as lying," Darla said.

"That's not true at all."

"My father knew he was going to leave us," Darla said. "He *withheld* that from my mother. From me. His secret was a lie."

"Not everything is as black and white as you want it to be. And neither am I."

Darla sighed. They sat there in silence, Darla unsure of what to say. Finally Jarko spoke.

"Speaking of questions, why are we at a swamp?" he said. "We could have gone back to your castle, or wherever it is the great Creature of Clear Creek dwells."

"You have a better chance of seeing me naked than you do of seeing where I live."

Jarko grinned. "Who says we can't do both?"

Darla groaned. "I think I just became the first monster in history to get the ick. I thought that was a human thing."

"What can I say. I'm a disruptor. But seriously. Swamp. Why?"

Darla sat back down. "My best friend and I used to come here all the time as girls. Gretl. Everyone knows her as the Gullet Gobbler."

"I've read about her," Jarko said. "Her Gobbler is quite deadly. Gross, but deadly."

"We still meet here from time to time. It's peaceful. Secluded. The only way humans can get here is if they row through several miles of sweltering gunk while being bombarded by mosquitos the size of a sedan. So, when Gretl and I meet here, we know we'll be left alone."

"So you're saying you wanted to make sure we'd be left alone."

Darla shrugged.

"Do you two still come here?" he asked.

"Not as often as we used to."

"Why not?"

Darla sighed. "Lives take different paths, I guess. She's settling down, found the monster of her dreams, now pregnant with her first, blah, blah, blah. If monsters had Instagram, her feed would be sickeningly sweet."

"You almost sound resentful."

"I don't know. Maybe? I was there before Tyrone. But Gretl found her monster. Their family is growing. And I'm on the outside watching and I feel like I practically have to beg her to stay a part of her existence. It's like, once you find the life you want, you don't have time for the life that came before it.

From the corner of her eye, Darla could have sworn she saw Jarko nod.

"So, what?" he said. "You never wanted that? A mate and a kid and all that?"

"I don't know," Darla said. "To be honest, I never really thought about it growing up. All I was taught to care about was the hunt. I spent all my time becoming the perfect hunter. I didn't want to be a nepo baby monster. I wanted to *earn* the title of Duchess of Death."

"You did," Jarko said. "And then some."

Darla was taken aback. Was that reverence in Jarko's voice?

"What do you mean by that?"

"I mean your mom made a name for herself. But you took it a step further. Older monsters may be considered legends, your mom included, but they were kind of rough around the edges. Their hunts were never clean. Too much collateral damage. Hunted too many innocents. And yes, I include people having premarital sex as innocents. I mean, did your mom's generation *really* need to skewer two consenting adults with a fishing pole just because they wanted to bone before they got a marriage license?"

"*Thank* you," Darla said. "That's what I keep telling her. You can scare everyone, you *should* scare everyone, but only kill the assholes. You want them to both fear *and* respect you. And nobody will respect you if you pluck out the eyes of some poor teenage girl just because she wanted to take some mushrooms and watch the solar system turn into a giant unicorn on the hood of her Camry with her boyfriend."

"If you notice," Jarko said, "my body count is still at zero. I haven't decided which, if any, of these kids deserve to have their head squeezed off."

As if to prove his ability, Jarko shot out a tentacle, wrapped it around the trunk of a slim tree, and shattered it with one squeeze.

"So why didn't you do that to me?" Darla said.

"I didn't come here to fight you," Jarko said. "I just want to hunt and be left alone."

The way he said those last two words, *left alone*, put a hollow feeling into Darla's stomach.

"You really want to be left alone? I don't think you mean that."

"I mean that more than anything I've ever said before in my life."

She felt an unexpected, unwanted, and yet intense desire to know more. Where Jarko had been before he came to Clear Creek. Why he wanted to be left alone. Darla had her issues, sure, but she never, ever wanted to be alone. And the way he said it didn't feel defiant, like he was a lone wolf preferring to live by his own rules. It sounded sad. It sounded resigned. It sounded...broken.

For just a fleeting moment, Darla wanted to climb inside

Jarko Murkvale's head, rummage around, and see what lay behind those piercing yellow eyes. She wanted to place her hand on his face, look into those eyes, and swim in them.

Stop thinking about his eyes, Darla thought. *They're not even that piercing.*

But the more she tried to convince herself, the more she realized she was lying to herself.

"Why are you staring at me? Do I have a bone in my teeth or something?" Jarko said. "I had a muskrat for lunch and thought I brushed and flossed."

"No. Sorry. Just zoned out for a second."

"Listen. Duchess," Jarko said. "I respect everything you've done. But I'm not leaving."

"Neither am I."

"Then I guess we're both screwed," he said.

"So is Clear Creek," Darla said. "I've seen you hunt twice now. You're sloppy. You make a spectacle out of yourself, flinging your arms everywhere like an octopus on meth. You know what you remind me of? One of those weird tall inflatable floppy guys you see on the side of the road at car dealerships. You're not scary. You're just a glorified rodeo clown in a cooler jacket."

"Well, excuse me, Duchess," Jarko said. "The eighteenth century called and it said it wants skulking around in the darkness and creaking floorboards and using whatever hot garbage your breath smells like to rattle curtains back. It's a new era. I'm a monster for the new millennium. You're stuck in the past. You're as scary as a loud fart under the covers."

A moment ago, Darla was transfixed by Jarko's eyes. Imagined touching his face, feeling the grayish skin, feeling his tentacle…

No.

He was an intruder. A menace. The only thing she wanted to do to his face was slash it with her scourge.

Then it occurred to her. Jarko might be stubborn, but he also had pride. If she could break that, she might just be able to get what she wanted.

"I have a proposition for you," Darla said.

Jarko's eyes perked up.

"I'm listening," he said.

"I have my methods. You have yours. My methods are like a knife's edge, delicate and refined. Yours are like a, well, like a bunch of tentacles flailing around like an octopus caught in a blender."

"That sounds less like a proposition and more like an insult."

"I'm getting to that," she said. "Here's my proposition. We each participate in one hunt using the other's methods. You say I'm too methodical? Then you hunt by my refined methods."

"And then you hunt using my...*less* refined methods."

"Precisely," Darla said.

"Be careful what you wish for, Duchess," Jarko said. "My limbs aren't the only things that are adaptable to their environment."

"I'm not too concerned. I think you're an out-of-control amateur who wouldn't know a real hunt if it snuck up behind him and lopped his head clean off."

"Your confidence will be your downfall," Jarko said.

"Whichever one of us does a better job hunting with the other's methods," Darla said, "will be the *sole* monster hunting in Clear Creek."

Jarko raised his eyebrows. "And the loser?"

"Loser leaves town. Forever."

She caught a twitch in Jarko's eye, something that told her he wasn't one to back down from a fight, but that he knew Darla wasn't a monster to be taken lightly.

"So, I hunt using your methods," he said, "meaning slow and boring."

"No. Meaning you ratchet up the fear and tension before finally unleashing your meager talents on your terrified prey, making the whole endeavor that much more malevolent and fulfilling and delicious."

"Fulfilling and delicious?" Jarko said. "You should be selling salad dressing instead of hunting."

"You perform a hunt the way I say. Meaning planned out and executed properly. And then I'll do one the way you say. Meaning slapdash and chaotic and messy."

"You mean thrilling and spectacular and explosive."

"And you sound like you should be selling used cars. Or condoms."

"So, if I execute a hunt your way better than you execute a hunt my way, you'll leave Clear Creek. For good."

"That's the deal. But there's a better chance of Godzilla fitting through the eye of a sewing needle than of you beating me at a hunt."

"Careful, Duchess," Jarko said. "Don't take this—or me—lightly. Because if you lose, you lose Clear Creek. For good."

"And when *you* lose—notice how I say *when* and not *if*—you'll just be another loser. A sad sack monster traveling from territory to territory with no home, no family, and no legacy."

The smile disappeared from Jarko's face. His brow furrowed. His thin lips pursed.

He held out a tentacled hand.

"You're sure about this," Jarko said. "The Drake family is legendary in Clear Creek. You'd risk that just to prove a point?"

It's not just to prove a point, Darla thought. *It's about proving that I'm still one of the most feared monsters around.*

"I'm sure," she said, her eyes meeting Jarko's. Neither of them blinked. "I just hope you bought a return ticket to wherever it is you came from."

"I don't plan on going back there," Jarko said. "Ever."

"I'll see about that."

Then she held out her hand and shook his, their grips firm and resolute.

"Deal," she said.

"Deal," he replied.

She could see resolve in his yellow eyes, but there was something else behind them. A twinge of anger. She'd clearly struck a nerve with her comments. She just didn't know which ones exactly, or why. But there was something else in his eyes. Behind the resolve and anger. She couldn't be certain, but it might have been a twinkle of fear.

"Meet me here tomorrow night," Darla said. "One a.m. sharp."

"I'll be here at twelve thirty."

"Great. Just one more thing."

"What?"

"Tell me how to get this goddamn slime off my hand."

CHAPTER 12

Darla and Gretl sat by the shore of Maker's Marsh, where Darla had just caught her best friend up on the arrival of Jarko Murkvale and their agreement. As expected, Gretl took the news calmly, with thoughtful consideration.

"Holy Bubbling Babadook," Gretl said. "You did *what*?"

She screamed so loud that the Gobbler in her mouth accidentally dropped a trout back into the marsh, where it swam away quickly, knowing how lucky it was not to be currently digesting in a monster's stomach.

"I made a bet with Jarko. And whichever monster loses has to leave Clear Creek."

"Okay," Gretl said, her normally pinkish skin turning redder, "let me get this straight. I want you to respond with yes and no. And only yeses and nos."

"Okay, but in my defense—"

"I said only yeses and nos!"

The Gobbler inside her mouth shot out and wagged a tiny

finger at Darla before going back inside.

"Okay. Go."

"Another monster is in Clear Creek."

"Yes, and—"

"What did I say?"

"Yes."

"Named Marko—"

"Jarko."

"Jarko Murkwater."

"Murkvale."

"Jarko Murkvale. And he's staked a claim to Clear Creek."

"Yes."

"And you met this guy."

"Yes."

"And he grabbed you by the neck with his tentacle hand and pulled you into his cave and you two fought and you whipped him with your scourge."

"Yes."

"Okay. That's kind of hot."

"Hot? I wanted to kill him."

"But you didn't. Think about that. There's a fine line between murder and sexual tension."

"Is there really?"

"Um, *yes*. My first date with Tyrone, he took me out to a college party in the middle of a cornfield and we chased around a bunch of frat douchebags. It was super fun, and afterward we made out bigtime in the middle of a raging fire because one of the frat boys tossed a lit cigarette at Tyrone thinking it would, I don't know, light him on fire or something? But the moron missed and accidentally lit up the whole cornfield and I will admit that it was pretty romantic once all the kids ran away.

Something about all the running and screaming and seeing Tyrone with his hatchet...ugh. Just thinking about it gets my blood pumping over ten beats a minute."

"The man does know how to wield a sharp implement."

"I love a guy who takes his work seriously. At first, I was annoyed because, I don't know, I wanted a little privacy on our first date. I mean, do we *really* need to be scaring the bejesus out of kids right now? I don't need to bring my work home, you know?"

"But you ended up liking it?"

"Yeah. By the end it felt like he was sharing a part of himself with me. Like, this is who I am and what I do and this is how terrifying I can be. Some monsters never want you to see that side of themselves."

"William never wanted me to watch him hunt," Darla said. "I thought I was helping him. Pushing him. But he said it made him nervous. If I made any noise he would get nervous and all his pores would open up. Nobody is scared of a monster who looks like they've sprung a leak."

"William Wendell was a good guy," Gretl said, "but he wasn't right for you."

"You were always nice to him."

"Of course I was! He was your boyfriend!"

"Don't call him that. You know I don't like labels."

"You have, like, nine nicknames. Duchess of Death, Creature of Clear Creek, Chick of Ultimate Disemboweling, She Who Cutteth Off Limbs. I feel like I'm forgetting a few."

"You made up most of those."

"Yeah, but they're still kind of catchy, right?"

"Labels are fine when we're talking about scaring the crap out of pockmarked teens. I'm all in favor of good marketing.

I just don't like using labels for monsters I'm dating. And, honestly, who really cares? It's not like there's a financial benefit to calling someone my quote, unquote boyfriend. It's not like we file our taxes jointly. Or pay taxes at all."

"I think all of that is just a big excuse. I think the Creature of Clear Creek just doesn't like to be tied down."

"Anyone tries to tie me down, they'll lose any and all appendages they try to tie me down with."

"You know what I mean, Darla," Gretl said, rolling her eyes. "You're just looking for any reason not to commit. *That's* what I mean about not wanting to be tied down."

"I'd be more than happy to tie Jarko down. To a railroad track."

"See? You're already thinking about tying him down."

"Yes, in the hopes he gets bisected by a train. So?"

"You, my dear, are flirting."

"Stop it," Darla said. "Talking about bisecting someone under thousands of tons of steel is *not* flirting."

"Depends who you're talking about bisecting," Gretl said. "There is a very fine line between murder and sexual tension."

"There's no tension. I just want to get rid of him."

"So, you really don't have an MFU?" Gretl said. "You had no idea that after six months of inactivity a monster technically relinquishes the rights to their hunting ground?"

"Do you think I'd be going through all this if I knew?" Darla replied. "And, to be fair, my mom turned them away thinking they were Jehovah's Witnesses."

"She's so old-fashioned," Gretl said.

"You have no idea. Any time I tell her that I saw two counselors making out, she wants to know why I didn't disembowel them on the spot."

"Um, because human birth rates are already plummeting and they don't need our help lowering them even further by scaring everyone into celibacy," Gretl said.

Darla brushed her scourge along the ground, making overlapping circles with the braids. As a girl, she would sit on the ground for hours, making pictures in the dirt of her favorite monsters, trying to recreate some of the most iconic stories in monster lore. She loved being a monster. More than anything in the world. She loved being a part of this world, of creating a legacy, of being feared by humans and respected and revered by her peers. How was that not enough? Gretl wasn't half the monster Darla was, and she was content. It wasn't fair.

"So you knew about it, the rule," Darla said. "That if I was inactive for six months, I could lose Clear Creek."

"Of course I did!" Gretl replied. "And I assumed you did too! You can request a continuance, another six months, for monsternity leave, mental health issues, etcetera. But it's a *ton* of paperwork. I figured you had your reasons. But if you just needed some time, you should have requested a leave. At least then you wouldn't have to worry about Dorkwood coming in and taking over Clear Creek."

"I would have if I'd known about it," Darla said. "I swear. Sometimes it's like my mom has lost her mind."

"I mean... Technically..." Gretl said. "So you fight this guy Jarko. Who, by the sound of it, is not *not* hot."

"I never said he was hot."

"No, but the way you described him, with intense yellow eyes and sharp cheekbones and tentacles that—"

"I did *not* describe it the way you're describing it."

"You might think you didn't, but you totally did. And so you fight this not *not* hot monster to a standstill, then interrupt his hunt and fight *again*? Oh my god, the tension is *killing me*."

"There's no tension!" Darla said. "He tried to pop my head off like a pimple with his tentacles, and I tried to sever his stupid gray head with my scourge."

"But you didn't," Gretl said. "I wonder why that is."

"Because monsters don't kill other monsters," Darla said. "Period. Besides, this is a way more respectable way to settle the issue."

"Also way sexier," Gretl said. "You're one of the most competitive monsters I've ever met. And it sounds like Jarko isn't going to back down. It's like that famous saying: the unstoppable fork meets the immobile object."

"You need to read more," Darla said.

"And you need to leave your cave more," Gretl said. "Gosh, even *before* your nervous breakdown—"

"It wasn't a nervous breakdown, Gret."

"Fine. Your *sabbatical*, even before, you never did much of anything."

"That's not true. I went out plenty."

"After your mother lost her head—"

"Technically, she lost the rest of her. She still has her head."

"Speaking of which, did you tell her about this plan?"

"I did."

"And? I can't imagine Dolores Drake was too thrilled with it."

"No. She wasn't. But I think part of her maybe was a little bit. She knows I'm competitive. Maybe she's hoping this gets me back into the hunting frame of mind."

"That wouldn't be such a bad thing. I'm glad you're doing it."

"Why?"

"After your mom got...separated...you broke up with William pretty much instantly."

"That relationship wasn't going to last."

"Maybe not. But I don't even think you waited a day. Breaking up with him wasn't about him. It was about you."

"Monsters aren't allowed to have closure?"

"I don't think you've had closure on anything in your whole life," Gretl said.

They sat there, silent, the words hanging over them.

"After that," Gretl said, "it felt like you just kind of withdrew. I'm your best friend and I practically had to hurl boulders at your cave to get you to acknowledge me, let alone hang out. And you definitely didn't make any efforts to meet anyone new."

"I had my mom to look after," Darla said. "And I had to keep hunting. That was all our family had left. How was I supposed to find time for dating *and* dismemberment?"

"Monsters find the time," Gretl said. "I did."

"Well, good for you," Darla said sarcastically. "I did go to a few Monster Mashes."

"Yeah. And you'd sit in a corner of the quarry drinking fermented swamp juice while looking like you'd rather have WereWalter gnawing on your feet than spend another minute talking to other monsters. Some of whom, you might be shocked to believe, are actually fun and cool and find time for dating and dismemberment."

"Wait, I always thought WereWalter gnawed on people's feet because that's just how he flirted."

"I think it's both? I know he dated Henna the Hateful Howler Monkey for a little while, and it *may* have ended after he chomped off two of her toes."

"I don't know, Gret, every time I went to one of those, I just felt like I should have been doing something else. I had all these responsibilities and I was sitting there getting tipsy when my mom was there alone. You don't know what it was like for her after my dad left."

"For you too," Gretl said. "Don't forget what it was like for you too."

Darla stayed silent. Looked down at the swamp. She could feel the fish swimming through the water. The frogs watching Gretl, waiting to see if her Gobbler would shoot out and try to make them an instant meal.

"Look, Dar," Gretl said. "I get that you want to be daughter of the year. But you can't live your life only for other people."

"Easy for you to say. Your parents both have their legs."

"I'm just saying that maybe part of the reason you had your *not breakdown* is because you didn't know who *you* were."

"That's ridiculous. I'm Darla Drake, the Duchess of Death."

"Yes. You are. Everyone in the world knows who Darla Drake is. But do *you* know who Darla Drake is?"

CHAPTER 13

Darla arrived at Maker's Marsh an hour early. To her great annoyance, Jarko was already there, waiting for her. He had a smile on his face like it had been plastered there for hours, just waiting for her to show up knowing it would make her blood boil. Literally. Darla could actually feel the temperature of her blood rising, and if she didn't do the breathing exercises her mother had taught her, steam would start emanating from her nose and ears. Which was far more humorous than threatening. And Darla would rather be pecked to death by Gretl's Gobbler than entertain Jarko Murkvale at the expense of her dignity.

Not only was Jarko there early, he was nonchalantly juggling half a dozen frogs, flipping them into the air with his tentacles, catching them before they hit the ground, and then tossing them back up again. When he saw Darla, he winked, continuing his juggling act, not even watching the amphibians as they came closer than they knew to a terrible (and embarrassing) death.

"I'm glad to see you here early and practicing for your secondary career working as a clown at children's birthday parties," Darla said. "Though little Jimmy and Sally might run away screaming when you get hungry and munch on one of your tools."

Jarko scoffed and one by one tossed each frog back into the marsh, watching them swim away before their captor changed his mind.

"If you think I eat frog, you are sadly mistaken, Duchess," he said.

"You live in a cave behind a waterfall. I've seen it. You don't have a fridge, and there's no Kwik-E-Mart near you. Plus, you're as subtle as a fireworks display, so if you'd been robbing the camp canteen or kitchen, I would have heard the screams from my house. And I live behind a literal rock."

"Just because you eat like a hobo monster doesn't mean I have to as well."

"What's that supposed to mean?"

"I don't eat raw frogs or stolen pantry items from a summer camp. I actually know how to cook, Duchess. Don't you?"

Darla was speechless. She looked at his tentacles, how they'd spun around almost gracefully at the campground. How they'd nimbly flung the fearful frogs into the air and caught them without smooshing one into frog pâté.

"I, um…I made oatmeal once. Okay, it was from a packet. Okay, I dumped it into a puddle of cave water and just drank that. But that counts as cooking."

"I don't know if you saw it," Jarko said, "but I just threw up in my mouth."

"Delightful."

"I mean, what do you do, just eat stale Pop-Tarts for

sustenance?" Jarko waited. Then he sighed. "Your silence tells me you do. Great Godzilla's eyeball, Duchess, I thought you were a *modern* monster."

"I am," she said. "My mother never cooked. So I never learned how."

"Neither of my parents cooked," Jarko said. "I taught myself. You live your life tethered to the way you were raised to do things instead of doing things the way *you* want to do them, you'll never really be living your own life."

Darla flinched. Jarko seemed to get he may have struck a nerve.

"Okay. We can insult each other all night, but I don't think that's what we really came here to do."

"Actually, I wouldn't mind insulting you all night," Darla said. "But you're right. Thanks for coming. I wasn't sure you would show up."

"I'm a monster of my word," Jarko said.

"Ah, right. You're one of those *respectable* monsters."

"Damn right I am." Jarko put his tentacled hands together and cracked his nonexistent knuckles. Instead, it sounded like he was pressing two wet sponges together. The sound was, frankly, rather gross. "So, Duchess, what's the plan?"

"Tonight, we'll be hunting a counselor named Randy Horvath," Darla said. "You met him briefly the other night when you did your octopus whirlwind thing in the middle of the campground. He and another counselor named Lewis Cawthorn nearly killed a few kids. Lewis got fired. Randy got promoted. So, he's already primed for the hunt."

Jarko rubbed his hands together with glee. "Sounds great. Tell me more."

"Randy is the counselor for the Starfish group at Camp

Clear Creek. And he's a bully. And I *hate* bullies."

"So, what's the plan? Crash through the window and filet him with a spoon? Break through the floor beneath him, pull him into the basement, hang him on a hook, and turn his insides out? Ooh, I know. Zip him up inside his sleeping bag and wallop him against a tree trunk forty or fifty times until he's basically tenderized. Which one, Duchess?"

"None of them."

Jarko's smile disappeared. "None of them?"

"No. Remember. You're hunting how *I* hunt. Slow. Methodical. Raising the tension. Raising the fear. The hunt is far more fulfilling when you bring the fear to a boil and *then* strike."

"To be honest, Duchess, that sounds...boring. Like, why waste all that time when I can wrap one arm around him and his bed, then use the other to swing high into the air and drop him from a really, really high height?"

"You'll have your chance to do things your way," Darla said. "Remember. If you can't do this, you're out of Clear Creek."

Jarko nodded. "A deal is a deal. I'll follow your lead."

"Okay. Stay quiet. I'll traverse over to the cabin grounds. You follow me with your octopus monkey swinging."

"My drift," Jarko said.

"I'm sorry?"

"It's not octopus monkey swinging. I call it my drift. As in, I drift through the trees."

"Huh," Darla said. "That's actually not bad."

Jarko smiled. It was an honest, genuine, surprised smile. Not a smirk. It took Darla aback. He actually looked...cute.

She shook it off. Too much time spent with Gretl.

"Follow me. And try not to rip any trees down while you're

drifting."

Darla began her traversal, zooming through the woods, her green tunic flowing as she hovered barely half an inch above the ground, the grass tickling the sides of her feet, twigs tugging at the cloth wrapped around her legs. She didn't go as fast as she could. She didn't want to lose Jarko, then have to wind back, risk him making a grand old mess of the woods and putting the camp on high alert before they even got to Randy's cabin.

She looked behind her. Her heart sank. She saw nothing. Jarko wasn't there. Had he already fallen behind so much? She felt bad for him. This sad monster, unable to keep pace with—

"Hey, Duchess," came Jarko's voice from above her. Darla looked up. He was drifting through the trees above her, swinging from branch to branch effortlessly, each tentacle latching on and swinging him forward with an odd sense of grace. "There a reason you're going so slow?"

Darla felt her blood temperature rise so fast a faint wisp of smoke snaked out of her nostrils and wafted into the sky.

"Whoa, easy there, Smaug," Jarko said. "Just making sure you didn't sprain an ankle or something."

"I do not sprain my ankles," Darla said. She traversed faster through the forest, faster than she usually went, so fast she barely had time to avoid the trees and rocks. She looked up. Saw Jarko drifting. He was struggling to keep up, his swings a little more erratic, but he was still right there above her, matching her pace. She could hear him breathing heavy. His tentacles barely gripping branches that were further and further away. She smiled. Jarko talked a big game, but he—

And then Darla's face smacked right into a tree branch, knocking her dizzy and probably coming close to making her more like her mother than she ever wanted. Darla righted herself, shook off the stars, and kept going.

"You all right there, Duchess?" Jarko shouted from above. "Almost took your head off there. Want me to take the lead?"

Darla didn't respond. Another tendril of smoke wafted into the air.

Finally, they arrived at Camp Clear Creek. Darla traversed behind the cafeteria, abandoned and dark at this time of night. Jarko landed beside her, his arms retracting into his sleeves. He pointed to a spot on his forehead, above his right eye.

"You got a nasty ding there, Duchess," he said. "I could go find some ice for you."

"I'm fine."

"No, really. I saw you go headfirst into that tree. Maybe we should take you to the ER, make sure you didn't suffer any permanent damage. Do you have health insurance? There's probably a walk-in clinic somewhere around here..."

"If you don't stop talking right now, I'm going to rip your arms off and serve them as sushi."

"Shutting up before I become a fancy meal," Jarko said, the smirk returning to his face, along with a twinkle in his yellow eyes. The look wasn't mean or condescending, it was...funny. It broke through Darla's defenses and made her head stop smarting.

"It was pretty clumsy," she said.

"It was," Jarko agreed. "If it makes you feel better, when I was first learning how to drift, I attached to a tree branch that was covered in sap. My grip stuck to it and didn't release when I tried, so I ended up flipping end over end about thirty feet in the air. I landed on a pinecone. And it was not horizontal at the moment of impact."

Darla snorted so hard a small black rock shot out of her

nose and pinged off the side of the cafeteria.

"Sorry," she said. "When I get worked up, my blood boils, and if it cools down too fast, it can solidify."

"So, basically, you sneeze volcanic rock," Jarko said.

"Pretty much."

"You should have opened up a souvenir shop. People would pay good money for Darla Drake snot rocks."

"Enough. Let's focus," Darla said. "Randy Horvath's cabin is right down at the end of this gravel trail. He shares it with one other counselor, Ramesh Agarwal. But it's Thursday night, and on Thursday, Ramesh goes camping with his girlfriend, Sarika Chatterjee, out at Turkey Rock Park. They don't come back until sunrise. So Randy is all alone for the next four and a half hours, give or take."

Jarko rubbed his hands together, his eyes glowing. "This is so exciting," he said. "I've never done this kind of hunt. I would have turned that cabin into my own personal maelstrom by now."

"Which, I'm sure, is loads of fun. But I think when you take your time, you'll see how satisfying it is when the whole hunt comes together."

"I'm all yours, Duchess."

Darla felt her face redden. Thankfully, they rarely changed the light bulbs around camp, so Jarko couldn't see her complexion change in the darkness.

"I have a checklist," Darla said, composing herself. "When I start a hunt, I go one by one. Humans are largely predictable, but you always need to be on your toes, just in case. Some scare easier, some harder. Some run. Some try to fight."

"I'd like to see them try," Jarko said.

"Careful," Darla said. "My mother was one of the most

feared monsters of her day. But she let her guard down once and now she never has to worry about clipping her toenails again."

"I hear you."

"Do you?" Darla said. "Because one wrong move and you could be on the receiving end of a—"

Jarko snapped to face Darla. There was something in his eyes, something both wild and pained that told her to stop talking. That her warning was not only received, but understood in a way she couldn't fully understand.

"I got it," Jarko said with a gravelly whisper. "Don't say it again."

She nodded. "Okay. You got it. Let's begin. Step one. You have to wake the victim."

Jarko smiled and raised his tentacles.

"But you want to do it *gently*," she added. "The key is waking them while making them think they were awakened by something that can be explained rationally."

"Like a tree trunk through the roof."

Darla smacked her head. "How could a tree trunk through the roof be explained rationally?"

Jarko thought for a moment. "Tsunami."

Darla nodded at him and cocked her head. "We're on a *lake*."

"Okay. Maybe not a tsunami."

"Maybe think about things that can happen outside of, you know, a natural disaster. Smaller things. I like to start by rattling the windows. Maybe one good thump against the cabin wall. Something that will wake them up, get their heart beating faster, but subtle enough they can blame it on the wind or an animal and try to fall back to sleep."

"And then?" Jarko said impatiently. He was into this. Darla

liked that.

"Then you ramp things up. Most of these cabins have lights on the porch. Smash one."

"Go on," Jarko said.

"Something like that will get their attention. They won't go right back to sleep. Usually, they'll want to investigate. They'll step out onto the porch to see what might have done the damage."

"And *that's* when you squeeze their neck until their head pops off like a grape."

Darla sighed. "No. You're still just ramping up their fear. Let them go back inside. Let them think those two occurrences are just a coincidence. Maybe they don't believe it, but they convince themselves of it because the alternative is too terrible to comprehend."

"I like terrible," Jarko said. Darla was amused. This fearsome monster was acting like a puppy being taught how to play fetch for the first time. It was even endearing. "Then what?"

"Odds are they won't try to go back to sleep," Darla said. "They'll be too ramped up. They don't *really* believe it's a coincidence. So they'll leave the lights on. Get under the covers, but they'll keep their eyes open. Try to take their mind off it with a book or an iPad. But they're waiting for the next bad thing to happen."

"And then?"

"And then you give it to them. But you start to ramp things up. If they've turned the lights on, you might cut the power. If they're sitting up in bed, now you can, you guessed it, toss a branch through a window."

Jarko nodded, eyes wide, irises gleaming yellow like

they were small stars embedded in his gray face. They were mesmerizing. Darla had to force herself to concentrate. She could hear Gretl's voice in her mind, how she was monster crazy as a girl, always falling for the guy with the most scales or with the largest wingspan. Until she met Tyrone and fell head over talons, she figured Gretl would bounce around her whole life. But then she met the right one and—*poof*—she was done for.

But this was not a monster she could look at that way. He was an interloper. A thief. She was going to run circles around him and send him away from Clear Creek—with prejudice. When Darla was done with him, nobody would ever know the name Jarko Murkvale.

But she was going to do it fair. She was going to give Jarko a hunting chance.

"Branch through a window," he said, nodding. "I can do that."

"By that point, he'll know this isn't a coincidence. This can't be explained. And it's definitely not random. Something is *coming* for him."

"This is delightful," Jarko said.

"We haven't even begun," Darla said. "Once he's good and terrified, he'll look to get away."

"Out the front door," Jarko said.

"Probably not," Darla said. "I've calculated that only about twenty percent of them try to run through the front door. Remember, you just shattered the light. They assume something is out there. They'll most likely try to go out the back. But be prepared either way. You have to be quick. You have to be nimble. Are you capable of being nimble without, you know, breaking the world?"

"Duchess," Jarko said, letting his tentacles extend ever so slowly, holding them out for her to see. "You ain't seen nothing yet."

"Then let's go hunting."

CHAPTER 14

Darla traversed over to the arts and crafts pavilion, which overlooked the six cabins in the Starfish group: four camper cabins, two counselor cabins. Randy Horvath's cabin was on the north end, next to the tennis courts. Darla watched intently. She didn't know where Jarko was. She didn't know where or how he was starting. Whether he would instantly make an enormous mess of things, or if he had listened and taken in her instructions.

The camp was quiet. Darla listened. She could sense faint vibrations in the cabins, as the campers' hearts beat slow and steady. She turned toward Randy's cabin. Slow. Steady. She wondered what Jarko had in store.

Then she heard it. The faintest rattling sound. It sounded almost like raindrops. Something pitter-pattering on the wooden sides of Randy's cabin. What was that? She strained to listen. A minute later, she could sense Randy's heart rate slowly creep upward. It was Jarko. He was using his tentacle fingers to *tap, tap, tap* around the cabin walls. Just heavy and consistent enough that Randy would know it wasn't rain or rocks.

Then the tapping stopped. All was quiet. Then Darla saw a light. A flashlight, she believed. Its beam shining through the window of the cabin. Then the light began to circle the cabin. Darla could just make out Jarko's figure as he swung his way around the cabin sides, like some sort of strange, hyperspeed lizard, the light circling the cabin windows almost like an alien ship was landing.

Darla heard a clatter, and the light flicked off. The clatter had come from inside the cabin. No doubt Randy had jolted out of bed and knocked something over. He was scared now.

Then Darla realized something: her own heart was beating fast. She counted. Twenty beats per minute. She laughed to herself. Her heart hadn't beat that fast in a long time. Maybe it was luck, or maybe Jarko actually had some skills.

Darla heard footsteps inside the cabin. The steps went to the windows at the east end. Then west. South. Then to the front door. Randy was petrified. Trying to find out where the light had come from and where it had gone. He knew there was no rational explanation. There was something out there. Something watching him. Maybe even something hunting him...

Then there was an enormous crash as a tree branch shattered the window right where Randy stood. The counselor screamed loud enough to stir Dolores's detached body, wherever it was buried.

Darla inched forward. She had a huge grin on her face. She'd watched hunts before. Gretl's were particularly enjoyable, especially the moment when she hovered over a downed victim, opened her mouth, and her Gobbler shot out, ready to either pluck out the victim's eyes, gouge their throat, or, if Gretl was in a more playful mood, just honk their nose.

William was hit or miss. Darla had wanted to be a supportive girlfriend and attend his hunts. But the first time she went with him, staying out of sight atop a telephone pole, the victim asked William (holding his weed whacker) if he was there to plant shrubs. Presumably humiliated at the knowledge that a) the victim did not know who he was, and b) his girlfriend had witnessed this humiliation, William's pores opened up and turned the ground into a literal puddle before having to chase down the very scared and very confused victim with his whacker.

Jarko did not seem to have that...whacker problem. He was playing Randy Horvath like an instrument, dialing up the tension and fear. And now he had Randy right where he wanted him. Darla was anxious to see how he followed through.

Boom, boom.

Darla stood up. It sounded like two thunderclaps at the same time.

Boom, boom.

There it was again. She peered at the cabin, her night vision illuminating the scene. Jarko was standing at the rear end of the cabin. Both of his arm tentacles were fully extended to fifteen, twenty feet. He was spreading his arms wide, like he was opening up for the mother of all hugs, then he swung his arms together, slamming them against the walls of the cabin.

Boom, boom.

The sound was deafening. It was terrifying. It was original. And Darla freaking *loved* it.

After the fifth *boom, boom*, the front door of the cabin opened and Randy Horvath, wearing nothing but boxer shorts, stumbled out into the darkness, screaming like he'd fallen front-first onto a cactus. He leapt off the front porch onto the ground, and immediately howled, likely now regretting not putting on socks or shoes before deciding to jaunt off into the forest.

Suddenly, one massively long tentacle shot out of the darkness, looped around Randy's legs, and pulled them out from under him. The counselor fell face-first into the dirt with a *whump*. Then the tentacle retracted into the night.

Randy stood up, shaking. He spun around, searching for where it had come from. Jarko was being patient. Darla didn't think he had it in him.

Then she saw one tentacle snaking along the ground behind Randy. He hadn't seen it yet. Darla watched in giddy anticipation as the tentacle slid closer and closer. Then, as Randy was facing the woods, the tentacle lifted off the ground and gently *tapped* Randy's shoulder.

Randy turned around. Slowly. He saw the tentacle hovering next to him and shrieked. Then he bolted into the woods.

The tentacle retracted, and Jarko appeared in front of the cabin, watching Randy run. He had a delighted smile on his face. He waited for Randy to get a head start. Just like Darla used to. Let them believe they were getting away. Then, when Randy was far enough into the woods, Jarko shot out an arm, latched onto a tree, and swung into the wilderness.

Darla hopped down from her perch and traversed behind Jarko, slowly, giving him space. This was his hunt. She was just a spectator. But her heart was hammering at nearly twenty-five beats per minute. She was living vicariously through Jarko and loving every second of it. She hated to admit it, but she missed this. Missed the hunt.

Jarko narrowed the gap on Randy, drifting effortlessly

through the trees. Randy kept looking back, a relieved smile seeing that nobody was following behind him, but unaware that Jarko was drifting above him, toying with Randy like a snarky cat with a douchey mouse.

Then, as Randy approached an embankment, Jarko flung himself through the trees and landed right in front of the young man. Randy stopped in his tracks, skidded, and fell right on his ass. Darla watched, riveted. Jarko's yellow eyes glowed in the moonlight. He looked imposing, terrifying in his long black coat, his gray skin looking almost bluish in the night. He towered over Randy, who tried to scuttle backward like a wounded crab.

"Hello, Randy," Jarko said. He moved forward deliberately. Methodically. His movements were fluid and calm.

"*Puh...puh...puh...please*," Randy sputtered.

Jarko held his right arm up. His tentacle slowly slid out from its sleeve, stopping an inch from Randy's terror-stricken face. The purple fingers unfolded, as Randy's eyes widened.

Then the tentacle wrapped around Randy's ankles and Jarko hurled the young man upward, wrapping his arm around a thick tree branch, still holding the half-naked teen, who dangled in the air from twenty feet up.

"Oh my god!" Randy cried. "Please don't drop me. Please!"

Darla had to hand it to Jarko. She'd never dangled a counselor from a tree that high before. Ten feet, maybe. But if he dropped Randy from that height, he'd be flatter than an omelet in seconds.

Then something truly astonishing happened. As Randy hung there, Jarko's neck extended out from the collar of his black jacket. Darla marveled. His neck was its own tentacle, his head at its apex. Jarko's neck lengthened upward, stretching and stretching, until his face was directly in front of Randy's, their noses almost touching—only on opposite ends of the gravity spectrum.

Darla wasn't sure how to feel about this. The excitement of seeing Jarko execute a proper—and quite original—hunt was breathtaking. Literally. Darla realized it had been several minutes since she'd taken a breath, her heart rate spiking to twenty-eight beats per minute. She couldn't remember the last time it was that high. Not even when she was dating William and he showed her his other weed whacker. Darla shuddered just thinking about it, pushing the rather unpleasant memory from her mind. But Jarko. Jarko seemed to know exactly what he was doing, and was in full control of his, well, faculties.

Despite the excitement, Randy was a run-of-the-mill douchebag. And Darla did consider herself a modern monster. Killing those who deserved to die and taking immense pleasure in that. But she wasn't sure about Randy. The terror in his eyes told her that if he was permitted to take any breaths beyond this night, he would appreciate those moments and realize that only monsters like Darla and Jarko could live forever. Monsters like Randy Horvath could die very, very easily.

But just because they could die didn't mean they all should. Darla had stayed out of Jarko's way until now. But she leaned forward, ready to step in if necessary.

"Randy, Randy, Randy," Jarko said, his head twenty feet in the air, saliva coating Randy's face. "You've been a bad boy."

"No, I haven't!"

Jarko cocked his head, the tentacle it was attached to quivering as he did.

"I've been watching you," Jarko said, his lips curled into a smirk, his already normally deep voice lowering several octaves, deep enough to make Darla's legs quiver. "I see everything. I see the kind of man you are. I'm not a monster, Randy. You are."

"Please," Randy said. "I swear I'll be better. I *swear*. I swear to God. I swear on my mom. I swear on all of my most valuable NFTs."

Jarko's smile disappeared. He brought his face even closer to Randy.

"I don't want you to swear to them, Randy," Jarko said, his voice deep enough to rumble the earth. "I want you to swear to *me*."

"I swear to you!" Randy said. "I swear to...who are you?"

"Jarko Murkvale," he said.

"I swear to Jarko Murkvale!"

"And if you break that promise," Jarko said, "I will peel your skin from your bones and let you see my Randy quilt before you die."

"I swear," Randy burbled. "IswearIswear*Iswear*."

"We'll see," Jarko said. Then he released Randy's ankles, letting him plunge toward the ground before the young man had time to scream. Darla jumped down, ready to traverse over to catch Randy, but at the last second, Jarko snagged Randy's waist, his head just a millimeter from a jagged rock. Then Jarko gently lowered Randy's quivering body to the ground in a heap.

Jarko latched onto a tree high above Randy. He gave the young man one final look, then vaulted up and disappeared into the darkness.

Randy lay there, shaking, covered in dirt and leaves. Then he stood up and, of all things, began to laugh. He patted down his body, as if checking for holes or broken bones, but other than a few scrapes from being dragged through the trees, he was unharmed.

He looked up in the direction Jarko had gone and said, "Thank you." And he began to walk back toward camp, arms folded across his chest, either for modesty or warmth.

When he was gone, Darla dropped down to the ground. Jarko appeared from above, landing in front of her with a grin on his face.

"So?" he said. "How'd I do?"

"Given that I expected you to hunt with all the subtlety and grace of a hippo on meth, you did...not bad."

Jarko seemed to consider this and said, "Not bad. I'll take it."

"That trick with your neck. I had no idea you could stretch it out like that."

"You think you know everything about me from a few conversations, a few confrontations, and a little whipping action with your scourge?"

"I don't know. I guess I thought I did," she said. "Are there any...other body parts you can extend like your arms and neck?"

"Just one," Jarko said with a grin, "but I only reveal that during a very different kind of hunt."

Darla felt a puff of smoke escape her nose and she waved it away.

"No monster shows all their powers and tricks at once," Jarko said, leaning in close to Darla. "Not to humans. Not to monsters. And *especially* not to monsters trying to run them out of town."

"I guess I underestimated you, then. My mistake. And I won't make another one."

"Maybe," Jarko said. "So, now that we've established what I

can do playing your game, it's time for you to play mine."

"All right. Who are we hunting?"

"Oh, Duchess," Jarko said with a wide smile. "Like I said. No monster shows their hand. Meet me tomorrow at my waterfall at eleven p.m. Be ready. And make sure your scourge is sharpened."

"No hints?"

"Nope."

"All right," she said. "I'll be there."

Jarko smiled. His smile no longer irritated her.

"Just one thing, Duchess," he said.

"What's that?"

"Your heart is beating way too fast for tonight to have been 'not bad.'"

Darla gasped in surprise. "You can hear—?"

"I'm a lot more than you think, Duchess. A *lot* more."

Then Jarko shot a tentacle upward and drifted away through the trees, a stupid smile spread across Darla's face, the blood thickening in her veins as her nine-chambered heart pumped an astonishing thirty beats per minute.

CHAPTER 15

Darla nearly tipped the boulder over as she entered her cave, having to grab it before it rolled down the hill, flattening the grass and potentially clueing humans in to their location, not to mention squishing a whole bunch of poor unsuspecting woodland creatures.

Pay attention, Darla thought, slipping inside the cave and gently repositioning the boulder at the entrance. She made sure it was steady and secured in its grooves. She felt drunk. And she hadn't been drunk in a long, long time. She hated to admit it—but she kind of liked it.

She walked through the cave, feeling the water running beneath the soles of her feet, cool and refreshing. She trailed her fingers along the smooth rock of the cave walls, feeling the moisture, the moss. She'd lived in this cave her whole life, but she had never really taken the time to *look* at it.

Her heartbeat had slowed. The first part of their challenge was over. Jarko had done spectacularly well. And she wasn't sure how she felt about it.

On one hand, the night had been exhilarating. She hadn't watched a hunt with that kind of tension (present company excluded) in years. Maybe ever. Gretl's hunts were always enjoyable, but something about the sight of her Gobbler shooting from her mouth made Darla laugh. Even if it scared the bejesus out of her prey, Darla would have to practically bite down on her scourge to keep from ruining the moment and the mood by laughing.

And William...poor, sweet William. He was a good monster. Dependable. Loyal. Eager to please her, to impress her. In fact, he tried so hard to impress her that she wound up having to applaud his every hunt just to avoid hurting his feelings. Darla did feel occasional guilt about how she'd ended it with William, but the truth was she couldn't commit to him. Couldn't commit to anything. He was a decent monster. There weren't a whole lot of those out there. And he deserved someone who *was* impressed by him, who could love him and be there for him and help cleanse his unusually large pores after he wept.

And that wasn't Darla. She'd had her doubts. But after everything happened with her father. Her mother. She only had so much of herself to give. And other people needed her. Darla had to be there. Even if it meant giving up some of herself.

"Darla?" came her mother's voice. "That you?"

"No, it's Jehovah's Witnesses."

"Well, hardy-har-har. Now that you're no longer a fearsome monster, maybe you can start a career as a terrible comedian."

"I'm still a fearsome monster," Darla said, walking into her mother's room. "That never changed."

Dolores looked up from her book and wrinkled her brow.

"Your hunting skills are like my torso," Dolores said.

"Pretty useless if you don't actually use them."

"Unlike your torso, I can use my skills whenever I want."

Dolores eyed Darla. "That was a low blow."

"You don't have anywhere low *to* blow, Mom."

Dolores looked at her daughter for a moment, then burst into laughter. Darla smiled. Then she joined in, the two of them laughing harder than Darla could remember them ever laughing. She brought a stool over so she could sit face to face with her mother and they both laughed until green tears streamed down their cheeks, Dolores's pooling below her chin.

"Hon," Dolores said between laughing gasps, "would you, please? It's starting to itch my neck."

Darla nodded, then used a tissue to mop up her mother's tears.

Finally, Dolores composed herself. "So?" she said. "How'd it go with Murkwater tonight?"

Darla sighed. "Actually, he did really well."

Dolores's eyebrows raised. "Did he now?"

Darla nodded. "Credit where credit is due. He surprised me."

"Hmph," Dolores said. "I didn't expect that."

"Neither did I."

"You don't seem...upset by it."

"I don't know. I thought I would be."

"What's he like? This Murkwater?"

"Murkvale," Darla said. "He's...I would have given you a different answer a few days ago."

"You like him?" Dolores asked with a mixture of surprise and skepticism.

"No. I admire that he performed well in the hunt," Darla said evenly. "Monsters have to respect the talents of other monsters."

"That they do," Dolores said. "That's how I fell in love with your father."

Darla's eyes perked up. "Really."

Dolores nodded. "A bunch of us had gathered at Barker Beach for a gathering. We didn't have names for those kinds of big gatherings then. I think you call them Monster Mashes now, right?"

Darla nodded.

"Anyway, back then, we didn't have to worry about social media or satellite imagery or any of that. We just had to look out for old-fashioned people with cameras, and they were easy enough to scare away by showing your claws or spitting acid at them. So we were all drinking, more and more monsters arriving from all over the place. I was using my scourge to create little whirlpools in the ocean. Then, out of nowhere, we hear this noise. It's one of those open-door Jeeps. Four or five men inside. And they're firing guns into the air. Doesn't threaten us, none of us can be killed by bullets, but there's a resort a few miles down the coastline and one of them could hit some poor kid out swimming. I was always happy to disembowel a couple of teens about to do the deed before marriage, but I drew the line at little kids."

"And Dad was there?" Darla said.

Dolores nodded. "I didn't even know his name yet. Just that he was called the Sand Shark. Soon enough, I knew why. As soon as that Jeep came near, your father's hands started whirring like small drills. He jumped up and dove straight into the sand, his hands spinning so fast he dug two holes in the ground. A few moments later, that Jeep was thrown into the air like a jack-in-the-box popping up. Those men went flying.

And I mean *flying*. Your father exploded out from the sand like some gorgeous creature rising up from hell. What he did to those men…" Dolores smiled like she was recalling a vivid dream. "I'll never forget. Darwinus Drake. When he told me his name, it sent chills down both my spines. From that moment on, he had me."

"Until he left us," Darla said.

Dolores's smile disappeared. "You never know how someone is going to act years down the road," she said. "I don't regret the time I spent with your father. Only how it ended. Darwinus chose his path."

"Literally," Darla said. "And made damn sure we wouldn't be able to follow it."

"That he did."

"And you still don't regret meeting him on the beach that night?"

"Not for a moment," Dolores said. "If I hadn't met Darwinus Drake, I wouldn't have you. I would be all right with feeling my heart split in two every day the rest of my life as long as you were still in it. It was all worth it just to see that little wisp of smoke coming out of your nostrils the day you were born."

"Even losing your body?"

"Even losing my body."

"I guess I've been a pretty big disappointment, then," Darla said.

"Not to me," Dolores said. "Never to me. Maybe to yourself."

"When I decided to hang up my scourge," Darla said, "you were pretty disappointed."

"I think every parent wants their child to do what they did. Thinking that the way they did it is the right way, and that there's no other way. But that's not true. Your way isn't my way. My way certainly wasn't my mother's way—ugh, she was *obsessed* with performing Blood Eagles on bearded men. And let me tell you, those things are *messy*."

Darla sniffed and sighed, then looked up at her mother's head. "So how did you know when you were happy?"

Dolores thought for a moment, then replied, "Ask yourself, 'Am I happy?' And whatever pops into your head is the answer. When I met your father, I was happy. When you were born, I was happy. Could have gone without the three-year pregnancy and four-week labor period, but the moment I saw those tiny little nubbins on your head, and knew they would grow into a bone crown, I was the happiest monster alive."

"Thanks, Mom," Darla said. She gestured at the e-reader in front of her mother. "How's the book?"

"Eh," Dolores said. "Not enough smut."

"Ew. Mom," Darla said, standing up to leave. "That just made me very *un*happy."

She was seventeen when her father left.

Darla's bone crown was nearly fully formed, and every morning she looked at herself in the cracked mirror in the cave and touched the tips of her incoming crooked bone and smiled with pride and thought, *I'm a monster.*

The world was opening up to her like an oyster. No, wait. The world was opening up to her like the rib cage of a psychopathic teenager who liked to tease little kids by tossing hairdryers at them while they were in the shower.

Her mother was taking her on more and more hunts. And while she had noticed a chilliness between Dolores and Darwinus, it never occurred to her that the earth was about to open up under their family.

Quite literally.

She awakened one morning to the anguished wails of her mother. Darla scrambled out of bed and ran into the cave, thinking some foolish, evil people had discovered their frailties and were looking to put an end to the Drake family once and for all.

But instead, she found her mother kneeling beside a large hole in the cave floor, tears streaming down her cheeks, pooling in the dirt as she punched the ground with such force that insects fell from the ceiling and skittered away, fearful of ending up as paste below Dolores Drake's fist.

"What's going on?" Darla said. "Are you okay? Where's Dad?"

Dolores looked up at her with such sadness it was like getting harpooned in the heart, only worse.

"Mom?" she said again. "Where is he?"

Dolores just looked at the hole and nodded. "Down there," she said. "Somewhere."

"What do you mean? Why would he burrow through our cave?"

Her father would often burrow under the earth while hunting, popping up underneath or behind an unsuspecting victim. But he had never burrowed underneath their cave.

"He's gone," Dolores said, wiping her face. "Darla, I am so, so sorry."

"Gone?" she replied. "What do you mean? He's just hunting, right?"

Dolores shook her head. "I'm sorry."

"He's not *gone* gone," Darla said. "He wouldn't do that to us."

Darla stood above the hole and looked inside. It was dark.

Nothing visible but rocks and earth.

"Dad!" she shouted. "Dad, are you down there?"

"I already looked," Dolores said.

"Let me," Darla said. "Dad, I'm coming!'

"Darla, wait."

But she ignored her mother and hopped into the hole. Darla slid down about twenty feet, her arms and leg scraping against the sides of the tunnel. When she hit the bottom, she blinked and allowed her still-developing night vision to focus. The tunnel stretched far out ahead of her. Darla followed it, crawling on her hands and knees. Her father was at the end of this tunnel. When she found him, they'd talk. If there was a problem, they'd work it out. They'd go hunting as a family that night, wake up tomorrow and fill this hole back up and cover it with a nice humanskin rug.

But when she reached the end of the tunnel, what she found make her gasp.

The one tunnel branched off into dozens of other tunnels, like some enormous monster-sized ant farm. Each separate tunnel appeared to go on for miles and miles. Darla couldn't see the end to any of them. Her father had clearly dug all of these. He didn't want to be followed. He wanted to disappear.

"Dad!" Darla shouted. "*Dad!*"

There was no response. So she sat there and cried. She didn't know how long she was down there. But when she crawled back out into their cave, her mother was waiting to gather Darla into her strong arms, holding her head against her shoulder, gently stroking her hair and bone crown.

"We'll be okay," Dolores said, her voice trembling enough to let Darla know that she was saying it for her daughter's sake, not because she necessarily believed it. "I promise."

At that moment, a terrible realization came over Darla. She knew in that moment that even if you loved someone, loved them with all of your heart, it didn't mean they would always be there when you woke up.

CHAPTER 16

The day she was scheduled to meet Jarko to participate in her side of the hunt, Darla spent half the day touching the center of her forehead. When she woke up, her heart was beating faster than she remembered it doing on most mornings. And so she touched the center of her forehead, where she received the strongest pulse reading. Eighteen beats per minute.

What the hell?

Her heartbeat rarely got above fifteen on a hunt—and those were the difficult ones. The hunts where she was chasing down a future Olympics athlete or, worse, some kid drunk or high in danger of offing themselves (or others) before Darla could get to them. And even then, she'd been on enough hunts like that where she was confident in her abilities. She knew herself. Knew her body. Her heart rate only rose to these levels when she was truly nervous. Or truly excited. And she hadn't been either in a long, long time.

And still she had no idea what Jarko's plan was. She'd told

him about Randy. He had time to prepare for the cabin. All Darla knew was that Jarko wanted her to hunt *his* way. Loud. Noisy. Chaotic. None of that was Darla. Clear Creek was at stake, and the Duchess of Death, the Creature of Clear Creek, was woefully unprepared.

She went from room to room in the cave, just trying to keep busy, trying to keep her mind off that night. Off Jarko. She tried reading some of her mother's books, which she was surprised to find actually had a fair amount of smut, so she had no idea what in the hell Dolores was complaining about.

She never used to get anxious before a hunt. Never used to pace. She would lie in bed, envisioning how it would play out. It was serene. Blissful. She'd always felt that hunting was what she was meant to do, and the day of a hunt was the calm before the beautiful storm.

But what if she got there tonight and felt the same nerves? What if she screwed up? What if Jarko proved better at her game than she was at his? Perhaps her biggest fear wasn't losing Clear Creek. It was losing her faith in herself. She'd been the one to challenge Jarko to this battle. But only now did she realize just how much she had to lose.

Backing down and backing out weren't options. When the sun went down over Clear Creek, Darla put on a clean dark green tunic, strapped her customary blue fabric around her legs and heels, and took her scourge down from the wall. She'd taken it on so many hunts. Had so many incredibly memories. Outside of Dolores, and maybe Gretl (though that was debatable), the scourge had been Darla's only constant companion.

It had been a year since she used her scourge for anything other than reprimanding Jarko. She ran her fingers down the smooth wooden handle. Caressed the long leather tails. Gently pressed the embedded ball bearings. Remembered all the memorable hunts, the look in the eyes of her prey when they saw the scourge at her side.

"You ready, old friend?" Darla said, hooking the weapon to her belt.

"Are you talking to me?" came Dolores's voice from her room.

"No, Mom, I'm just...talking to the scourge."

"You know that thing can't talk, right?"

"I know, Mom."

"Okay, just making sure. For all I know, spending so much time inside this cave has driven you a little bit crazy."

"I think you've driven me a little bit crazy."

"That's my job."

"Maybe you should get a new job."

"Maybe if you found my body, I'd do just that."

Darla sighed. "I'm gonna go meet Jarko."

"Good luck, hon. Show that guy how the Drakes hunt."

"I'll do my best."

"And, Dar?"

"Yeah?"

"Don't talk to your scourge while you're hunting. You want to *scare* your prey. Not freak them out."

Chapter 17

Jarko was waiting for her in front of the waterfall. Small droplets of water slid down the shoulders of his black coat, shimmering in the moonlight. His yellow eyes gleamed like polished citrine stones. His hair was damp, and his skin looked like slate, slightly more bluish than gray, as if it changed hue depending on the light.

He was smiling in a way she hadn't seen before. Not a smirk. Or a grin. But just…she didn't know what to make of it, other than that he seemed genuinely happy to see her. She felt a flush creep over her skin, her blood heating up inside her veins.

"Hey, Duchess," Jarko said. He tapped his nose.

"What?" Darla asked. Then she saw the faint wisp of smoke drifting upward from her nostrils. Embarrassed, she turned around and fanned it away.

"You okay?" Jarko asked.

"Yeah. Fine. Had chili for lunch."

"Chili," he said. "Right. So, are you ready?"

"Of course I am," Darla replied. "Even though I have no idea what we're doing."

"You're a monster," Jarko said. "And not just any monster. You are the Duchess of Death, one of the most feared monsters around, responsible for innumerable deaths, decapitations, and dismemberments. Your legend and your family's legacy are known far and wide. I'm pretty sure you can handle a surprise hunt."

"Oh, I can handle it," Darla said.

"I know you can, Duchess," he said. His voice softened. "I had fun last night."

Darla didn't know what to say. Her tongue felt thick in her mouth. Finally, she said, "Good."

"Good?" he said, raising a thick eyebrow. "That's all?"

"All right. I did too."

"I thought you did. It's all right to admit you had fun."

"I admit that it was not quite as awful as I expected it to be."

"Then I'm thrilled to have cleared the very, very low bar for your expectations."

"Barely," Darla said. "Barely cleared it. Almost tripped on it."

Jarko laughed. "Hey, let me ask you a question."

"Shoot."

"You've been hunting in Clear Creek for, what, twenty years?"

"Twenty-two," Darla said.

"And your mom hunted here for fifty before that, right?"

"That's right. Right up until the day she was decapitated by a counselor named Franklin Shine. That was fifteen years ago."

"Decapitated, huh," Jarko said with a whistle. "That's

rough. And you never found her body to reattach it?"

"Nope. It could be anywhere. I suppose Franklin Shine would know where it's buried, but I don't even know where he is. And my bone crown doesn't exactly make it easy to blend in anywhere to look for him."

"So, fifteen years without a body," Jarko said. "Your mom must be *pissed*."

"You don't know the half of it. I mean, every kid disappoints their parents in some way. Not being able to find the rest of your mother's body is some *pretty* big baggage to carry."

"I can imagine," he said. "So, you've hunted for twenty years, right?"

"Give or take."

"Which means between the two of you, you've done terrible things to a *lot* of camp counselors."

"Yes, but at least on my end, they all deserved it."

"Fair enough. So why do parents keep sending their kids here if monsters have been hunting the campgrounds for the better part of a century?"

"Parents would send their children to camp inside an active volcano if it meant they got to have a kid-free summer," Darla said.

"Ah. And even after a monster attack, they still wouldn't bring their kids home?"

"Clear Creek has a no-refund policy," Darla said. "Parents would rather keep their kids here and take their chances with the terrifying monsters than have to entertain them for all of July and August."

"Makes sense," he said. "Speaking of terrifying people who deserve it, shall we begin the night's festivities?"

"We shall. So, are you going to tell me where we're going

for said festivities?"

"Nope. Just follow me." Jarko shot an arm into the sky, latched onto a tree, and drifted out into the woods.

Darla followed, traversing behind him. He wasn't swinging very fast, moving at an almost leisurely pace. Darla had plenty of time to navigate through the woods. He wasn't headed toward the camp. He was going somewhere else.

"Are we not hunting at Clear Creek?" Darla shouted.

"Nope," Jarko said.

"So then where are we going?"

"You ask a lot of questions."

"Just want to make sure you don't get us lost, or that we don't wind up falling into a volcano or something."

"I didn't realize there were volcanos around here."

"There aren't. I'm just saying, don't get us lost."

"Have faith, Duchess," Jarko said. "Just a little while longer."

Darla continued to follow Jarko. After several miles of Jarko drifting through the woods and Darla traversing underneath him, Darla saw a clearing up ahead. The woods were ending. She saw a road running parallel to the woods, cars speeding by intermittently. Where the hell was he taking her?

Jarko swung onto a high branch among the last row of trees before the highway began. Darla joined him, leaping onto an adjacent branch. They were hidden by the foliage, twenty feet above ground, out of sight of the cars passing by.

"Where the hell are we?" Darla asked.

"You know," Jarko said, "considering you've lived in Clear Creek your whole life, you really haven't explored much beyond the camp."

"That's not true. I meet Gretl at Maker's Marsh all the time.

And I've been to a bunch of Monster Mashes at the quarry in TohoTown."

"But you've never hunted out here," he said.

"No."

Darla surveyed the road and the land on the other side. Jarko pointed out in the distance. Darla could see a squat, square building with a large neon sign atop it that read **BEER**. Several cars were parked in the lot, along with at least twenty or twenty-five motorcycles. She could see several men out in the parking lot, smoking cigarettes and drinking beer from bottles. The men were large, tattooed, with unkempt beards. Two of them wore sunglasses even though it was after midnight. She could see bulges in their vests that surely concealed weapons and concealed them poorly.

"It's a bar," Darla said.

"Yes, it is," Jarko said. "But do you know what kind of bar?"

Darla shook her head.

"It's called the Absinthe Bar," Jarko said. "But they don't serve absinthe here."

"Then why do they call it that?"

"The initials."

"AB."

Jarko nodded. "Know what else those initials stand for?" When Darla paused, he said, "Aryan Brotherhood."

Darla's eyes widened. "It's a Nazi bar."

"Neo-Nazi, to get all technical," Jarko said. "But yeah. Let's just say the people who drink at this bar have very particular ideas about who is and is not welcome and what they would like to do about it."

Darla felt her blood begin to boil. A wisp of smoke drifted out from her nostrils. This time, she did not bother to wave it away.

"How did I not know about this?" she said with a mixture of embarrassment, anger, remorse, and shame.

"Sometimes when you're a part of something, you can be so close to it that you can't see it as a whole. You see the pieces you want to. Because you love it the way you love Clear Creek. But sometimes love means not seeing everything. Or ignoring the things you don't want to because they don't fit the picture you have in your mind. And then things…slip. And you can lose track of what matters the most."

Jarko turned away for a second. Something about the way he'd said it made Darla believe he wasn't just talking about her and Clear Creek.

"You…okay?" Darla asked.

He turned back around. His face was a dark gray in the shadows. He nodded. Features placid.

"Before I came here, I learned everything I could about Clear Creek," he said. "When I found out about this bar, let's just say I knew it wouldn't be long before I paid its denizens a visit. But now I'm kind of glad that I ended up paying it a visit with you. Mayhem is just a little more fun when it's with someone."

Darla looked at Jarko. His eyes were brilliant, reflecting the moon, his lips turned upward in a slight smile. The wind blowing out his long jacket just enough that she could see the rest of him underneath, almost like an invitation.

They locked eyes, her night vision unnecessary with the glow of the streetlamps along the road. She didn't know how to respond to his comment. When she went out with William, Darla had always felt like she was playing a role. The doting monster girlfriend. Cheerleader. Roles she took on for him, even if inside she felt like they diminished her.

Somehow, Darla knew it wasn't that she didn't want those things. It was that she wanted them with the right monster.

Jarko looked away, and the moment snapped apart like a taut rubber band.

"So, what's the plan?" Darla asked.

Jarko shrugged. "I don't have one."

"You don't have one?"

He shook his head and grinned. "My dad wrote a book once," he said. "A novel, actually."

"Wait, your *dad* wrote a novel?"

"Yup," Jarko said. "There are some really good monster-owned publishers out there. I have a copy if you're interested. About a lone werewolf monster who travels across the country with nothing but a pair of stretchy pants—for when he turns into a werewolf—and a folding toothbrush. Because you really can't just use mouthwash to get bad guy flesh off your canines. He was half French. Jacques the Reaper, that was the character's name. Anyway, my dad used to always tell me that there are two types of writers: plotter and pantsers. Plotters plan everything out in advance. They know the story, how it's going to unfold, and all the twists and turns. You're a plotter, Darla."

"I take that as a compliment."

"You should. Plotters rarely make mistakes."

"And the other ones, what are they called, pantsers?"

"Yeah, pantsers. Pantsers might have a general idea of how things might unfold, but they like to wing it. Let the story unfold naturally, see what comes to them. To me, pantsing allows for a little experimentation. Surprise. I'm a pantser, Duchess. In case you hadn't noticed."

"I'm still stuck on the 'there are good monster-owned

publishers' comment."

"You really don't get out much, do you, Duchess?"

"I think we've established that by this point."

"When this is over, I'm going to broaden your horizons."

"Is that so?" Darla said, smiling at Jarko. *Wait…was she… flirting?*

"That's so," he said. "You might even enjoy it."

"Maybe."

"I'll take a maybe."

"Unless I do better tonight than you did last night. In which case, you promised to leave Clear Creek."

"I did," Jarko said. "But I guess you could always change your mind."

Darla didn't respond. Jarko seemed to take the hint.

"All right. Here we go. You ready?"

"I was born ready."

"That you were," he said, pointing to her bone crown. "Now let's go say hello to the Aryan Brotherhood."

CHAPTER 18

They waited until the stragglers outside the bar went back in. That was Darla's idea. No need for them to cause some commotion outside that would alert the people inside and give anyone time to prepare, or even duck out a back door or window.

When the parking lot was clear, Darla traversed across the road and knelt in a shadow beside the front door. Jarko latched onto the streetlamp above the road and swung over, landing next to Darla. They knelt there, a millimeter apart. Darla could hear him breathing. It seemed just slightly elevated, slightly faster than normal. She wondered if it was because he was nervous about what they were about to do—unlikely—or because he was nervous about being this close to Darla without her trying to separate his limbs from his body.

Her heart thumped inside her forty-six ribs. She wasn't nervous about what they were about to do. She was excited for it. She was nervous about something else. She just didn't quite want to admit what that was.

Just then, they heard loud music emanating from inside the bar. Loud enough that the walls seemed to shake, the glass in the windows rattled, the very ground itself vibrated underneath them.

Darla smiled at Jarko. "Well, they're going to be in a good mood for another three-point-two seconds."

Jarko extended his hand toward the door and smiled at Darla. She felt her blood rise several degrees. A faint puff of smoke drifted up from her nose. Jarko pretended to catch it between his fingers. Darla laughed. It was high and real and pure, and Jarko smiled, as though he was taking true joy from seeing that he'd made her laugh.

"After you, Duchess," he said.

Darla nodded. Then she stood up and walked over to the bar's front door. Jarko followed behind her.

She unstrapped the scourge from her belt and looked at Jarko.

"I've been waiting for you to use that on someone besides me," he said.

Darla began to whip the scourge in a circle, creating a windmill, the tails and bronze studs moving so fast they couldn't be seen by the naked eye.

Then Darla raised the scourge above her head and brought it down on the wooden door, cleaving it in two right down the center. She looked at Jarko and nodded, and they each kicked one half of the door into the bar, sending the halves flying twenty feet, flattening several patrons in their wake.

The entire bar stopped what they were doing and turned to look at the doorway. The music kept playing, an odd contrast to the absolute silence of the patrons. Several patrons crawled out from underneath the door halves, dizzy and confused. Darla could see a few pairs of arms and legs underneath the doors that were not moving. Good.

The two monsters stood there in the doorway, the moon illuminating them from behind, casting their shadows across the floor. Darla held her scourge at her waist, flipping it around nonchalantly. Jarko stood there, arms folded across his chest, nearly as tall as the doorway itself.

There were about forty people in the bar. They were all men, mostly bearded and heavily tattooed, with markings that Darla recognized as not particularly friendly. A good portion of them were thick, muscular men who looked like they knew how to handle themselves.

They would be the most fun.

One man stepped forward. He was enormous, six foot five or so, a slab of a man two hundred and fifty plus pounds, with a beard down to his navel and a shaved head that bore numerous cross tattoos that most definitely did not denote his adherence to Jesus's teachings.

Several men fell in line behind him, forming a hefty triangle of ignorance. The man pulled a knife from a sheath, approached the monsters, and said, "Who in the hell do you think you are?"

Darla stepped forward. "Darla Drake. Duchess of Death. Creature of Clear Creek."

Jarko stepped forward, next to Darla. "Jarko Murkvale."

Darla waited. When Jarko didn't speak, she turned to him and whispered, "And?"

"And what?" he whispered back.

"Don't you have an, I don't know, cool nickname?"

Jarko looked irritated. "Uh, no. We don't all go around inventing fancy nicknames for ourselves like Duchess of Death."

"I didn't *invent* that nickname. It was my mom's and then

she passed it to me when I took over and—"

"Shut the fuck up," Beardy McBigot shouted, holding the knife out. "Leave now or die."

Darla looked at Jarko and shrugged. "I can think of a third option," she said.

"Oh yeah? What's that?"

Darla brought the scourge down in a wide, arcing motion. Beardy's knife clattered to the ground. His forearm landed next to it.

Beardy screamed and fell down, while the rest of Beardy's Bigot Troupe stepped back, their eyes wide in fear. Several bolted for the back door. Before they could reach it, Jarko latched onto a rafter and swung himself over to the far side of the bar, landing in front of the back door.

"Sorry," he said. "You know what they say about roaches. Once they go in, they don't go out."

Everyone in the bar who was still moving picked up some sort of weapon: broken bottle, pieces from the splintered door, pool sticks, napkin holders, flagpoles. Some had come with their own weapons: knives, brass knuckles, batons—even a few guns.

Darla could see Jarko at the other end of the bar, his citrine eyes gleaming with anticipation. She had to be honest: she was already having fun.

"All right, everyone," Darla said, beginning to whip her scourge in a blur. "Let's dance."

The first group of Beardy's men came at her wielding sticks and knives. Within seconds, both the weapons and the appendages that wielded them were scattered all over the bar.

Half a dozen tried to push their way toward the back door, hoping to go through Jarko. But Jarko's tentacles shot out from his jacket sleeves and he swung them in a wide, sweeping motion, like a pair of slimy purple scythes. Half a dozen of Beardy's men flew through the air, crashing into the walls, arms and legs splayed everywhere.

"Kill them!" Beardy shouted, still holding his maimed arm.

Darla jumped into the middle of the fray, spinning her scourge like a fan, as Beardy's men shrieked and lost some weight the old-fashioned way. Jarko flung his tentacles around the bar, wrapping them around various patrons and flinging them with wild, joyful abandon. Some flew behind the bar, some got spun out by ceiling fans, and a few more found themselves hanging from the rafters.

Darla had to admit it: mayhem a la Jarko was kind of fun.

"I think I like being a pantser!" Darla shouted as one of Beardy's men lost his mind—literally.

"Embrace the chaos, Duchess!" Jarko shouted, popping one of Beardy's friend's heads like a hateful blueberry. Bodies and weapons and parts flew everywhere. The bar looked like it had been wadded up and shoved into a blender, pieces of wood and glass and metal hurling through the air like a tornado was sweeping through the four walls.

Jarko picked up a half-empty bottle of tequila and took a long sip, his other arm curled around three patrons, as he plucked out their beard hairs one by one. Then he tossed the bottle down and let loose an enormous belch.

"Human drinks are awful," Jarko said. "Give me fermented swamp water with a mulled tree root chaser any day of the week over this stuff."

Darla brought her scourge down, cleaving the bar itself in two, revealing a thin bearded man huddling beside the sink, holding a shotgun. Before she could raise her scourge, the man emptied both barrels into Darla's abdomen. The blast knocked her back and drove the breath from two of her three lungs. She looked down. Black blood trickled from dozens of small holes. But just as soon as they appeared, the holes closed up. The blood, however, remained.

Darla looked at the man, smoke pouring out of her nostrils. He skittered back across the floor, trying to reload the shotgun but dropping the shells on the floor.

"You're going to pay for my dry-cleaning bill," she said, bringing her scourge down.

Darla and Jarko danced through the bar, Darla swinging her scourge like a majestic windmill, Jarko's arms sweeping up and down and side to side like a deadly mop, cleaning all manner of detritus—both living and not—from the floor. Darla could not remember the last time she'd had this much fun.

Half an hour after they'd broken down the door, Darla and Jarko stood in the middle of the bar, surrounded by the bodies of Beardy's bigoted friends. She looked into Jarko's eyes and saw her reflection, saw the enormous smile on her face, and felt her blood temperature begin to rise. Then she stepped forward.

"If anyone here is still drawing breath," Darla said, "remember to be kind to your fellow humans. Otherwise, those who are very much not human will be very, very unkind to you."

One of the men on the floor raised an arm weakly, hand clenched around a broken bottle, which he waved at Darla and Jarko with all the menace of a cute, fluffy bunny waving a carrot. Jarko slapped him upside the head with a tentacle and the man dropped to the ground.

"I could go for a drink," Jarko said.

"I know a place," Darla said. "Follow me."

They left the bar, stepping out into the moonlight, the sound of sirens far off in the distance, and by the time law enforcement arrived, Darla was traversing through the woods, Jarko swinging above her, every part of her body alive and electric.

CHAPTER 19

Darla traversed five miles east of the bar and stopped by the banks of the Lugosi River. Jarko landed beside her, and they both stared out at the running water, the stillness a lovely contrast to the madness they'd just left.

"So, Duchess," Jarko said, "I would have to say that when you put your mind to it, you can create some absolutely beautiful chaos."

"Is that what you'd call pantsing it?" Darla asked.

"I'd say so. I mean, we could have always made an even bigger mess. Hit a gas main. I've hunted a few devil worshipping cannibals at their secret churches and I have to say, causing a little mayhem with hundreds of lit candles around gives the hunt this, I don't know, *je ne sais quoi*."

Darla's eyebrows perked up. "French," she said. "I wouldn't have guessed that."

Jarko smiled. "*C'est une belle nuit pour le chaos.*"

"I heard a chaos in there," she said. "What did you say?"

"I said it's a beautiful night for chaos."

"Where did you learn that?" Darla asked.

Jarko shrugged, but she saw a glimmer of something in his yellow eyes, something he was holding back.

"Nowhere special," he said, clearly lying. "Just picked it up along the way."

"Along the way."

He nodded.

"If you want to tell me…"

"It's really not that interesting," he said.

"Maybe you could let me be the judge of that."

"Maybe," he said, but didn't offer more. Darla realized this was as far as this particular line of conversation was going to go at the moment. But the more she learned about Jarko Murkvale, the more questions she had.

She smiled. "Come here."

Jarko followed Darla over to a downed tree. She used her scourge and gently carved out two large pieces of wood, then hollowed them out with a delicate spin from her weapon until they looked like two wooden cups. Then she went over to the banks of the river, knelt down, and filled each makeshift cup with river water. She gently pressed her fingertip to the point of her bone crown, allowing a single drop of blood to fall into each cup. It turned the liquid an amber color. She handed a cup to Jarko. He took it.

"It's warm," he said. "Is that from you?"

She nodded. "Don't worry. I don't have cooties."

"What are cooties? A type of monster?"

"Never mind," she said. "Fresh river water with a layer of silt at the bottom. And a drop of plasma to give it a little kick. Let me know what you think."

Jarko brought the cup to his lips.

"Oh, and be careful of splinters."

He smiled and took a sip. He pursed his lips and smacked them together.

"Not bad, Duchess," he said. "Not bad at all. I mean, it's no tequila from a broken bottle inside a Nazi bar."

"Well, nothing can compare to that."

Jarko took another sip. Darla smiled, watching him drink. Another sip and he held the cup back out to her.

"Can I get a refill?" he asked.

"Why of course," she said. Darla filled his cup again and handed it back. He downed the contents greedily. She sipped hers, listening to the sounds of the river as they drank.

"So," Jarko said after draining the last of his second cup, "is this where you take all the monsters after you've hunted with them?"

"Oh yeah," she deadpanned. "All of them. Thousands. I have them stand in an orderly queue."

Jarko laughed. She could feel him standing there, even though he was several feet away. There was a soft vibration coming from underneath Jarko's feet. Even though he looked like he wasn't moving, it was definitely there. He was shifting his weight imperceptibly. He was nervous. And now she was too.

"I had fun tonight," Darla said, breaking the silence.

He looked at her with a smile wide across his grayish-blue face. She thought back to the moment she saw him, standing in the middle of the campground, flinging counselors around like bocce balls. She'd *hated* him at that moment. Who was this monster causing a ruckus on her home turf?

"I did too, Duchess," Jarko said.

But now that they'd been on two hunts together, Darla couldn't remember the last time she'd had this much fun with another monster. Gretl notwithstanding. Hell, even with Gretl, it was a different kind of fun. This fun felt dangerous. Forbidden. Like she was straying off the path and venturing out somewhere strange and exciting and, well, intoxicating.

"Can I ask you a question?" she said.

"Of course," Jarko replied.

"Why did you come here?" she said. "For real."

Jarko looked down. He shook his cup, as though hoping to find one last drop he could put to his lips to avoid her question.

"It's a long story," he finally replied.

"I have nowhere else to be tonight," she said. "Unless you have another Nazi bar for us to dismantle."

Jarko laughed softly. "Unfortunately, there are always more where those people came from," he said. "I recommend keeping your scourge at the ready."

"I always do," she said.

"When you split that door in half with the scourge, that was so damn cool," he said.

Darla felt her blood begin to warm. "Really?" she said. She couldn't remember anyone ever calling anything she did "cool". She was pretty sure "noteworthy" was the best she'd ever gotten from Gretl. And "almost as good as me" from William, which made her want to dunk her head in the water just thinking about it.

"Really," he said. "It's been a long time since I've hunted with anyone."

"Me too," she said. "Who did you hunt with before this?"

Jarko stayed silent.

"Come on," she said.

"You first."

"All right," Darla said. "Since I asked. Ex-boyfriend."

Jarko's orange eyes lit up and his lips curved into a surprised smile.

"Really," he said, more as an amused statement than question.

"Yeah, why? Does that surprise you?"

"Not the ex part," he said. "Frankly, I would have been shocked if you hadn't left a trail of exes' bodies in your wake. It's the idea of you hunting with someone. You...don't seem like the type to do tandem hunting."

"Oh, and you are?"

"Like I said, Duchess," Jarko replied, "you really don't know very much about me."

"So tell me," she said.

"Come on, Duchess," he said. "The challenges are over. You don't have to pretend to want to know more."

"I'm not pretending," Darla said. "I really did have fun. Speaking of which, there's a Monster Mash at the TohoTown quarry next week. You should come."

Jarko seemed to consider this. "I haven't been to a Monster Mash in a long time."

"Well, then, you have to," she said. "Monsters come from all over the area. I want you to meet my friend Gretl."

"Gretl the Gullet Gobbler?" Jarko said.

"You've heard of her?"

Jarko made a *pssh* sound. "Of course. Before I came to Clear Creek, I made it my business to know all the monsters in the area. Not just the ones in Clear Creek itself."

"So you'll come."

"I'll think about it."

"Come on. There will be drinks. Music. Tons of cool monsters. And, okay, some annoying ones too, but you can avoid them."

"Will you be there?" he asked.

"I will.

"Then I will definitely, absolutely, maybe come."

"I'm going to need a more definitive answer than that," Darla said. "Just say yes."

"You're working hard to sell me on this," he said.

"I think you'd have fun."

"You think I'd have fun, or you think *you'd* have fun?"

"I think we'd both have fun."

Jarko nodded. "All right, then. I'll be there. Assuming we haven't decided that you won the challenge and you're throwing me out of Clear Creek like an annoying counselor into the middle of the lake."

Darla smiled and moved an inch closer to Jarko.

"Even if that happens," she said, "and I throw you out on your ass and reclaim Clear Creek for the Drake family, I'd still want you to come."

Jarko smiled, but there was something behind it. As though he didn't know how to react to the enthusiasm, the kindness.

"Tell me," Darla said. "Why did you come here? To Clear Creek? Tell me the truth."

She could feel Jarko withdraw even if he didn't move. It wasn't just that he didn't want to answer her question. It was that even thinking about the answer brought him some sort of discomfort or pain.

"I'd rather not talk about it," he said. "I had fun tonight. Let's let the night end on that note. All right if we do that? Just have a few drinks and go our separate ways?"

Darla felt a fingernail scrape along her heart.

"Oh, crap, Duchess. I didn't mean it like that."

"How did you mean it, then?"

"I just meant...hell, I don't really know. I just don't want you to feel any obligation to be my friend after all this. Here's some truth for you. I didn't come to Clear Creek to make friends, to meet other monsters, go tandem hunting, or do anything else of the sort. In fact, I came here for the opposite reason."

"The opposite reason?" Darla asked. "What does that mean?"

"Don't you get it, Duchess?" he said. "I came to Clear Creek to be left the hell alone."

Darla sat there for a few minutes, letting that statement sink in. He didn't seem to want to add to it or illuminate it any further.

Finally, she said, "Looks like I messed your plan up pretty good."

Jarko turned to Darla and said, "I'd say so. Messed it up completely. Just ruined it."

"Just absolutely destroyed it," she added, her heart beginning to beat faster.

"Took your scourge to my plan and annihilated it," he said, his smile widening millimeter by millimeter.

"Put it into a blender and put that plan on frappé."

"Took that plan and put it on a rock and beat on it for a week straight."

"With your tentacles *and* your weird, elongated neck."

"Smashed that plan until it was flat out unrecognizable," Jarko said, and he slid one inch closer to Darla.

"Crushed it into paste."

"Mashed it into molasses."

"Beat it into plan pulp."

"It was a really, *really* good plan," Jarko said, leaning toward her, close enough that Darla could smell him. His scent was something sweet, unidentifiable. Swamp water mixed with citrus, maybe a hint of pine needles and tree sap. It was intoxicating. She breathed it in.

"And then what happened?" Darla asked softly.

"And then you came along."

Before she knew what she was doing, Darla had placed her hand on Jarko's cheek, feeling the rough texture of his skin, then leaned in and gently pressed her lips to his. The kiss felt like fire, literally and figuratively. His lips made her feel dizzy, but she also felt her blood begin to ignite. She could feel the smoke coming out of her nostrils, drifting upward against his face.

Then she felt his hand on her face, a slightly moist sensation given that his hands were part tentacle, but if anything, it drove her crazier knowing she was essentially suctioned to him. He ran his fingers over her head, gently sliding up and down her bone crown, sending an electric current down the nape of her neck and her wishbone-shaped spine into her legs.

He pressed his lips back against hers and moved closer, their shoulders touching, for the first time Darla realizing how big and solid Jarko was, how it felt like he could engulf her, wrap himself around her (he would have to be careful, of course, not to impale himself on her bone crown).

She brought her hand down to his neck, feeling the coarseness of his skin, feeling his arm wrap around her waist once, twice, three times. She went to unhook her scourge from her belt and then, suddenly, Jarko stopped. He unwrapped his arm from around her. Pulled his face away from her. Moved back so that there was a foot of space between them that may as well have been a canyon.

"I...I'm sorry," Jarko said. He was standing up straight, arms at his sides, both fully retracted. He shook his head and said, "I can't."

"I shouldn't have done that," Darla said, now hideously embarrassed. "I just got caught up and the hunt was so much fun and the drinks and...it was a mistake."

Jarko nodded. He was still looking at her, his eyes saying that he didn't believe what he said. That it wasn't a mistake. That he wanted to have his arms back around her. But despite that yearning, he didn't move.

"Thanks for coming tonight," he said matter-of-factly. "It was enjoyable."

Then Jarko latched onto a tree above and drifted back into the woods, his wooden cup clattering onto the stones where he'd stood just a moment ago, leaving Darla staring out into the darkness wondering what the hell had just happened.

Chapter 20

"Wait, so after all that, he just...left?"

Darla nodded and sipped her drink. Gretl looked at her incredulously and shifted on her tree stump. Her abdomen had doubled in size since the last time Darla had seen her—which wasn't all that long ago—and every few minutes a low growl would emerge from its general vicinity. Darla was reasonably sure Gretl was either going to give birth very, very soon, or be eaten alive from the inside by her own progeny.

"He just left," Darla said.

"So let me get this straight," Gretl said. "You went with Jarko to a Nazi bar."

"Correct."

"You turned the bar into your own personal blender."

"And set it to frappé."

"You had fun doing all of this. With Jarko."

"More fun than I've had in years."

"Then the two of you went for a romantic drink."

"We went for a drink. I did not anticipate the romance part of it."

Gretl offered her friend professional-grade side eye. "Sure, you didn't."

"I swear on your Gobbler I didn't!"

Gretl opened her mouth and her Gobbler came out, offered a sarcastic *hmph*, and went back inside.

"Even he doesn't believe you."

"Is that thing actually a he? Because I don't see any—"

"Stop changing the subject," Gretl interrupted. "So during this romantic interlude—"

"More like a beverage gathering."

"Whatever. During this...thing...you two ended up making out."

"I wouldn't call it making out."

"So, what was it, then?"

"My face and his face ended up in the same general vicinity."

"Was there any other touching than of the face variety?"

Darla thought for a moment. "My hand *may* have touched him a little bit."

"And?"

"And he *may* have wrapped his tentacles around me. A few times."

"That is making out," Gretl said.

"But then he ended it before it went any further."

"Which means you would have preferred it to go further."

"Absolutely not," Darla said. "I was going to stop him if he hadn't stopped me first."

Gretl laughed in disbelief. Her Gobbler shot out of her mouth and laughed as well, then retracted back inside.

"See. None of us believe you that you didn't have anything

romantic in mind when you went with Jarko for the drink."

"Okay," Darla said. "I considered the possi*bility* that something might happen. But we went for the drink to commemorate the end of the challenges."

"I've never heard of sex referred to as 'commemorating the end of the challenges.'"

"I was *not* going to have sex with him. I don't even know how that would work physiologically."

"Who won those challenges, by the way?"

"I...I don't know. Me?"

"You don't even know who won."

"I guess not."

"Know why that matters?" Gretl asked, munching on a leaf.

"Why?"

"Because it was never about the challenge."

Darla looked at her friend. "Then what was it about, Ms. I Forgot You Had a Degree in Monster Psychology?"

"It was about the companionship," she said. "You both needed it. And you both got it."

"I didn't need companionship," Darla said. "I have you and my mom."

"If we're your only companionship," Gretl said, "then no wonder you were ready to jump Jarko's tentacles the moment the two of you were alone."

"I wasn't ready to jump his tentacles."

"You live near Maker's Marsh," Gretl said, "not near *denial river*."

"You didn't just *denile river* me," Darla said.

"I did. You are wading deep in denial and I'm here to rescue you."

"If you send your Gobbler out for me to grab on to, I'm

going to tie it in a knot behind your back."

"Stop it," Gretl said, covering her mouth. "You're going to hurt his feelings."

"Sorry, Gobbler," Darla said.

"Tell me honestly," Gretl said. "How do you feel about what happened? Not the challenges. That he left right as you two were getting close."

Darla ran her fingers along her bone crown. The memory of gently pricking her finger and letting a drop of blood fall into his drink, seeing him greedily down it, replayed in her mind. He seemed like he was enjoying himself. Forget *seemed*. He *was* enjoying himself. So, what happened?

"I think it has something to do with why he came here," Darla said.

"Why *did* he come here?"

Darla shook her head and sighed. "I still don't know. I've asked him, but I think he'd rather me whip him with my scourge a few thousand times before answer the question. But I've thought about it a lot. Not to sharpen my own bone crown, but my family has a reputation. *I* have a reputation. We're legends in Clear Creek."

"I wouldn't argue that for a second," Gretl said. "What's your point?"

"Why come here?" Darla said. "If he needed a place to hunt, why come to a territory where there was already a legendary monster? Why not find somewhere truly unclaimed? Where he could make a name for himself?"

"Maybe," Gretl said, "he didn't *want* to make a name for himself."

Darla thought about what Jarko had said during their first conversation at Maker's Marsh.

I just want to hunt and be left alone.

And again, right before they kissed.

I came to Clear Creek to be left the hell alone.

What if Gretl was right? What if Jarko's entire purpose for coming to Clear Creek was *because* there was already a legendary monster here? He knew he would remain in the shadows of the Drake family. He could hunt in relative anonymity. It would be like the next guy to hunt in Haddonfield. He would always be considered second fiddle to Mr. William Shatner mask.

"Maybe you're right," Darla said. "Maybe he came to Clear Creek because he knew he would always be in my shadow. And that's exactly what he wanted."

"Can you ask him about it?"

Darla shook her head. "That's for him to tell me if he ever wants to."

"I understand," Gretl said. "Oh no, that's really bad."

"What's really bad? That he left mid-kiss?"

"Oh no, that's so, so bad."

"Was it really? Now you're making me feel really self-conscious, Gret."

"Oh my god. *Bad.*"

"What, that I won't ask Jarko about his past? Is it really that bad?"

"*No!*" Gretl shouted, standing upright and gripping her abdomen, which was roiling and rolling beneath her hands. "Baby! The baby is coming!"

"Now?" Darla said.

"No! Next week! Yes, *now*!"

"Holy crap! What can I do?"

She went over to Gretl, who draped an arm around Darla's shoulders. She was panting heavily. Inside Gretl's mouth, she could see the Gobbler with his hands to his cheeks, mouth open, like a tiny monster version of Edvard Munch's *The Scream*.

"Tyrone," Gretl said, gasping. Her stomach appeared to be growing by the minute. "Get me to my Hatchetman."

"You got it. Hold onto me."

Darla wrapped Gretl's arms around her neck and lifted her up so that her legs were draped across Darla's arms. She had no idea how much of the weight was Darla, and how much of it was the baby monster growing inside Gretl like a living sponge soaking up water.

"Get me to my boyfriend," Gretl gasped. "Oh my god, our baby is coming! Hurry!"

"I'll go as fast as I can. Just please try not to let your Gobbler sever my carotid artery while we're traversing."

"No promises!" Gretl shouted, clinging to her friend.

Darla felt her heart aching as she sped through Maker's Marsh to take her best friend home, knowing their friendship would never be the same.

CHAPTER 21

"That is a big goddamn baby," Darla said.

Gretl lay on a bed of rock and tree bark. Sweat coated her face. Tyrone stood next to her, his arm around her, a smile as wide as Clear Creek itself on his face. Cradled in Gretl's arms was Baby Binks. Though calling it a baby wasn't quite fair to babies. This baby was the size of a decent sized goat—and quite a bit louder. It had a full head of hair, one side black and the other orange, and its body was coated in fine tufts of white fur. When it cried, Darla could see the teeniest, tiniest Gobbler inside its mouth, and her heart swelled with joy for her best friend.

"Her name is Manticore Myers Binks," Gretl said, her face flushed with love and pride. "She'll be our little Manti, for short."

"Decided against Shatterspine?"

"You know," Gretl said, "I just saw this beautiful, vicious baby and thought, 'she's our little Manticore.'"

"She's not so little."

"No, she is not," Gretl said. "Daddy's going to have to use his hatchet to cut some more wood because our stroller is gonna need major reinforcement."

"Mommy and Daddy love you, Manti," Tyrone said, gently stroking Gretl's head. She looked up at him with absolute, boundless love, and he leaned down and gently kissed her on the lips. Tyrone still had his hatchet by his side, having used it to cut the umbilical cord, which was about the thickness and density of a braided rope. Manti cooed and opened her mouth wide.

"She has her daddy's canines," Gretl said with pure love.

Tyrone looked up at his wife and said, "I wanted to wait until Manti was here to give you this."

He reached into his pocket and pulled out a small cloth wrapped around something. He gave it to Gretl. Her eyes grew wide.

"Is this what I think it is?" Tyrone merely smiled as Gretl unwrapped it. A small toe fell into her palm, and Gretl squealed with glee. "Is that from SlothMan?"

"It is," Tyrone said. "I've used my hatchet thousands of times, baby. But none of them have meant as much as hacking off that toe."

"That means you've completed all five Hell Tasks," Gretl said.

"It does." Tyrone knelt down. He took a ring from his pocket. It was gold with a blue gem in its center. Gretl gasped. "This is the ring my father took from the captain's safe of the *SS Albacore* after he bit the propeller off and sunk it in 1964. It's been in the Binks family for over fifty years. I would like you to officially be a Binks. Gretl Sneed, will you marry me?"

Tears sprung from Gretl's eyes. "Yes," she said. "With all my heart, yes."

She opened her mouth and her Gobbler came out, crying its tiny eyes out. It took the ring from Tyrone's hand and put it gently onto Gretl's before retracting.

"It's beautiful," Gretl said. "I love you."

"I love you too."

They kissed, their baby in Gretl's arms, and Darla felt tears springing to her eyes. She wiped them away with the hem of her tunic.

"You okay, Dar?" Gretl asked.

"Oh yeah. Fine. Got impaled by a harpoon in the eye in this morning, you know how it is."

"Those smart," Tyrone said. "Need some Neosporin? The humans seem to think it cures everything."

"No, I'm good. But I should leave."

"Why?" Gretl asked.

"This is a family moment," Darla said. "You and your daughter and your fiancé need a little family time. You have a new monster, you're newly engaged. We'll celebrate another time."

"Absolutely not," Gretl said.

"You're Gretl's family," Tyrone said, "which means you're my family. And now you're Manti's family."

"You're my sister, Darla," Gretl said, "and I want you here."

"I'm the luckiest monster alive," Darla said, just as Manti spat up and coated Gretl's head in viscous blue saliva.

"Aw," Gretl said as Tyrone wiped the muck from her eyes. "She's just like her mama."

So Darla stayed. Watching Gretl give birth to her ginormous baby was something she would never forget as long as she lived, and seeing her get engaged to the monster of her dreams gave her feels she'd never experienced before. She looked at the way Tyrone stared at Gretl, and something about the sight of their love made a faint wisp of smoke drift up from her nostril. She turned away before they noticed it.

"Dar?" Gretl said. "Are you sure you're okay?"

Darla nodded. "Yeah, just my eye again."

"Is it still the harpoon? Because if it's not, it could be Drogeur spores," Tyrone said, reaching for his hatchet. "I'm incredibly allergic, those spores turn my bones to jelly. It's possible a Drogeur flew overhead and released its spores and some got into your eyes. If so, I might need to call in some backup, Drogeurs can release millions of spores on every pass and they can be hard to take down unless you have flight capability and—"

"Ty," Gretl said, putting her finger to her fiancé's lips. "Enough with the spores. Take the hint, love."

He looked at Gretl, then at Darla, and said, "Oh, gotcha. Yup. Still the harpoon in the eye. That'll do it."

"Ty, be a doll, go cut me some bark for Manti to chew on, would you? Oh, and a few frogs for me and the Gobbler. I just lost seventy percent of my body weight and I'm hungrier than the fires of hell."

"You got it, babe." Tyrone got up and went over to Darla. "I'm glad you're here. We're glad you're here."

"I'd be here for Gretl in half a heartbeat," Darla said.

"I'm not just glad you're here for Gretl," Tyrone said. "You've been Gret's family since long before I came skulking around. And now Manti is going to grow up with the most amazing women monsters to not only show her the ropes, but show her how to use those ropes to tie people to railroad tracks.

You're basically her Aunt Duchess of Death. You should be here for you as much as you are for her."

Darla blushed, a deep magenta glow rising in her cheeks. "Auntie Duchess does have a nice ring to it," Darla said. "Thanks, Hatchet. I hope Gretl knows how lucky she is to have met someone like you."

"Eh, depends on her mood. Not to mention her Gobbler. I've caught that thing trying to eat my nose while I was sleeping more times than I can count," Tyrone said. "Just think about how lucky Manti is that she'll have you and Gretl to teach her how to hunt. I mean, I've never met anyone so single-minded about the hunt as Auntie Duchess."

"Until last year," Darla said. "Now I'm not so sure I should be teaching anyone anything."

"You'll get back on it," Tyrone said. "I mean, nobody is as obsessed with the hunt as you. And it's not like you have a little monster at home to take care of, right?"

Darla felt a pressure on her chest, and a wisp of smoke drifted away from her face.

"Right," she said. "I certainly don't have that."

"See? Nothing holding you back," he said. "Hey, I'm gonna get Darla and Manti some chow. Happy, well-fed monster wife, happy life, am I right?"

"I wouldn't know," Darla said.

Tyrone laughed and said, "Right, of course not." Then he jogged off into the forest to get Gretl and the baby their food.

"Hey, Dar, why the long—er, longer—face?"

Darla turned to see Gretl looking at her, the enormous newborn baby monster dozing peacefully on her lap, mouth open, its tiny Gobbler curled up on its shoulder also asleep. It was such a peaceful, loving sight, it made Darla think that if

William the Weed Whacker was there, every single one of his pores would open and begin gushing simultaneously and risk drowning the entire lot of them.

"Hey, hon," Darla said, kneeling beside Gretl. The baby smelled like a combination of pollen, fresh cut flowers, and roadkill. Darla breathed it in and smiled. "She is really beautiful."

The baby's eyes fluttered open. They were almond-shaped, the irises red and orange like a freshly lit flame. It uttered a soft, mewling cozy sound. Then it reached out and curled its tiny fingers around the scourge at Darla's waist and tried to pull it off. Gretl laughed.

"Less than a day old and she already wants to start maiming," Gretl said.

"The size of this baby, she could filet half of Clear Creek in an afternoon."

"Seriously," Gretl said. "Do you see those nails? We're going to need an iron fence to keep little Manti from burrowing through walls."

"Not to mention burrowing through other monsters," Darla said. "You and Ty are going to be amazing parents."

"I hope so," Gretl replied. "Part of me is ready. Part of me has no idea what the hell I'm doing. I feel like it was just yesterday I was going to Monster Mashes and drinking so much quarry water I would wake up the next day with my skin sloughing off and promise the next day to never drink again."

"And did you ever keep that promise?"

"Not once," Gretl said. "But I do promise we'll still have time for us to hang out. That's a promise I'll keep."

"Manti comes first," Gretl said. "Then me. Then *maybe* Tyrone. I was in your life first, after all."

"Oh, he's fully aware that once I'm back on my feet, he's on little monster duty so we can have girls' nights out to scare the living hell out of some crusty camp counselors."

"Whenever you're ready," Darla said. "I'm really happy for you."

"Thanks, Dar."

"Can I ask you something?"

"You know you can."

"Do you feel...I don't know...content?"

Gretl thought for a moment, then said, "I think I am. I'd never really considered it, but yeah. I'm happy. I have a family I love. I have friends I love. And I suppose being happy makes you content. I think I was always happy with myself. I knew what kind of monster I was and I was happy. But I also wanted someone to share myself with. I wanted someone to share themselves with me. Tyrone gave me that. He was the piece I was missing."

Darla nodded. Baby Manti wrapped her fingers around Darla's wrist and squeezed.

"Holy crap she's strong." Manti released Darla's wrist, leaving indents in her skin.

"Tell me about it. I'm worried when I breastfeed, she's going to tear my boob clean off."

Darla and Gretl both laughed. Then Gretl said, "I know you've been alone most of your life. And I also know you've preferred it that way."

"Except for William."

"Except for William," Gretl said. "Ugh, one time, he cried so hard he ruined my favorite pair of boots."

"I got you a new pair!"

"You got me a pair of crocs. And I *refuse* to hunt in crocs,"

Gretl said. "Maybe your taking time off wasn't because you didn't want to hunt any more. Maybe it was because you were tired of being alone."

"I'm not alone. I have you. And Dolores."

"Your best friend and your mom's head don't count. You need your own life."

"Maybe I'll start by getting my own place," Darla said. "I think I've shared too many meals with my mom's head."

"Seriously. If you can't find Dolores's body, you need to graft her head onto, like, a bat or a llama or something. Find a way to get her outside without you having to toss her in a backpack. You know, Tyrone has a cousin who's a warlock who might be able to help out."

"I don't know about warlocks. There's a fifty percent chance she'd end up with a shrunken head, and I can't even fathom the level of guilt she'd lay on me if that happened," Darla said. "I'll just deal with it. After a certain age, parents don't change who they are."

"In eighty or ninety years, Manti will be the one complaining about us," Gretl said. "Just think about the warlock option."

"Dolores doesn't even like to eat dinner after five o'clock. I really don't think she would go for her head being grafted onto a bat."

"Llama?"

"Doubtful. Plus, way noisier."

"Just a thought."

At that moment, Tyrone emerged from the tree line carrying a basket filled with various types of tree bark. When he got close to Gretl, baby Manti's Gobbler lashed out and grabbed a two-foot-long piece of bark, brought it into the baby's mouth, where it was promptly shredded into frothy pulp in less than three seconds. Manti then let out a loud, satisfied belch and cooed in Gretl's arms.

"Aw, honey," Tyrone said lovingly to his fiancée. "She takes after you."

Chapter 22

Each night, Darla traversed to the Clear Creek campground and waited. Waited to see if Jarko would show up, flail his tentacles this way and that, flinging counselors and campers around like a child throwing french fries during a temper tantrum. But he didn't come. Three nights she waited in the hopes he would show. She wanted to talk to him. *Needed* to talk to him. But she didn't want to, once again, show up uninvited to his waterfall and risk getting dragged into his cave and having to fight for her life, or at the very least her dignity.

She didn't think he would do that again. It did feel like they'd reached an amicable détente at the very least. But he had left her mid-kiss with no explanation, and there had to be a reason for that. She could still feel his tentacles around her waist, his fingers caressing her bone crown, both strong and gentle at the same time. A warmth spreading through her veins like lava. And she knew he had wanted her touch as much as she had his. So why did he run from her like she was a human who had discovered his frailty?

After three days of waiting for Jarko to show up at the camp and cause mayhem, Darla grew tired. Not only was she tired of waiting for him, but angry at herself for doing it. She was the Duchess of Death, for crying out loud. She was one of the most feared and legendary monsters around, striking fear into the hearts of millions around the world (in person, via Halloween mask, and a low-budget unauthorized Netflix miniseries where they cast a tiny British actress the size of a blueberry scone to play her. However, they did cast Helen Mirren to play Dolores, so Darla's mother was thrilled).

But one thing Darla Drake did *not* do was wait around for men. And she would not start now.

That night, Darla traversed through the woods of Clear Creek in a foul mood, cutting through trees and bushes with her scourge rather than sidestep them. She realized the silliness of taking out her frustrations on shrubbery, but she couldn't understand what had happened with Jarko, and she needed to get out her anger on something, even if it was inanimate.

When she arrived at Jarko's waterfall, she didn't wait to be let in, and didn't wait for a purple tentacle to shoot out and drag her inside. She traversed right through the water and into Jarko's cave—where she saw him sitting on the floor, naked except for a pair of faded gym shorts, stirring something in a bubbling pot over an open flame.

When he saw her, Jarko yelped, shot up, and grabbed a shirt from a rock outcropping.

"I'm so sorry!" Darla said. She turned around and covered her eyes. "I had no idea you'd be—"

"No idea I'd be what? Potentially not clothed in my own cavern, where I live in secret and solitude and generally don't have to worry about people coming through my waterfall when I'm half naked and cooking dinner?"

"I should have knocked."

"On what, the waterfall?"

"Okay, I could have...thrown a rock or something inside here to let you know I was here," Darla said. "Hey, whatever you're cooking, it smells really, really good."

"First off, that's not the point. Second off, I know."

"Next time I come here, I will make sure to announce my presence with a rock or a deer or something along those lines."

"Why would there be a next time?" Jarko said. Darla felt like she'd been tentacle-whipped in the stomach. Jarko seemed to get that he'd hurt her and said, "I'm sorry. I didn't mean it like that. I just didn't expect you, that's all."

"So, you figured after the other night we'd, what, just never see each other again?"

"I really don't know," he said, stirring the pot with a thin branch. "I hadn't much thought about it."

Something about the way Jarko said it let Darla know he wasn't quite being honest. Still, that wasn't why she came. She breathed in the air. Steam rose from Jarko's concoction. It smelled absolutely delicious.

"Can I ask what's in that?"

Jarko looked at her. His face softened. "Seasoned muskrat, with fresh pinecone, tree sap, and shredded cattails. Want a taste?"

"Don't mind if I do."

She walked over to Jarko's DIY kitchen. He picked up a homemade ladle, dipped it into the pot, then held it out for Darla. She put the ladle in her mouth, chewed, and swallowed the stew. The food was heavenly, especially given that her food intake was 25 percent Pop-Tart.

"Gotta say, I did not see that coming," she said, savoring the flavors. "How do you season your muskrat?"

"I found some salt and pepper left at a Clear Creek campsite," Jarko said. "Plus a little paprika and cumin I 'found' near the cafeteria. Add some ground pine needles, moss, and acorn, and that'll hide some of the sourness of muskrat meat."

"Where'd you learn all of this?"

"Me."

"You taught yourself how to cook?"

"My parents were happy to eat moldy bread and drink whatever was left in discarded soda cans. But just because you were raised a certain way doesn't mean you're tethered to those ways for the rest of your life."

"Whatever you did, it works," Darla said, licking her lips. "Thanks for the taste. Now, can we talk?"

"Sure," Jarko said, returning to his stove.

"Can I have your undivided attention?" she said, with no small amount of irritation.

"But my dinner—"

"There are plenty of muskrats in Maker's Marsh," Darla said. "If you overcook this one, I'm pretty sure you'll survive."

Jarko nodded. He stood up and went over to where Darla stood.

"All right, Duchess," he said. "Let's talk."

"Why did you leave the other night?"

"We finished your challenge," he said. "You beat up Nazis like you'd been doing it your whole life. I was impressed."

"That's not what I'm talking about, Jarko, and you know it."

Jarko looked down and said, "I know."

"If that was a mistake, and we both want to pretend it never happened, just say the word. But I deserve to know why you drifted away without any explanation whatsoever."

"I never said that."

"Never said what?"

"That I want to pretend it never happened."

Darla felt a flame ignite within her chest. "Then I don't understand. Why did you leave?"

"I can't explain it," Jarko replied. "It's just something I can't do. Not to you. Not to me."

"So, you don't have any interest."

"Again, I didn't say that."

"Then tell me why. There has to be a reason for why you left. You owe me an explanation."

"Duchess, please," Jarko said, pleading with her. "Just leave it."

"No," she said. "I won't. Just be honest with me. I don't care what the reasons are. I just deserve to know what they are. No judgments."

"No judgments?"

"None."

"What if I ate a baby?"

"Oh my god, please don't tell me you ate a baby. Did you? Eat a baby?"

"No, I didn't eat a baby, what kind of monster do you take me for? I'm just using it as a hypothetical. What if I *had* eaten a baby?"

"But you just said you didn't."

"You said no judgments. I was using baby-eating as a hypothetical, because if I had, in fact, eaten a baby, you absolutely would have judged me."

"Fine. If you had eaten a baby, I would have judged you."

"So, then you can't honestly ask me that question and say no judgments because if you had found out I ate a baby, you would have passed judgment."

"Can you cut the shit?" Darla said. "You didn't eat a baby. And unless you did something in the *realm* of eating a baby—which I'm reasonably sure you didn't, because you might be a huge asshole sometimes but you're not a baby-eater—then I want you to tell me the truth, Jarko. You owe me that."

"No," he said. "I don't."

Darla felt her blood temperature rise. Smoke rose from her nose.

"You came to Clear Creek," she said. "The territory my family has hunted in for decades. Screw your MCU or MFU or whatever it is. This is *not* your territory. But I let you stay. I gave you a fair shot to prove yourself. You did well. Really well. Better than I thought you could. *You* impressed *me*, and I don't get impressed easily. And then I hunted with you and we disemboweled some scumbags and it was the most fun I've had in years. Maybe ever. And I started to *feel* something for you, despite my better judgment. And I know you did the same. Am I wrong?"

"No," Jarko replied. "You're not wrong."

"Then tell me," she said. "Why did you leave?"

Jarko stood there, silent. He wasn't ignoring her. He seemed to be gathering the courage to give her what she had asked for.

Finally, he said, "I lost someone. A monster who was very close to me."

"Oh, Jarko," she said. "I'm so sorry. Who did you lose?"

"A monster I loved. Very, very much. Her real name was Frederica Fimmel. Her monster name was the Frost Witch. But to me, she was just my Freddy."

"What happened to her?" Darla asked, her voice soft, understanding. She was treading on thin ice now. She was encroaching on Jarko's territory. She could see the pain etched in his blue-gray face when he said Freddy's name. That saying it brought back memories and pain he had tried to push away.

"For years, I hunted in the Humboldt Redwoods State Park in California," Jarko said. "I would hunt loggers and parasitic humans who tried to destroy the redwoods. Some of those trees grow up to three hundred and fifty feet tall. Let me tell you, Duchess, there is absolutely no better feeling in this world than drifting among three-hundred-foot-tall redwoods. It's breathtaking."

"Go on," Darla said, stepping closer to Jarko.

"One day I was too slow. I was distracted. And while my mind was off god knows where, some pyromaniac managed to set a blaze at the base of one of the redwoods. The whole thing went up in flames in minutes. The entire forest was going to burn down. There was nothing I could do." He held up his tentacles. "These are great for batting around bad guys like wiffle balls. Not so much for dealing with a massive forest fire."

"So, the Frost Witch came to help," Darla said.

"The Frost Witch came to help," Jarko said with a sad smile. "Freddy lived in the town over and saw the blaze from her frozen lake. Before I knew what had happened, she'd stopped the fires in their tracks. Saved I don't know how many trees and lives. And after she finished, we hunted down the guy who set the blaze. Let's just say there are few things more satisfying than freezing a pyromaniac and *then* whupping them with a tentacle. Guy must have shattered into a hundred pieces."

"That sounds very cathartic," Darla said.

"You have no idea," Jarko replied. "I was tentacle over

heels for Freddy. She was my everything. I think that's why I was distracted that day among the redwoods. We'd been getting a little more serious, talking about starting a family, and that's all I could think about. I forgot why I was there in the first place. And it cost me everything."

"What happened?" Darla said. "I understand if you don't want to talk about it."

"It's all right," he said. "I have nothing to hide from you, Duchess."

"Then go on."

"We didn't know that pyro had a brother," Jarko said, taking in a deep breath. "And that brother had friends. And one of those friends had money. *Real* money. And used a lot of it to hire a team of monster experts and archaeologists and historians. And they were able to discover Freddy's frailty."

"Oh no. Jarko, I..."

"Of course, we didn't know what her frailty was so we couldn't prepare. As it turned out, her frailty was a bottle of her mother's old perfume, which had been buried with her mother in the Fimmel family mausoleum. The brother found out about it and dug it up. Then they set another fire as bait and waited. Sure enough, Freddy and I came to put it out and deal with the arsonists. The brother dipped a knife in the perfume, heated up the blade so it would cut through Freddy's frozen skin, and when she went to put out the flames, he slid it between her ribs."

"Animals," Darla said.

"I hunted each of them down and made them pay for what they did to her. But I couldn't bring Freddy back. If I hadn't been distracted that day, I would have prevented the fire, which means Freddy never would have had to come put it out, which means they never would have gone looking for her frailty. It was my fault she died."

"There's no way you could have known."

"It doesn't matter. What's done is done. Afterward, I just couldn't stay there. I had to get away. Somewhere without the memories. This all happened about two years ago. I just drifted for about a year. There weren't a lot of open territories with decent hunting. And even less that had trees. If I'm not able to drift around, I'm not all that fast. I can't traverse like you. Not quite as scary when a monster just…jogs after you."

Darla laughed, then covered her mouth. "I'm sorry," she said. "Just, the mental image of you kind of loping after someone with your tentacles flailing about."

"I mean, that's pretty much what it would look like," he said. "And then you took your sabbatical or whatever it was and Clear Creek was listed as an open territory. I figured it was perfect. Miles and miles of woods for me to drift in. Incredible hunting that would replenish every year thanks to parents with disposable income and an apparent dislike for their children. And, most importantly, I could live in your shadow."

"What do you mean by that?" Darla asked.

"I was ashamed after what happened to Freddy. I didn't want to go somewhere and have to think about making a name for myself. Here, I could just be me. Jarko Murkvale would never be as well-known as the Duchess of Death. And that's exactly the way I wanted it. I just didn't expect you to come back. I already have no one. And if you kicked me out of Clear Creek, I'd have nowhere else to go."

"I'm sorry," Darla said. "I didn't know."

"So, the other night when we…"

"Kissed," Darla said.

"I just don't want to do that again. I can't do that again. I can't risk jeopardizing another life of someone I care about."

"I'm not going anywhere."

"I didn't think Freddy was either," he said. "Do you know what your frailty is? Or where it is? Or who might be looking for it?"

"No. I don't."

"Then I can't risk doing something that would encourage someone to start hunting you," Jarko said, tapping his chest. "I'm sorry. For a moment, I thought I could. But I can't."

"This is my choice too," Darla said. She reached out to touch his face, but he stepped back.

"Don't," he said.

"I want you to stay in Clear Creek," she said.

"But you'll be here too."

"We'll coexist," she said. "Trade off hunting weeks."

"I don't know..."

"We'll have nothing to do with each other's hunting lives. Nobody will come for me because of you. Trust me, I'm plenty good at making enemies myself."

"I could teach you how to cook," he said.

"Hey, I've made muskrat before."

"How did it come out?"

"My mother didn't speak to me for a week. But let me try again. Come over for dinner. Meet Dolores. I'll cook."

"I don't know, Duchess."

"Jarko," she said. "I'm not her. You're not putting me at risk. This is my choice. Honor it."

He looked at her, and finally a small smile spread across his lips.

"Okay," Jarko said, "but no muskrat. Try something... simpler."

"I can do that," Darla said.

"Then it's a deal. Dinner it is."

"Dinner it is," Darla said. She gave him the location of their cave.

"I'll be there."

"Just beware of Dolores," Darla said. "She can be…cranky."

"I would be too if I was just a head."

"I'll let her know you're coming, otherwise she's apt to try to bite your legs off."

"Duly noted," Jarko said with a laugh. "When was the last time she left your cave?"

"Left the cave? Probably the last time she had legs."

"She must be going quite a bit stir crazy."

"Or just crazy crazy."

"I'm looking forward to dinner," Jarko said. "As friends."

"As friends."

Jarko looked at Darla, his yellow eyes gleaming, a wide smile on his face. "I'd like that."

"Me too," she lied.

CHAPTER 23

"**W**hat in the blue man-bull hell do I know about cooking?" Darla asked herself, rather audibly, which scared away half the creatures in Maker's Marsh. Unfortunately, Dolores had been little help, which was not a surprise given that 99 percent of the Drake family meals growing up consisted of food that fell off trucks or were stolen from the Clear Creek cafeteria or were not even food, despite Dolores's insistence. It also meant Darla was easy to impress, given that at least 25 percent of her diet was made from powdered taco meat and two-week old milk.

So, she took a page from Jarko's book and decided to wing it. But winging it seemed easy when you were hunting humans whose odds of killing you were about the same as being eaten by a shark while being struck by lightning in the middle of a tsunami made of ketchup. Winging it may not have been the wisest route when whatever concoction she whisked up could potentially turn a monster's stomach inside out.

In her hands she held a basket of fronds and wood, and inside she'd tossed a number of flora, fauna, insects, amphibians, and anything else within her grasp. If it wasn't edible, she could simply boil it until it was.

She saw a frog sitting on a lily pad, staring at her. Frogs were not known to be the most expressive creatures, but she could have sworn it was looking at her with a healthy dose of skepticism.

"Can it," Darla said, aware of the ridiculousness of her scolding a small amphibian. "If you don't get that smug look off your face, I don't care if she just had a baby, I'm going to get Gretl down here and her Gobbler is going to dunk you into her digestive juices."

The frog hopped into the water and swam off. Darla looked at her basket. It was full. She had no idea if the meal would be good, but at least there would be a lot of it.

By the time she finished, the sun was starting to go down. As she traversed back to the cave, Darla thought about her conversation with Jarko. She had never lost someone the way he had. And given that the vast majority of monsters lived for hundreds of years, if not more, the emotions seemed foreign. Impossible to even consider.

When her mother had been decapitated, Darla had been a wreck. Yet even then, she knew Dolores would survive. Not in the same way she had fifteen years ago before Franklin Shine and his lucky shovel. Her anger and sadness there was not so much that she'd lost her mother—she hadn't—but that she'd failed her.

Franklin Shine had come along just months after Darla's father had left them. Darla was starting to come into her own as a monster. Dolores was a shell of herself. Her hunts were sloppy.

She left victims alive, got photographed, only ate seven meals a day, let her scourge rust and fall apart, and was basically a walking disaster of a monster.

And then Franklin Shine got lucky, cut Dolores's head off, not realizing without her frailty it wouldn't kill her. Still, Franklin and his pals buried Dolores's body somewhere in Clear Creek, and despite digging up half the territory, Darla had come up empty.

It had occurred to her that maybe Franklin Shine hadn't actually gotten lucky. That perhaps a part of Dolores actually wanted him to dispatch her. That she blamed herself for her husband leaving, and getting decapitated was penance for not being able to keep him.

Darla had broken up with William Wendell shortly after her mother's "incident." Since then, she'd devoted herself single-mindedly to two things: the hunt and Dolores. There had been no room for anything else. No room for any*one* else.

And until Jarko arrived, she hadn't even considered letting anyone else in. William Wendell was not her monster. She knew that long before they actually broke up. And Dolores's needy head cemented her decision: Darla Drake simply did not have time for Darla Drake.

When she arrived back at the cave, Darla was shocked to find that the boulder at the entryway was sitting off to the side. Given that Dolores wasn't quite able to nudge the giant rock aside with her nose, it meant someone was there. Darla gently placed the basket of ingredients down, unhooked her scourge from her belt, and stepped inside.

She walked through the corridors slowly, listening, feeling the ground for vibrations. There were none. Either nobody was here, or they were able to hide their movements to a degree that no human could, and very few monsters could.

"Hello?" Darla shouted, reaching the main atrium. "Mom?"

No answer. She went into Dolores's room and gasped.

Her mother's head was gone. She looked for signs of a struggle, but then remembered that Dolores didn't exactly have the appendages necessary to struggle with.

Darla felt her blood thicken, her internal temperature rising. Smoke drifted upward from her nostrils. If someone had taken her mother's head, they could be anywhere. Done anything with it. Dolores could be gone for—

"Darla?" came Dolore's voice from the cave's entrance. Darla breathed a sigh of relief. It was her mother.

Darla traversed over to the entrance, only to find Jarko standing there, holding her mother's head in the crook of his arm like a human might carry a baby, or a bowling ball.

"Mom?" Darla said. "Where the hell have you been?"

"Mr. Murkvale here offered to take me for a stroll," Dolores said. "Seeing as how I haven't been outside of this cave in, I don't know, years, I took him up on it."

Darla looked at Jarko, unsure whether to be angry or incredulous.

"You took my mom...for a walk?"

"I got here a little early," Jarko said. "Dolores and I started chatting."

"You and my mom...started chatting?"

"That's right," Dolores said. "At least *someone* is interested in talking to me."

"I've lived with you here for over thirty years, Mom," Darla said.

Dolores looked up at Jarko. "Can you lift me so I can look my daughter in the eye?"

"Sure thing."

Jarko lifted Dolores's head up so she was at eye level with Darla. "You know how much I've missed the outdoors," Dolores said.

"Mom, I kept you in here to protect you. To keep you alive."

"Sitting on the same dresser year after year smelling like Murphy's Oil isn't much living. So, Mr. Murkvale here—"

"Jarko," he said. "Please."

"Jarko offered to bring me to Maker's Marsh to watch the sun set. Then we went over to the Clear Creek campground. It was the first time I'd laid eyes on the camp since I still had my body." A tear streaked down Dolores's cheek. "Jarko, can you get that?"

Jarko removed the tear from Dolores's eye with his finger and wiped it on his jacket.

"It's just nice to know there are still gentlemonsters out there who care about a lady's feelings," Dolores said.

"Jarko," Darla said, picking up her basket. "Could you please bring my mother inside before I throw up all over both of you?"

"Is that for tonight?" Jarko asked.

"It is."

"What are you making?"

"Food," Darla said.

"Well, good, then. I happen to enjoy...food."

"Move it, gentleman."

Jarko carried Dolores's head back inside the cave and placed it on the communal table in the atrium. Darla placed the basket on the table and hung her scourge from an iron hook. Then she looked around the atrium.

"You don't know what to do next, do you?" Jarko asked.

"Yes, I do. You start a fire."

"Okay. Do you have kindling?"

"Do I have what now?"

"Or a pot?"

Darla's silence seemed to let Jarko know that she perhaps hadn't thought all of this through.

"I'm sorry, Mr. Murkvale. Jarko. The Drake family isn't exactly known for its haute cuisine."

"If you don't shut up, Mom, I'm going to duct tape your mouth closed," Darla said.

"See how she speaks to me? I'm sure you don't speak to your mother that way."

"May I?" Jarko said, pointing to the basket.

Darla sighed. "Fine."

Jarko emptied out the contents of the basket and picked through it with his tentacles.

"Okay, not a total loss. But unless you're planning to make grass soup, you're missing a few ingredients."

Jarko looked at Darla, waiting for her to respond. Finally, she said, "You're asking if you can cook."

"I mean, I'm a big fan of grass soup, but I feel like after a long week it won't be very filling."

"He's telling you very politely that you can't cook for crap and unless you want to get swamp poisoning, you should let him do it," Dolores said.

"Mom. Duct tape."

"Darla is really good at a lot of things," Jarko said. "She's the best hunter I've ever met."

Darla felt her heart swell. She brushed a trail of smoke from her nose.

"This is just one thing that maybe I can do a little bit better,"

Jarko said. "But it's your cave. I'm not here to impose. I'll only co—"

"Do it," Darla said. "Stop trying to sell us on it and just make dinner."

"Thank god," Dolores whispered under her breath. Darla shot her mother's head a glare and Dolores closed her mouth.

"Let me just run out and get a few more things. Back in a couple."

Jarko took the basket and left the cave. Darla took a seat.

"Can I speak now?" Dolores asked.

"Depends on what you're going to say."

"He's not what I expected," Dolores said.

"Join the club," Darla said, stretching her legs.

"So, are you two…friends now?" Dolores asked.

Darla breathed in deeply and said, "I don't know. I don't know what we are."

"But you like him."

"It doesn't matter if I like him," Darla said.

"He likes you."

Darla sat up. "What did you say?"

"I said he. Likes. You."

"How do you know that?"

"When he was taking me around Clear Creek," Dolores said, "all he wanted to talk about was you. What a thrill it was to hunt the way you'd laid out for him, how he'd never really taken his time like that. He said you opened up a new world for him."

"He really said that? You're not just blowing smoke?"

"I don't have lungs to blow smoke with," Dolores said. "But yes. He said it. And he also said you were a natural at—how did he put it?—tearing shit up."

Darla laughed. "We did tear shit up."

"Your father was like that," Dolores said.

"Like what?"

"Preferred to hunt with a little bit of chaos, a little bit of anarchy. You have some of him in your blood."

"I don't want to talk about him."

"Never be ashamed of who you are," Dolores said. "He had good qualities. You got those. The rest, well, you're still here. So, I guess those other qualities weren't passed on."

"Or I'm just better than he was."

Dolores smiled. "That you are."

They heard a noise from the cave entrance, the sound of suctions, and Jarko drifted into the atrium carrying the basket in his free hand. When he landed, he placed the basket on the table.

"Is it...moving?" Dolores asked.

Sure enough, something inside the basket was trying to get out.

"That's our main course," he said. "Don't worry. It won't bounce around after I'm done with it."

"What is it?" Darla asked.

"That, Duchess, is a surprise."

"Just cook it before it escapes," Dolores added. "I don't need whatever is in there getting loose and chomping on my nose in the middle of the night."

Jarko laughed and slung a knapsack onto the table with a clank. He untied it and removed a large iron pot and several fitted logs to hold it over the flame, along with kindling and small stones to keep the fire contained. He set up his makeshift kitchen at the far end of the atrium and quickly got a fire going. Darla and Dolores watched in awe.

"I feel like I'm watching Picasso paint," Dolores said. "Or Michael Myers use a kitchen utensil."

"Come on, Mrs. Drake," Jarko said. "Hold off on the superlatives until you actually taste it. I'm sure Darla has made some delicious meals here over the years."

"My daughter is many things," Dolores said. "A brilliant hunter. A terrifying monster. A master of the cleaning arts. And while I love my daughter with every fiber of, well, what's left of me, no offense to her, but, unfortunately, culinary wizardry is not one of her skills."

"No offense taken," Darla said. "If I tried to do this, I would burn the cave down. And rock isn't even flammable."

They watched Jarko work, his tentacles moving around like a painter with a brush. He let the flame heat up the pot, then he tossed in a number of plants and flowers, along with some spices that smelled heavenly. While that cooked, he went outside and got a bucket of swamp water and poured it in as well. Once it was boiling, he took the basket, along with whatever was causing all that commotion inside, and dumped it into the pot.

He stirred, then let the pot simmer. After a few minutes, he took a spoon and tasted his concoction. He smiled, then refilled the spoon and brought it over to Darla.

"Taste," he said simply.

Darla opened her mouth and closed her eyes and felt him place the spoon on her tongue.

"Oh wow," she said. "That is amazing. What is it?"

"Trade secret," he said.

"Gimme, gimme, gimme," Dolores whined. Jarko brought her another spoonful and fed it to the elder Drake. "Oh. Mr. Murkvale. You are invited to come cook for us any time you like."

"Appreciate it, Mrs. Drake."

"Dolores. You put all those amateur chefs on the television to shame. And they don't even cook with live ingredients."

Jarko laughed and said, "Just a few more minutes and it'll be ready to serve. Darla, do you have anything to drink?"

"That," she said, "I can do."

Darla made a batch of the same drink she'd made for Jarko the other night, adding a few drops of her plasma to give it the right amount of smoky flavor.

When Jarko was finished, Darla placed three bowls on the table. She also got a curved dish from the shelf and placed her mother's head in it. When she caught Jarko looking at the setup, she said, "When she drinks, it makes a bit of a mess since it just kind of, well, comes out her stump."

"Ah, gotcha."

Jarko filled the bowls with his stew and Darla filled three glasses with her drink.

"To new friends," Jarko said.

"New friends," Darla said with feigned enthusiasm.

"To my new favorite chef," Dolores said.

"Yeah, like you have a huge sample size to compare him to," Darla said. She brought a spoonful to her mouth. The moment the stew touched her tongue, she felt a warmth spread through her body, her blood temperature rising, a wisp of smoke rising to the top of the cave.

"Some people burp when they have a good meal," Jarko said, "some people literally appear to be catching on fire. I'll take it."

"It's amazing," Darla said. She sipped her drink. They paired together perfectly.

"Forgetting someone?" Dolores said.

Darla sighed and spoon fed her mother. Dolores licked her lips and moaned with delight.

"Drink?" she said. Darla poured some of the cup into her mother's mouth. The dish below her head began to fill with a mixture of Jarko's food and Darla's drink as it went down her throat and then out her neck.

"Honestly, I should just put your head in Depends," Darla said.

"Everything okay, hon?" Dolores said as Darla fed her another spoon of the stew. "You seem extra grumpy tonight."

"No, I don't."

"Yes. You do."

"Jarko. Do I seem grumpy?"

"Not especially?" he said. "To be fair, the first few times we met you tried to lop my arm off with your scourge, so this is relatively polite."

"Okay. I'm sorry. Let's just have a nice meal." She ladled more soup into Dolores's mouth.

"Ooh, bone, bone," Dolores said, opening her mouth wide. Darla stuck her finger into her mother's mouth and pulled out what appeared to be a fully intact spine from whatever Jarko had cooked in his stew. Darla unwedged it from her mother's epiglottis and tossed it onto the floor.

"Sorry about that," Jarko said.

"Please don't be," Dolores said. "Bones add flavor. I just can't floss as easily as I used to."

Jarko laughed. "You're all right, Mrs. Drake. Dolores."

Darla saw a flush rise in her mother's wrinkly cheeks, a color she hadn't seen in a very long time. She looked like a mummy blushing.

They ate and drank and sat for hours. Dolores regaled them

with stories from her early hunting days.

"I swear," she said, "the shorts the counselors wore back then, when they ran from you, you could practically see everything the lord gave them. Now, they wear shorts that are basically pants."

"What was your favorite hunt of all time?" Jarko asked.

"Ooh, that's a good question," Dolores said, arching her eyebrows in thought. "I would have to say...summer of 1964. Some members of that white hooded Klan came up here to Clear Creek, trying to recruit some of the young boys. Taking them apart with my scourge was just a pure joy. Much more fulfilling than teaching a lesson to some counselors who couldn't keep their hands to themselves."

"Seriously," Darla said, "what did all you monsters have against sex?"

"It was a different time," Dolores said. "Social mores aren't what they are now. You're taught right and wrong and you follow those teachings and don't know any better. That's not an excuse, it's just the way it was. And you hopefully learn and grow and teach the next generation of monsters that two consenting adults who want to play grabby hands or smoke some potty should be left alone as long as they aren't hurting anyone else."

"Did you just say 'grabby hands' and 'smoke some potty'?" Jarko said, laughing so hard a masticated toe shot out of his nose.

"Ha-ha, everyone laugh at the old monster," Dolores said. "We didn't have it easy back then, we had to—"

"I know, I know, Mom," Darla said. "You had to ride a dinosaur thirty miles in the freezing snow just to disembowel teenagers."

They laughed and ate and drank and even Darla had to admit that her mother was pretty darn good company. Her stories were hilarious and gruesome and Jarko seemed mesmerized by them. And not in an ironic way, like Darla usually was, but he asked questions, stared wide-eyed, this huge monster seeming more like a monster fanboy than someone she had just seen tear apart an entire bar of Nazi scum.

Jarko was having fun. And almost despite herself, Darla was too.

Several times throughout the meal, however, she caught Jarko looking at her. And not just while she was talking. Dolores would be in the middle of a story about smushing two teens with a plastic kayak and Jarko would be staring at her, a silly, imperceptible smile on his face. And the moment he saw her notice, he would look away, turn back to Dolores, pretend nothing had happened.

Every time she caught it, Darla's blood rose several degrees. She'd been around enough monsters to know that the way Jarko was looking at her was decidedly *not* the way you looked at a friend.

She didn't know what to make of it. He was also far more charming than she remembered, and seeing joy in her mother's face brought her a mixture of happiness and remorse. Dolores's life had been so small since Darla's father had left and after Franklin Shine cleaved her in two. And as overbearing as she could be, Darla rarely did much to make her life better. It was mostly finding things like books and TVs and e-readers that would occupy her attention. Attention Darla had grown tired of.

Darla rarely asked about her mother's past, about her hunts, about her life. But Jarko couldn't get enough of it, and

Darla could tell that Dolores was eating up the attention. Quite literally. Dolores ate and drank so much that every so often Darla had to lift her mother's head out of the dish and clean it and her stump before she ended up to her nose in drink and stew.

After a while, Darla could see Dolores's eyelids start to droop. This was the longest dinner Darla could remember, and her mother was clearly struggling to stay awake.

"I think it might be time for bed, Mom," Darla said.

Dolores blinked. "Nope. I have plenty of energy. I'm getting my second wind." Then Dolores yawned so wide her chin touched the bottom of the dish her head rested in.

"I think that yawn was your second wind leaving your body. Er, face," Darla said.

"I know, I just haven't had this much fun in a long time. Jarko, promise me we'll do this again soon."

Jarko smiled and said, "I'm glad you had fun, Ms. Drake. I can see why you're a legend."

Dolores uttered a high-pitched laugh Darla had never heard before. "You, sir, are a charmer. Hon, think you'd better put me in my room before I start to drool."

Darla picked up her mother and took her into the bedroom. She placed her carefully on the table and extinguished the candles with the tips of her fingers.

"He's a good one," Dolores said, her eyes beginning to close. "Don't you think?"

"I do," Darla said softly, as her mother closed her eyes and began to gently snore.

She watched her mother sleeping peacefully and wiped her mouth where a little dribble of saliva had begun to slide down her lips. She couldn't remember the last time Dolores had been so animated. With or without legs.

Darla went back into the atrium. Jarko sat there, sipping his drink.

"She asleep?" he said. Darla nodded. "Okay. Time to go, I suppose."

He put his cup down and stood up.

"You can stay," Darla said.

Jarko hesitated. There was something in his yellow eyes that seemed at war with itself.

"Please," Darla added.

Jarko merely nodded and sat back down.

"Another round, then," he said.

Darla smiled and poured him a cup. He watched as she pierced her finger on her bone crown, allowing a few drops to plummet into his cup. Darla shook the cup and held it out to him. He took it and drank.

"Damn, that's good," he said. "I'm going to need the recipe."

"Part of the recipe is literally me, so unless you plan to drain me of all my blood and take it with you, I'm not sure how that's going to work."

"I know a few vampires who could help with that," Jarko said. "But they're generally not fans of just holding on to blood, if you know what I mean."

"You know where I live," Darla said. "You can come by any time for a refill."

Jarko smiled sadly and twirled his cup in his fingers.

"What's wrong?" she asked.

Jarko looked up at her. There was something in his eyes she'd never seen before. And it felt like a lead ball had implanted itself in her stomach. Sadness.

"You look like you just found out a human discovered your

frailty," Darla said. "Please tell me they didn't."

Jarko laughed quietly. "Nope, thankfully, to the best of my knowledge, it's still hidden."

"So, what's up, then? Why do you look like you just found out that your tentacles are about to fall off?"

Jarko looked up at her and said, "I'm leaving Clear Creek."

The lead ball in Darla's stomach caught fire. She felt her blood temperature rise. Steam poured out from her nostrils. She didn't bother to wave it away.

"You're joking," she said. "Right? This is a joke."

"No joke."

"I don't understand."

"I checked my MFU. There's a territory that just opened up in Maine that runs from Bangor down to Bucksport and the Gulf of Maine. Tons of woods so I have plenty of room to drift, and the gulf has plenty of fishermen and lobstermen who get drunk and do terrible things to the mainlanders. Lobstra has been hunting in that territory for a long time, but, apparently, she's retiring to her home in the gulf. I put in a claim for her soon-to-be old territory this morning."

"You did *what*?" Darla said. "No. You can't do that."

"I have to do that, Duchess."

"You said you would stay," she said. "We agreed that we would work this out."

"They're just words, Duchess. We can't predict what will happen. Or if I might do the wrong thing thinking it's the right thing. What if one night I think you need help and smite the wrong person? You could end up with your frailty exposed. And that would be on me. I decided I just can't risk that. I can't risk you."

"I told you this is my choice. I made it. Please respect it."

"I'm making this decision because I respect you. Because I…"

Jarko trailed off.

"Please," Darla said.

"Before I came here," Jarko said, "I lost the monster I cared about more than anything in the world. And when it was over, I promised myself I would never let that happen again. I'm not going back on that promise."

"I'm not going anywhere," Darla said. "I can take care of myself. Anyone who comes for me will end up in pieces. I'm willing to open myself up for this. For you."

"Then maybe I'm not," he said. "Maybe some monsters are just meant to be lonely."

"Loneliness is a choice," Darla said, "not a sentence. I've been making that choice for too long. I'm willing to make a different one."

"Then loneliness is *my* choice."

"So make a different one."

"I can't."

"You could stay," Darla said. "You could hunt in Clear Creek. We don't have to even see each other."

"You know that's not realistic," Jarko said. "You don't need me. You're a hunter. I saw the look in your eye when we turned that bar inside out. I saw how excited you got when I hunted Randy Horvath. You were *born* to be a hunter. That's your destiny."

"Maybe that's not the only destiny I want," Darla said.

"Whatever destiny you want, I can't be part of it. I came to Clear Creek to be alone. If I can't be that here, then I need to be somewhere that I can."

"And I can't convince you to stay."

Jarko shook his head. "I'm sorry, Duchess."

"So, when do you leave?"

"Next week. Lobstra scheduled a final hurrah for this weekend. Some big corporation opened up a chain seafood joint and they're pushing out all the local shacks by threatening their families and bribing officials. She's sharpening her claws for one last hunt. Then she's off and her territory around the Gulf of Maine is mine."

Darla ran her hand over her bone crown. She felt like a balloon had inflated inside her chest and her dozens of ribs were going to burst and impale her heart.

"So that's it, then," she said.

"That's it."

"Next week," Darla said. "The Monster Mash is this weekend at the TohoTown quarry."

"Should I still come?"

"It's your life," Darla said. "You know what? Come. We'll drink some quarry water and toast to your fresh start."

Jarko looked at her with narrow eyes, as though he didn't fully trust this magnanimous offer, and said, "You sure?"

"Of course. It's a great idea. Toss a few back, and we'll say goodbye on good terms. Then you'll be gone and it'll be just like you were never here. A final goodbye before the good riddance."

"Duchess, I—"

"No. It's okay. I get it. A monster's gotta do what a monster's gotta do. Just so we're clear, I never felt anything. I had a little fun, but that's all. If you misinterpreted that kiss as more, then I apologize for the miscommunication."

She sensed a wound behind Jarko's eyes, but she didn't much care.

"You don't feel anything either now, right?" Darla said.

"Just so we're clear and on the same page. Tell me you feel nothing so we can both move on."

Jarko hesitated, then said, "I felt nothing."

"Good. Then it's settled. I'll see you at the Monster Mash this weekend. And then I'll never see you again."

"Duchess, I—"

"Good night, Jarko. Thanks for dinner. Don't bother leaving the recipe."

He stood there for what seemed like an eternity. Darla waited, wondering, hoping he might say something, anything. Then, when he didn't, she watched as Jarko turned around and walked slowly toward the entrance to the cave. She waited until she heard him slide the boulder out of the way, and then back in. Then she sat there in the dark, willing herself not to feel anything. And then Darla Drake, Duchess of Death, lay in bed, wide awake, until morning.

CHAPTER 24

D arla only left the cave once over the next several days, and that was to dump the remnants of Jarko's stew into Maker's Marsh and then kick dirt over the puddle as it congealed atop the water. She hated herself for what she'd become. For what she'd allowed herself to feel. She should have known better. Jarko Murkvale was *exactly* who she thought he was the moment she laid eyes on him: a selfish interloper who was hell-bent on destruction and chaos. Unfortunately for Darla, she hadn't known at the time that he could cause that kind of chaos inside her, as well as outside in Clear Creek.

She moved like a monster whose brain had been removed but was still alive. Like a reverse Frankenstein's monster, only angrier and more bitter. She cleaned Dolores's table, wiped off her face when she coughed or drooled in her sleep, and generally walked around with smoke trailing from her nostrils like she was permanently on fire.

One morning, Dolores, after nearly being knocked off her

perch by an errant dust rag, said, "I don't understand, Dar. We had such a good time the other night with Jarko. Didn't we? And now you're back to being a mopey monster. I don't get it. Can you explain it to me?"

"You liked being outside so much with Jarko?" Darla replied. "How about I dig a hole out there for you in the dirt and let some woodchucks roll you around in it for a few days."

That was the last time Dolores asked Darla why she was acting mopey.

She spent a full day oiling the leather straps of her scourge. Polishing the brass studs. She'd been wrong in her decision to give up the hunt a year ago. Her challenges with Jarko had proved that. She'd felt *alive* watching him terrify Randy Horvath. Felt the blood heat up and thicken in her veins as they ransacked the Absinthe Bar. She'd always enjoyed the hunt, but those nights took it to another level.

And for a few fleeting moments, Darla saw what her life could have been like. Giving up the hunt wasn't the solution to her problems. Her problems were, as Gretl said, that she wanted more than just the hunt. Now, she would just have to find it another way. Some day. And she had the rest of her—possibly infinite—life to figure it out.

Joy.

When the evening of the Monster Mash arrived, Darla cleaned her tunic, polished and sharpened her bone crown, and strapped her oiled and glistening scourge to her leather belt. She went over to the cracked full-length mirror in her mother's room and took inventory of herself. Her appearance on the outside hid how she felt inside. She looked strong. Confident. Like she could tear the head off a rampaging lion and look good while doing it.

She replayed her last conversation with Jarko. Asking him to make a different choice. And how he'd refused. For the first time in Darla's life, she'd felt like her life might take a different path than the one she'd seen. That there could be more than just the hunt. But when Jarko refused, he'd taken that choice away from her. Scrubbed the path clean.

"I'm glad you're going tonight," Dolores said from her perch atop the table.

"Gotta keep living, I guess," Darla said.

"I think you'll have fun," she said. "I miss going to Mashes. Seeing all the monsters I'd grown up with. Meeting the new ones. Chatting with my girlfriends about which monsters looked like they'd be the best hunters and trying to get them to flirt with us a little bit. Before I met your father, of course. Do you know one time I was talking to the Boston Basher and the Sheepskin Man came up from behind him, stole his wooden mallet, and tossed it into the lake? He never found it. We thought he was going to bash *our* brains in! Thankfully, I was pretty good with my scourge. Not on your level, but I could hold my own."

"Yeah, well, I'll always have the scourge, I guess. Least I have that going for me."

"You have the world going for you," Dolores said. "You are an exceptional monster. And you don't need anyone to tell you that."

"*You* just told me that."

"I'm your mother. You don't listen to me anyway."

Darla laughed, and it felt like a crack in a cement wall.

"Sorry if I've been a mope lately," she said.

"You used that word. Not me."

"Yeah, well, maybe I have been a mopey monster."

"You have been," Dolores said. "But I understand. So go

have fun tonight. Dance a little. Drink too much. Flirt with the wrong type of monster."

"Look at you being a bad influence."

"Sometimes being a good influence means being a bad one."

"Maybe it does," Darla said. "See you later, Mom. Don't wait up for me. And let me know if you go anywhere."

"Where could I possibly—oh. That was a joke. Har-har."

Darla winked at her mother and left the cave. She was going to have fun tonight, even if it killed her. Or, preferably, someone else.

CHAPTER 25

The TohoTown quarry was filled with dozens upon dozens of monsters. The limestone-lined pit itself was fifty feet deep, half a mile wide in every direction, with a small, green-tinged lake in its center. Monster Mashes had been held once a year at the TohoTown quarry for at least the last hundred years, and Darla herself had been going since she was in her early twenties.

She still remembered her very first Monster Mash. She'd met Gretl by Maker's Marsh, where they'd pregamed with Gretl's then-boyfriend, Simon Scythe, drinking fermented swamp water until they were sufficiently lubricated for Darla to leave her inhibitions on the banks of the marsh.

Though Darla had met a few monsters over the years—her mother's friends, Gretl's various boyfriends, and a few nomad monsters who came through the area—the Monster Mash was like nothing she'd ever seen. And tonight, the quarry was packed to the walls with monsters of all walks of life (and death), all shapes and sizes, from all over the country and beyond. It was the biggest Mash Darla had ever seen, and when she took it all in, she forgot about Jarko and Dolores and even the hunt and just marveled at how incredible the monster world was, and how much she loved being a part of it.

To the left of the entrance, she saw the familiar sight of ZAPruder Man, white electricity coursing all along his skin. He'd been in charge of Monster Mash security and secrecy for as long as Darla could remember. Rather than participating in the Mash, ZAPruder Man would stand there and send electrical currents into the sky, shorting out all electronic devices and surveillance equipment, making it impossible for there to be any surveillance of the Mash from either humans, satellites, or turncoat monsters. Planes couldn't fly through the electrical storm, cell phones would fry the moment they came near the electrical field, not to mention the electrical current sparkled in the night air, like millions of miniature explosions. Sadly, ZAPruder Man did not do monster birthday parties.

Dozens of monsters crowded around the quarry lake, dipping cups into the green water. They would then either drink it right then and there or add garnishes such as powdered limestone scooped out from the quarry, plant life from the lake, or their own bodily fluids (or the bodily fluids of other monsters, depending on how smashed the monster in question was).

Music filled the air as a Slayer cover band made up of monster musicians played atop a makeshift rock stage. Their instruments were all acoustic, guitars carved from trees, strings made from animal hair, and drums from the skin of...well... Darla wasn't quite sure where the drum skins had come from and knew better than to ask.

Dozens of monsters were gyrating and frolicking on a dance floor of smooth limestone. PorcuPaul stood in the center, dancing alone, as other monsters wisely avoided the hundreds of foot-long spikes that protruded from his body.

Out in the center of the lake, Darla could see Fin swimming beneath the surface, dorsal fin skimming through the green with a rope wrapped around it as Eunice Englund, aka Minnie Mouth, waterskied behind him, her jaw open two feet wide as she screamed with excitement.

Darla walked through the party, instantly forgetting the past week as she caught up with friends she hadn't seen in years. She hugged Klondike, then brushed the icicles from her tunic. She learned that Mitchell Marks, aka Machete Boy, was engaged to Stephen Scorpius, and that an invitation for their ceremony to take place at the local pet cemetery would be arriving at Darla's cave within the next few weeks.

She saw Kathleech in a corner full-on making out with Ivory Man, leaving massive hickeys all over his neck as she appeared to be trying to suck all the blood out of him in one slurp. RhiNora looked to be in competition with Dozer to see who could ram their heads into the limestone walls at the fastest speed without knocking themselves unconscious. Darla walked through the party with a huge smile on her face. These were her people. This was where she belonged. Jarko could go to hell. When he left to go to Maine, he would never come back. And good riddance. She had all the monster friends she needed right here.

She got a drink from the lake and watched Fin and Minnie Mouth circle for a few laps. Minnie's mouth was open so wide Darla saw all manner of insects—and maybe even a small bird or two—disappear into her maw. The drink immediately began to cool Darla's blood. And after a week where it felt like she was on the verge of boiling the entire time, it was a welcome sensation.

She watched as Fin leapt out of the lake, taking Minnie into the air with a joyful shriek so loud it could have shattered glass, when Darla heard a familiar voice.

"Dar! I'm so glad you made it!"

Darla turned around to see Gretl and Tyrone approaching. Tyrone had several chains wrapped around his shoulders, and behind him attached to the chains was a large metal box. The box had several holes punched into it. Every so often a growl would emanate from the box and it would bounce around, what was kept inside it clearly not too happy about being there.

Gretl ran up to Darla and wrapped her arms around her. She opened her mouth and her Gobbler shot out, wrapping its tiny arms around Darla's earlobe. It then went to take a bite of her earlobe, but Gretl retracted it before it could leave with a chunk of Darla's head.

"Hey, Darla," Tyrone said. He lugged the box over and gave Darla a kiss on the cheek.

"Hey, Ty. Um, where's your hatchet?"

Tyrone sighed. "Manti stole it the other day and hacked down half the forest before I was able to put her back in her enclosure."

"So that's Manti in there presumably?" Darla said, pointing to the bouncing box, which either held a ticked-off baby monster or the world's most aggressively popping popcorn.

"That is Manti," Tyrone said. "We both wanted to come tonight and, well, the last sitter we got for her got her leg bitten off. So, we had to bring her. Had to weld a couple extra metal plates on to keep her from busting out. This girl is *strong*. I'll tell you, when she's old enough to hunt, she's going to break some people in half. Literally."

"So, how's the brand-new mom feeling?" Darla asked.

"Actually, pretty good!" Gretl answered cheerfully. "Took about a day, day and a half for my body to sew itself back together after this chonker practically ripped me in half."

"Oh wow, that long?" Darla said.

"I know. Took *forever* to feel like myself again. You know, I heard that human women can take *weeks* to heal after giving birth. Sometimes months, even. And some of them *never* fully heal. Isn't that insane? How do they do it?"

"I have no idea, but if that's true, then I hope human women get at least a year or two off from work to recover."

"Can you imagine having to go back to work a few weeks after squeezing something the size of a bowling ball out of your body?" Gretl said.

"No way humans make each other do that," Darla said. "They aren't that sadistic. I bet humans treat their moms pretty well."

"To moms," Gretl said, raising her glass. "Old and new."

"To moms."

Darla looked at Tyrone cooing at Manti through her cage and felt a pang in her chest. She knew she didn't *need* a partner. She could go through her life without one and be mostly satisfied. But it would also be nice to have someone there to take care of her in the event she got decapitated on the job.

Gretl's eyes widened. "Oh, hell. You've got to be kidding me."

"What is it?" Darla said. She turned around to see what Gretl was looking at and saw it instantly. Or saw *him* instantly.

He stood over seven feet tall, his black body covered in fine hair. He wore only a skimpy pair of brown briefs, no shirt or shoes. His two incisors were twice as long as the rest of his teeth and moved back and forth as he talked. Oh, and he had eight long, hairy legs sticking out from his abdomen.

"Fucking Mantula," Gretl whispered. "Who even invited him? I haven't seen him since we..."

Gretl mimicked a whole bunch of fingers going through a hole.

"Ugh. Does Tyrone know that you and Mantula...I can't even say it."

"He does. I mean, it's not like Tyrone was ClericMan before we met. He had partners. They were all skankmonsters, but I don't hold it against him. He knows Mantula and I had a thing, and that it didn't go anywhere, and that he's the love of my infinite lifespan."

"So, you're not worried that Tyrone will get jealous?"

"Bitch, please," Gretl said. "I've done things with Tyrone that would make Mantula's arms fall right off his body."

The box containing Manti bounced right off the ground, falling back to earth and leaving a six-inch divot in the limestone.

"Is she hungry?" Darla asked.

"I don't think so. I fed her someone off the sex offender registry right before we came here. But who knows with babies."

Darla watched as Mantula talked with several other monsters. They were feeling his legs, which he flexed like he was entering a monster bodybuilding competition. When he saw Darla looking at her, he winked. Darla felt her stomach lurch.

"I'm glad you're here," Darla said. "It's been a hell of a week."

"But now you're back, right? In the hunt?"

"I am. The hunt wasn't the problem."

"I know, Dar. I know."

Before Darla could say anything else, Gretl put her arm around Darla and started to drag her quickly away from the lake.

"Come on," she said urgently. "There are much cooler monsters over this way."

"Where are we going?" Darla said. "I was just going to refill my drink."

Darla untangled herself from Gretl and turned back to the lake to get more quarry water when she saw what Gretl was trying to prevent her from seeing. Or more specifically, *who* Gretl was trying to prevent her from seeing.

"That monsterfucker," Darla said.

Standing at the other end of the lake, talking it up with half a dozen monsters and appearing to have the time of his life, was Jarko Murkvale.

CHAPTER 26

"Dar," Gretl said. "Dar, talk to me. You look like you might dismember someone right here."

"Why don't you give me your scourge?" Tyrone said. "You know, just for the rest of the night."

Tyrone reached for her scourge, but Darla slapped his hand away with such force that if he were a human, that hand would be on the ground without the rest of him.

Darla figured Jarko might still come to the Mash. Every monster was, and he did say he'd be here until he took over Lobstra's territory. But seeing him here, seeing him...*laugh* it up like he was the happiest monster alive, it made Darla's blood boil. Apparently literally. Because Tyrone said, "Uh, Darla, I think you're on fire."

She saw thick trails of smoke snaking out from her nostrils and waved them away. But they just kept on coming.

"Dar," Gretl said, "don't do anything you might regret. Because one time when I thought Tyrone was going to break up with me, I had my Gobbler punch a hole in his throat."

Tyrone nodded, wincing at the painful memory. "It healed. But man did it hurt having a baseball-sized hole in my esophagus for a little while."

Darla smiled. She looked at Gretl. Then at Tyrone.

"I'm not going to do anything I'll regret," she said.

"That definitely sounds like you're going to do something you'll regret," Gretl said.

"Not in the slightest. I'm here at the Monster Mash with my best friends in the world. I'm here to have fun. That's all I'm going to do. Have fun."

"What exactly does fun entail?" Gretl said. "Should we warn the other monsters?"

Darla looked around the quarry. She didn't quite know what she was looking for. All she knew was that out of the corner of her eye she could see Jarko laughing with Sawmill Stacy *and* The Blackened Sailor, and every molecule in her body felt like it wanted to do something terrible, something stupid, something...

Mantula.

There he was. Standing at the lake. By himself, filling up eight cups with lake water, one in each leg. He then proceeded to down one after another before wiping his lips with one hairy limb.

Gretl must have seen this, because she said, "Oh no. Darla. Don't even *think* about it."

"Think about what?" she said, starting to head toward the lake. "I'm here to have fun. So, I'm going to go have some fun."

"*That* is not fun," Gretl said, grabbing hold of Darla's arm. "*That* is a bad, bad, *bad* decision."

"I'm a grown monster, Gretl," Darla said. "And you're not

my mother. Or her head."

Then she headed down toward the lake, ignoring Gretl's shouts from behind her.

She walked up next to Mantula, dipped her cup in the water, filled it to the brim, then drank it all in one gulp. She leaned down and refilled her cup. She could feel Mantula watching her, a sly, crooked smile on his face.

"Thirsty?" he said.

"You have no idea."

Mantula turned to face her. He was enormous, well over seven feet tall, dwarfing even Jarko. His body was wide and covered in fine tufts of black hair. She could see herself reflected a thousand times in his eyes. When he spoke, the small protruding teeth on either side of his mouth wiggled, as if he was trying to trap a small creature with every word.

"Darla Drake, right?" Mantula said. His voice was like sandpaper being rubbed on rocks. "The one and only Duchess of Death."

"That's me," Darla said, taking a healthy swig. She dribbled some lake water down her chin and wiped it off with the sleeve of her tunic. "Creature of Clear Creek. At your service."

"At your service," Mantula said, scratching his chin with one of his eight hands. "Now what exactly does that entail?"

Darla looked across the lake. Jarko was still there. He was surrounded by monsters: men, women, non-binary, non-living, every form of life and afterlife. They all seemed to be enjoying his company.

But Jarko wasn't paying attention to them. He wasn't even smiling. He was looking right at her. At Darla. And he did not seem to be enjoying what he saw.

Good, she thought. *The hell with him.*

"I don't know," Darla said. "What do you want it to mean?"

Mantula's eyes glistened in the night. "Let's go for a walk," he said. "Hard to hear monsters talk, it's so noisy."

"A walk," Darla said.

"Just a walk," Mantula said. "Good company and good conversation."

Maybe Gretl was wrong, Darla thought. Maybe Mantula got a bad rap.

"Sure. Lead the way."

Mantula extended three hands in a direction away from the lake. Darla walked slowly, Mantula trailing just behind her. She couldn't tell if he was being gentlemanly or if he was gazing at her ass. She wanted to believe the former. She'd give him the benefit of the doubt. Maybe his situation with Gretl was more complicated than it seemed.

They threaded their way through the Mash, Darla stopping briefly to make small talk with monsters she hadn't seen since the last party. She noticed that Mantula wasn't greeting anyone. He just walked through the crowd, single-minded. He turned back and looked at her and said, "We've never really had a chance to chat, you and me. I'm such a fan."

"Thanks," Darla said. "I didn't know that."

"I told Gretl that when she and I..." Mantula paused. "I know you two are close. And there are things I wish I'd done different. But I'm glad she's happy now. Hatchetman seems like a hell of a guy, and a mighty hunter."

"He is both," Darla said. "That's big of you not to be jealous."

Mantula made a *pfft* sound. "Every monster has a monster that's right for them. We weren't each other's monster."

They walked through the quarry and found a trail that led

through the limestone rock, near a cave that had been boarded up years ago. Mantula sat on an outcropping of rock, and beckoned Darla to take a seat next to him. She hesitated, but then sat.

"I heard you took, what's the term, a little sabbatical from hunting?" Mantula said, stretching four legs above his head.

"You heard right."

"Wow. Guess it hits all of us sometimes."

"What do you mean?"

"We've all felt that way from time to time," Mantula said. "A little bit of the, I don't know, *monster doldrums*. Wondered what else is out there. What you might be missing."

"*You've* had that too?" Darla asked, surprised.

"You kidding?" he said. "Just a few months back, I finished eating some hitchhiker and I was sitting there thinking, how many times have I done this? I have a lot of years left. How many more of these things am I going to regurgitate? Do I even enjoy it anymore?"

"Sounds familiar," Darla said. "Kind of gross, but familiar."

Mantula shrugged. "So, I've thought about it. Taking a little time off. Seeing what else is out there."

"Really?"

Mantula nodded. "Being a monster isn't always as easy as it seems," he said. "Sure, you're pretty much invincible, and you'll live forever unless some lucky human discovers your frailty. But other than that, you have a *lot* of time to think about what you want."

Darla nodded. Was she agreeing with *Mantula*?

"So, what do you want?" he asked.

"Honestly?" she said with a sigh. "I'm not sure anymore. I wasn't sure I wanted the hunt, so I took time away, but I don't think that was it. I still enjoy it. I still get a thrill from it. It's still what I believe I'm meant to do. It's just not *all* of what I'm meant to do."

"What else do you think you're meant to do?"

Darla looked up. The night was so beautiful, the rocky walls like white paintings against the lush, navy-blue sky. "Guess I'm hoping to find my monster," she said. "Hunting is fun. Sharing it with someone might make it better."

"I agree," Mantula said.

Then she noticed that two of Mantula's legs had propped his body up ever so slightly, then moved him just a little bit closer to Darla.

"What are you doing?" Darla asked.

"I'm agreeing with you," Mantula replied. "Sharing the hunt, sharing a life with someone would make everything that much sweeter."

He scooted over several more inches. She felt several of Mantula's legs brush up against her back.

Darla shrugged them off and stood up. "I'm going to go back to the Mash," she said. "Thanks for the conversation."

"But we've barely scratched the surface," Mantula said. He stood up as well, his massive body towering over hers. "I have the Duchess of Death to myself and I want to get to know her. *Intimately.*"

"I think you've had too much to drink."

"I think I haven't had nearly enough."

Darla reached for her scourge, but before she could grip the wooden handle, one of Mantula's legs shot out and closed around her wrist. Darla went to rip the leg away, but three more legs grabbed her other hand and held it tight.

"Get the hell off of me, you hairy psychopath," Darla

shouted.

Mantula just smiled.

"I know about your past love. Mr. Weed Whacker. You have some taste. What a sad excuse for a monster he was. You deserve a strong monster. A monster who won't turn into a puddle every time you look at him the wrong way."

"William Wendell is a hundred times the monster you are," she said. "Now get the hell off of me."

"Not yet," Mantula said as two more legs went for the hem of her tunic. "Come on, Duchess. We have the whole night ahead of us. You're not going anywhere. Tonight, you're mine."

Before Darla could say another word, a shape shot out of the night like a bullet and slammed Mantula right across the face, sending him to his knees. Mantula's eyes narrowed as he saw a monster walking towards him from out of the gloom, his burning yellow eyes locked onto Mantula like a cat cornering a mouse.

"Who the hell are you?" Mantula asked, wiping a trace of blood from his lip.

Darla turned around. Her breath caught in her throat when she saw him.

"My name is Jarko Murkvale," he said. "And Darla is most definitely not yours. She's nobody's property. So if you touch her again, the next thing you see will be the backs of your ankles because your head will be resting comfortably on the ground. I will pop it off like a teenager's pimple."

Mantula stood up with a smirk.

"Never seen you before," Mantula said. "It takes a lot of courage and some mighty big balls to land a sucker punch."

"Takes a monster with no balls to touch someone who didn't ask for it."

Mantula swung two legs at Jarko, who deflected them with one of his tentacles. Jarko unleashed a guttural growl that sent a shiver down Darla's spine, then shot out his other tentacle and punched Mantula in the abdomen, knocking the monster back.

He shook off the blow, anger rising in his eyes.

"First I'm going to kill you," Mantula said, saliva dripping from his sharp teeth. "And then I'm going to eat you. Slowly. I'm going to *chew* you. And then I'll make the Duchess here watch when I throw you back up."

Jarko stepped forward. He shot out one tentacle, which Mantula caught with several legs. But while Mantula was distracted, Jarko wound up and swung the other tentacle in a wide arc, slamming it against Mantula's head with an audible *thunk*. The blow flung the monster to the side, where he smacked against the rock and crumpled into a heap.

Jarko walked over to Mantula, who was trying to stand back up. Jarko wrapped both of his tentacles around Mantula, pinning all eight of his legs against his torso. Mantula struggled, but Jarko was too strong.

"Look at you," Jarko said. "Wrapped up like a bunch of bacon around a pig-in-a-blanket."

"I'll disembowel you in your sleep," Mantula said.

"Lucky for me, I don't sleep," Jarko replied. "Now, the way I see it, you have two choices right now."

"If you—"

"Stop talking or I'll make the choice for you. And you might not like the one I pick. You gonna shut up?"

Mantula remained silent.

"Good. Choice one: leave this quarry now and never come back. If you do, I'll know. Choice two: you stay here, and I can't promise you leave this quarry in one piece."

Mantula squirmed, but realized soon that Jarko was in control.

"One," Mantula spat.

"I'm sorry," Jarko said, leaning forward, "I didn't quite catch that. Can you speak louder?"

"I said *one,* you ugly monsterfucker!"

"All right, then," Jarko said. Slowly, he unwounded his tentacles.

Mantula shrugged them off and stood up.

"You got lucky," he said. "If I got in a good shot before you were ready, that fight would have gone very differently."

"Keep telling yourself that," Jarko said. He turned to leave. As soon as Jarko's back was turned, Mantula shot out two legs and grabbed a pair of large rocks from the quarry, then aimed to bring them crashing down on Jarko's head. But before they reached Jarko, Darla brought her scourge down like a scythe and cleaved both legs clean to their joint. The severed limbs and the rocks they held fell to the ground. Mantula wailed and fell to his knees, holding his maimed appendages.

Jarko looked at Darla, her scourge at her side, dripping with Mantula juices. Then he looked at Mantula and shrugged.

"Guess you made choice number two," Jarko said. "Now stay down, or we'll leave more pieces of you in this quarry."

Mantula spat at Jarko, but the green glob flew well to the side.

Jarko shook his head as if to say *pitiful*. Then he turned to Darla.

"Are you okay?" Jarko asked.

"I had that under control," Darla replied. "Why the hell are you here?"

"I couldn't just stand there knowing someone was trying to

hurt you."

"Why?" Darla said. "Why do you care?"

"I don't know to explain it," he said. "It's like when I'm near you there's this electricity inside of me and it runs through my bones. And it surges through my blood. And I can feel it in my fingertips. And when I'm with you…I feel like I'm on fire. I feel alive."

"That sounds more like a rash than electricity," Darla said. "Lucky for you there's a lake in the middle of Camp Clear Creek. That should help with the itching. But I can take care of myself."

"I know you can. The only time I've ever felt this alive is when I was hunting," Jarko said. "I would tear apart a thousand monsters and cut off my own limbs before I let anyone else touch you."

"I didn't need your help," she said. "I don't need you. I don't want you. Leave now. Go to Maine. I don't care if your claim hasn't started yet, go rent an Airbnb until it's time to take over for Lobstra. Or you just can stay here in the quarry with Mantula. Or whatever's left of him."

"You cut off my *legs*!" Mantula wailed.

"Only two of them. Quit whining, you giant hairy baby," Darla said.

"Darla," Jarko said. He reached out for her. She stepped back and gripped her scourge.

"Don't," she said. "I don't want to hurt you, but I will cut you limb from limb just like our friend if you make me."

"Darla—"

"I'm leaving, Jarko. And so are you."

"It's not that simple."

"Yes. It is. I'm on my own. The way it's meant to be. And I

can take care of myself. The way it should be."

Then Darla traversed out of the quarry and headed back to her cave, leaving Jarko and Mantula behind; the last, lingering thought as she sped by was that despite the agony Mantula appeared to be in, the pain on Jarko's face as she left was far more agonizing.

CHAPTER 27

When morning came, Darla realized, with great remorse, that she was not hungover. Not in the slightest. In fact, she felt quite good. No headache, no dry mouth, no skin that had sloughed off her body (the quarry water had a tendency to break down skin cells at a fairly alarming rate, and every time Darla had woken up with all the skin having dripped off her legs, she swore never to drink quarry water again, a promise she of course broke at the very next Monster Mash).

If she'd woken up hungover, at least she would have known she had a good time. She would have had a great conversation with Gretl about their childhoods, being two single, terrifying monsters together, all the monsters they grew up with crushes on: BackScabber, InsecTina, Albert Adams. Seeing all the monsters she only saw once a year. Fanmonstering over whatever celebrities might show up unannounced. Monster Mashes were the highlights of the year. And Darla had gone and woken up wishing she'd never set foot in that quarry.

Next year would be better. Jarko wouldn't be there. She could concentrate on what made her happy. And right now, the only thing she could think of that made her happy was the hunt.

It was time for Darla Drake, the Duchess of Death, to pick her scourge back up and return to doing what she did best: hunting.

But first, she needed breakfast.

She'd drank *just* enough of the quarry water that her legs felt a little drippy, so she went into the pantry and ate four boxes of cold Pop-Tarts, so fast she didn't even taste them. Once she did, she could feel her cells regenerating. All was well with the world.

"Darla?" Dolores called. "Are you there?"

"In here, Mom," she said, tart crumbs spilling onto her tunic.

"So? How was last night?"

Darla sighed and wiped the mess off of herself. She went into her mother's room and brought a chair over to face her head's table. Dolores had a smile on her face, as if expecting to live vicariously through her daughter.

"Tell me," she said. "Who was there? Any monsters I would recognize? Was BarkDaddy there? Does he still look as handsome as I remember?"

"I didn't see him," Darla said. "But I wasn't really paying attention."

Dolores frowned. "It doesn't sound like this year's Mash was the exciting and memorable soiree you were expecting."

"No, it was," Darla said. "Just not for the reasons I was hoping for."

"What do you mean?"

"Maybe I've just outgrown them," Darla said. "I'm too old

to be drinking quarry water and making a fool of myself and waking up with my body feeling like it got shoved into a giant blender."

"Nonsense. I was going to Mashes until I was...I don't even know, but certainly older than you. Sometimes it's the only way to see our fellow monsters. To really be a part of our culture. Being a monster can be isolating, hon."

"I know it can," Darla said. "More than you know."

"Whatever's eating you, Dar, it'll pass."

"Nothing is eating me. If anything tried to eat me, I would cut it into bite-size chunks and eat it myself."

Dolores smiled. "Only a fool would try to eat you. How are you feeling?"

"Me? Fine. Thousand percent. Like I could cut the population of crusty teenagers and neo-Nazis in half in less than a week."

"You sure?" Dolores said. "You seem a little down. If you want to talk, I'm here."

"I'm sure," Darla said without hesitating. "In fact, I'm going hunting tonight. Feel like I got my fire back. Ol' scourgey is rusty and needs some playtime."

Dolores's eyes brightened. "I'm so glad to hear that. When you put your mind to the hunt, there's no more terrifying monster working today than Darla Drake."

"No," Darla said. "There isn't. And there never will be."

. . .

Darla was perched atop a large oak surveying the Clear Creek campgrounds and surrounding areas when she saw the car. It was parked about a quarter mile from the camp entrance, on the side of the road, nowhere near a parking lot. As Darla watched, the driver turned the headlights off and killed the motor. *Strange*, she thought. The driver wasn't headed to the camp, but didn't appear to be having car trouble either. He had just parked on the shoulder...and stopped. She swung around to the other side of the tree to get a better view.

Then, Darla saw movement inside the car. Nothing violent, just a shuffling. She needed to get a closer look.

She leapt down from the pole and traversed through the woods until she was about fifty yards away from the parked car. She could see it through the trees. Using her night vision, she saw the driver through the windshield and watched.

He was a middle-aged man, white, late forties, with an awful combover and chalky skin, his face red and flushed like he'd been sweating recently. Something about him made Darla's skin crawl—and it wasn't just the aftereffects of the quarry water. No, something about this guy and where he'd parked felt wrong. Very wrong. And she knew it for sure when he leaned toward the passenger side door and held a pair of binoculars to his eyes.

Darla traversed to the far side of the car, across the road. She wanted to see the driver's sight lines. Find out what he was looking at through those binoculars. She lined up her vision with his own eyesight and scanned. It didn't take long.

There was a clear-cut path through the woods all the way to the campgrounds. Specifically, the cabins where the youngest campers slept. It wasn't an accident the driver had parked right here. He must have scouted the area to find the *perfect* spot, where he could have an unobstructed view of the cabins through the trees. Where he could see right into the window of the Starfish campers. Their cabin lights were on. The campers were getting ready for bed. And this driver was watching them.

Who knew how many times he'd done this, parked in this very spot and sat here, watching the children?

However many it had been, tonight would be his last.

Darla didn't need to look to know that copious amounts of smoke were drifting upward from her nostrils.

She traversed over to the car and ran her scourge gently over the trunk. The driver bolted up. He dropped the binoculars on his lap, opened the window, and looked outside. He saw nothing. Darla made sure of that.

He surveyed the road. There were no other cars. No people. It must have been his imagination. Or a bat, or a large pinecone. Something explainable.

He raised the window and brought the binoculars back up. When he did, Darla brought the scourge down onto the back left tire, shredding the rubber with an audible *bang*.

The driver threw the door open and bolted out of the car. He spun around but saw nothing. He went to inspect the tire and gasped when he saw the damage. He ran his finger along the destroyed rubber, the dented hubcap. A frightened and confused look on his face that said *what the hell could have done this?*

He took his phone out of his pocket, then stopped. Darla watched. She knew what he was doing. Why he was hesitating. Obviously, the man had a record. A past. Something he'd done where, if he called AAA or 911, they would find him in a place he was not supposed to be.

Instead, he went around to the trunk and popped it open. He lugged out a spare tire and stared at it. Then he scratched his head. It was clear he had never changed a tire and had no idea what he was doing. Then he closed the trunk. And when he did, he saw Darla Drake, Duchess of Death, standing there, infamous scourge in hand, moonlight glinting off her needle-sharp bone crown, smoke drifting upward from her nostrils like a dragon who'd just eaten four-alarm hot sauce.

The man's mouth opened wide, and a high-pitched shriek like a train whistle came from his throat. He fell backward into a mud puddle, which splashed up around him, soaking his pants in brown. Darla unhooked the scourge from her belt and slowly walked toward him.

"You…" he said, gasping for air. "You're Darla Drake."

Darla said nothing. Just took step after step.

"I…I thought you were a myth."

No words. Step. Step. Step.

"I don't know what you think you saw," the man stammered, scooting backward, as though somehow his awkward muddy crab walk was simply too fast for the legendary Duchess of Death. "But I was just here because I got a flat. I was about to call a tow truck. Honest."

Step. Step. Step.

"Stop it!" he shouted, holding a hand out. Darla brought the scourge around in a windmill motion and instantly he was no longer holding the hand out.

The man screamed and looked at his arm and scrambled to his feet and stumble-ran off into the woods. As always, Darla wondered just what he thought this might accomplish. As though generations of victims had managed to escape Darla Drake with their sloth-like forty-yard dash.

Darla stood there. Watching him run. She was going to take her time with this one. He didn't deserve for this to end quickly. This wasn't just going to be a hunt. This was going to send a message: Clear Creek had a legendary monster stalking its grounds who would protect the innocent with every fiber of her being. And if you were a predator considering coming here and putting any of those lives at risk, you would soon learn the hard, *hard* way that the only predator allowed in Clear Creek was Darla Drake.

· · ·

Darla didn't traverse through the woods back to her cave; she walked. She didn't want to rush this night. This feeling. After ending the driver, she'd gone back to where she'd left the part of him that still had his pants and pulled out his wallet. His driver's license said his name was Kenneth Saddler. Inside the billfold, she found photos that were clearly taken on Clear Creek grounds from the very spot he'd parked in. The photos made her blood boil.

She took them all and put them near his car and struck the gas tank with her scourge and watched the vehicle explode in a massive orange fireball, and she watched from a distance as the counselors called 911 and the police came and they found Saddler's car, along with a piece of him to let them know they'd have to play a little 'find the body part.'

But tomorrow the news would report on Saddler's grim death, along with the truth about who he was, and it would serve as a warning to anyone else who even considered coming to Clear Creek to follow in his footsteps.

Darla could see the flames and smoke in the sky as she walked home. Then she realized this was her first solo hunt in a year. The first time she'd finished a hunt since before then. And it felt *good*. She was back. She felt it in her extra-dense bones. Once again, the scourge felt like it was a part of her, an extension of her.

The Duchess of Death was back in business. The last few

weeks had been a distraction. Nothing more. She was ready to put her mark back on Clear Creek. To forget about everything that had happened. Forget about the anger and sadness and longing which had blinded her and made her feel like for the first time in her life that she could have a life *alongside* the hunt.

But it wasn't to be. She had the hunt and she had Dolores and she had Gretl and that was enough. *More* than enough. The last thing she needed was some conceited interloper who blinded her from her true purpose. The last thing she needed was...

Jarko Murkvale.

She had to blink to realize she wasn't hallucinating or dreaming, and it had been long enough that the quarry water would have left her system by now.

No, it was real. Standing at the entrance of her cave was Jarko Murkvale.

"What...what are you doing here?" she said.

"I needed to talk to you," he said. "About last night."

"There's nothing to say."

"There's everything to say."

"I agree. And you were saying it to every monster with ears or extrasensory perception. You were even saying it to a few undead ones. So, congratulations, I've never had a guy who kissed me follow that up by flirting with a goddamn corpse."

"I wasn't flirting with anyone," Jarko said.

"Could've fooled me."

"Excuse me, you were the one who left the party to go gallivanting off with some Shelob wannabe."

"First off, what are you, a thousand years old? Who uses the word gallivanting? Second, I wasn't doing any such thing. I was looking for conversation because the monster I've been talking to is leaving and, well, I was just trying to…"

"Trying to what?" Jarko asked.

"I don't know."

"You wanted to make me jealous."

"I wanted you to know I would be just fine without you here," Darla said, "just like I was fine before you got here."

"You weren't fine before I got here," he replied. "You gave up on the hunt."

"And tonight I went back on the hunt and it was stupid glorious and fun and I turned this guy into more pieces than a Lego set and ceasing to hunt will never, *ever* happen again."

"Maybe not," Jarko said, "but the feelings you had when you did might also never leave."

"Maybe not," Darla replied. "But there's nothing I can do about that. You don't find your path by abandoning the one thing you have that makes you you."

"That's the funny thing about you," Jarko said. "You're never made up of just one thing."

Darla stood there before her cave, her mind swimming with so many emotions, many of which she'd never experienced before, and certainly not all at the same time. Emotions were like quarry water: nobody was *really* sure what all the ingredients were, and there was a very fine line between having just enough of it to make you feel good and having too much of it to make your skin peel from your body.

Darla felt like she was tilting toward the latter.

"So, what?" she said. "You came here to clarify that you weren't flirting with half the monsters at the Mash? Fine. I believe you. It doesn't matter. You're gone anyway. Go sire a whole litter of little monsters with whoever you want. Just go already and let me get on with my life."

"I don't want to leave on this note," Jarko said.

"You're leaving," Darla replied. "It doesn't matter what note you go on."

"What if…" Jarko said, scratching his head with a tentacle, "…I didn't go?"

Darla laughed. "Go back to your cave," she said. "I need to get some rest."

"I'm serious," Jarko said.

Darla stopped. Moved toward Jarko. For a moment, she found herself lost again in his brilliant yellow eyes and a tingle ran from the nape of her neck all the way down her wishbone-shaped spine, reminding her of the way his kiss felt. And then she closed her eyes and it was gone.

"Go home," Darla said. "Wherever your home is. Because it's not Clear Creek."

"What if I did?" Jarko said. "Want to stay?"

"Then I'd say you're just words," she replied. "Just another monster who talks and talks. I'm done talking to you. I'm a monster of action, Jarko. You say all these things but they don't mean anything because you won't back them up. Now excuse me. Let me inside, and don't follow me. I don't want to cut any of your limbs off, but I will."

Jarko hesitated for a moment, but then stepped aside.

"Thank you."

Darla rolled the boulder out of the way, looked at Jarko for what would likely be the very last time, then rolled it back into place, shrouding herself in the darkness.

CHAPTER 28

Getting back into the hunt was like riding a bicycle. Only Darla had never ridden a bicycle, so the metaphor wasn't quite apt, and, in fact, she probably wouldn't be very comfortable sitting on a bike given that her pelvis was six interlocking pieces, none of which were made for a bike. All of which to say once she began hunting again, it was like she'd never stopped.

No more depraved individuals like Kenneth Saddler showed up—hopefully the sickos had gotten word that if they ventured anywhere near Clear Creek, they would need several caskets for their funeral—but thankfully Darla's hands were full with sociopathic counselors probably all named Kyle, as well as other dregs of humanity.

Saddler was the only one she dispatched with—the counselors deserved one really good fright to try to get their act together. But Darla let them know under no uncertain terms that if they failed to see the error of their ways, the last thing they would see was smoke tendrils, and the last thing they would hear was the whistling sound as her scourge sailed through the air to meet its target.

She woke up each morning and oiled her scourge, polishing its brass studs to a shine. Then she cleaned and fed Dolores and set up her television—she had gotten into Hallmark movies, always pining for the big city girl to realize that she needed to dump her shallow Wall Street beau and instead go with the ruggedly handsome, flannel-wearing, bearded small-town single dad slash homemade jam maker.

She visited Gretl and Tyrone and baby Manti, who could now chew through an entire tree trunk in under thirty seconds. Less if it was a juniper. She displayed this talent for Darla, and when she was finished, both Gretl and her Gobbler gave the little one a cheery ovation, at which point Manti grabbed her mother's Gobbler and tried to rip it out of Gretl's mouth before Tyrone managed to calm Manti down with her favorite baby toy, a taxidermy black bear Tyrone had "borrowed" from a nearby hotel lobby.

This was her family. Dolores and Gretl and Tyrone and their ravenous, forest-destroying baby. These were the people she would spend the rest of her existence with, and they all made her happy. She would return to the next Monster Mash, this time not caring about anyone else who was there—other than Mantula, and if he had the nerve to show his now-truncated self, Darla would make sure he would have to be rolled back limbless to his stanky web.

On the day Jarko had told Darla he was leaving to go take over Lobstra's territory in Maine, Darla found herself traversing through the woods. She didn't know why she was going there. She supposed she needed to see for herself. Get some final, final, *final* closure.

When she arrived at the waterfall, she hesitated. Stood outside the entrance, feeling the droplets cascading off her crown, dripping off her tunic, soaking her feet. She stood there for what seemed like an hour but in reality, was probably only a few minutes.

She wondered if a tentacle would shoot out from behind the sheet of water, curl around her neck or body, and drag her inside. She didn't know what she would do if it did: fight it or succumb to it. In the end, she didn't have to worry about either, because nothing came.

She walked through the waterfall slowly, on guard. But she didn't need to be. Nobody was there. The cave was empty. Jarko was gone.

For a moment, Darla felt an emptiness inside her, a hollow feeling in at least two, maybe even all three of her stomachs. She stepped inside. There was a small, circular patch among the dirt and charred debris where Jarko had kept his fire pit and cooking pot. A large, monster-sized shape in the leaves where he had slept. Then a gust of wind came and blew the leaves around, and the shape was gone. It was as though nobody had stayed here. The memories of their time together fleeing faster than a stoned camp counselor being chased through the woods.

And then, Darla turned and left the waterfall and went back home.

CHAPTER 29

Darla had the honor of being the Godmonster at baby Manti's Catastrophism ceremony the following week. When Gretl asked her, tears welled up in Darla's eyes and she could barely speak over the nostril smoke. But she happily accepted, on the one condition that if Manti ever got loose, she would have backup when it came time to bring her home.

The ceremony was held at Maker's Marsh. The Cardinal led proceedings, his red-plumed feathers dipping into the water to let the droplets fall on Manti's forehead. Manti cooed at the sensation, then traced the Cardinal's black cheeks and plumage as Gretl and Tyrone watched, beaming with pride.

"Manticore Myers Binks," the Cardinal said, feathers rising into the air, a low, sonorous voice emanating from within its old, wrinkled beak. "The monster community welcomes you with open arms, and claws, and fangs, and fur. May your hunts be deadly, may your justice be swift, and may you create a legend that will be known far and wide. May your frailty never be discovered, and may your parents, Gretl and Tyrone Binks, watch over you with pride and protection from now until eternity."

Gretl began to cry. When she released a massive sob, her Gobbler came out of her mouth and wiped the tear away.

"And now, little Manti, as your parents call you, begin your Catastrophism."

The Cardinal let Manti loose into the marsh to complete the Catastrophism. Within seconds, the marsh was practically frothing as Manti ate everything she could get her growing hands and teeth on. A few minutes later, Manti came out with half a dozen frogs and several squirming fish in her mouth, plus about twenty pounds of marsh muck and fauna. Manti chewed it all and swallowed, then let out a burp that could wake the dead—or at least alert them to her presence.

Then the crowd erupted in applause, or a wet smacking or fluttering for those in attendance who had fins or other appendages. Then it was time to celebrate.

Unlike the Monster Mash, baby Manti's Catastrophism was a relatively formal affair. Stumpkins walked around with drinks and food atop their smooth heads, and other Birds of Prey flew around refilling cups when they ran dry. There was no insanity or making out and the dancing was PG at most. Darla stood there, looking at the smiles on her friends' faces, wondering how in the hell she'd gotten so lucky.

"Hey, Godmonster," Gretl said, sidling up to Darla. Her arm was wrapped in tree bark and mud.

"What happened there?" Darla asked.

Gretl sighed. "Manti was so excited she tried to chew my arm off. You know kids."

Darla laughed. "I did way worse to my mom," she said.

"Dolores loves to tell the story about how when I was two, I found her scourge and sliced off both of her legs while she was asleep and before my dad could stop me. She reattached them, but you should have seen her trying to chase after me on just her torso."

"To be fair," Gretl said, "you were just preparing Dolores for what was yet to come in terms of losing parts of her body."

Darla looked at her and raised an eyebrow.

"Too soon?" Gretl asked with a smile.

Darla returned the look. "Nah. If you can't laugh about your mother's severed head, what can you laugh at?"

They both laughed heartily. Gretl rested her head on Darla's shoulder. Manti had caught one of the Stumpkins and was chewing on it while the other Stumpkins tried to pry open her mouth.

"Isn't she beautiful?" Gretl said as Manti spat the Stumpkin into the marsh, where it swam away as fast as possible. Manti then went after the other Stumpkins, who dropped their appetizers and fled into the forest.

"There are no words," Darla replied. "You're one lucky monster mama."

"I can't wait to teach her how to hunt," Gretl said.

Darla watched as Manti leapt onto a muskrat and swallowed it whole. "I'd say she's already a natural."

"She is, isn't she? And the truth is, humans really aren't that much harder to hunt than muskrats. Maybe a little taller, a little less hairy, but that's pretty much the only difference."

"After a few decades hunting them, I'd have to agree."

Gretl nudged Darla with her elbow. "Want to see something cool?"

"If you're going to walk around and let your Gobbler take

chunks out of people's faces, I've seen it before."

Gretl laughed. "No, this is way cooler."

"All right. Let's see it."

Gretl reached into her bag and pulled out an MFU unit, almost exactly the same as the one Jarko had (only Darla could see Manti's bite marks on the metal). Gretl turned the unit on, and it displayed the map of Maker's Marsh. She tapped the screen, then tapped **Search By Monster**. She typed in her name, and **Gretl Binks, aka Gretl the Gobbler**, appeared. She tapped her name.

Two photos of Gretl appeared: one where she looked pretty normal, and the other with her mouth open and her Gobbler shooting out, arms open, teeth bared, as if to grab something or someone.

"Look here," Gretl said. She tapped an icon that read **Known Family**. Two thumbnail images opened up. The first was Tyrone Binks, aka Hatchetman. The photo showed Tyrone wielding his signature hatchet, gleaming metal plate covering his face except for two eyeholes, from which inside burned two bright turquoise irises. "Gotta say, even when he's about to cut someone in two, I'd still jump him. Hatchet and all."

"Maybe wait until he puts the hatchet down?" Darla asked.

"Uh-uh. No way. Hatchet comes to bed with us."

"I'm taking it you didn't open this up to tell me about your sex life with Tyrone, because if so, I have a quarry's worth of toxic chemicals to pour into my ears."

"No, not that. But I have to say, he is—"

"*Gretl.*"

"Okay. Sorry. Here. This is what I wanted to show you."

She closed Tyrone's page and scrolled down. A thumbnail appeared with the words **Manticore Myers Binks**.

"It's my daughter," Gretl said, a tear in her eye. The Gobbler stuck an arm out of her mouth and dabbed it away.

"What does it say?"

Gretl tapped the thumbnail and several pictures of Manti appeared. In one, she was sleeping peacefully, nestled in Tyrone's arms. In another, she was playing with Gretl, tossing a tree trunk high into the air and beaming. In another, she was peeking out of a thirty-foot-deep hole she'd dug in the ground. In another, she was in the air, mid-leap, about to land on a mountain lion which looked absolutely petrified.

"There are no words for how adorable she is," Darla said.

"And look." Gretl tapped the screen again. An icon appeared that read **Maker's Marsh – Hierarchy**. It read **1. Gretl Binks, 2. Tyrone Binks, 3. Manticore Binks**. "See that? Manti is officially listed as heir to the territory of Maker's Marsh. How freaking cool is that? She's like our Prince Harry, just less ginger and more homicidal."

"So, if you ever retire or—"

"Don't even go there, talking about frailties," Gretl said. "When we *retire*."

"She'll be the main monster of Maker's Marsh."

"Manti the Mauler," Gretl said. "I like the sound of that."

"Hey," Darla said, pointing at the MFU unit. "You can look up any living monster on that, right? Or see who's hunting in which territory?"

"Sure can," Gretl said. "Before Tyrone, I may or may not have used this thing to stalk other monsters I had crushes on."

"Even Mantula?" Darla said.

"I plead the fifth. Why do you ask?"

"Can you look up a territory for me?"

"Sure. Which one?"

"Bangor, Maine," Darla said.

"Sure. One sec."

Gretl tapped the screen a few times and zoomed in on a territory in south-central Maine. She tapped one more time.

"Okay, looks like this territory is manned, er, womaned, er, *lobstered* by Lobstra. Is that who you were looking for?"

"I thought Lobstra was retired by now," Darla said. "What does it say?"

"Let me see. Oh, yeah. Looks like a retirement proclamation was placed a few weeks ago but seems like it was rescinded until further notice."

"Wait, so Lobstra is still in charge of that territory?"

"Apparently."

"Nobody else?"

"Nope," Gretl said, "nobody else."

"And that thing is accurate?"

"It had Manti's profile up the day after she was born and nearly ripped me in half."

"Weird," Darla said, scratching her bone crown.

"Weird, how?"

"Jarko. He said he was leaving to take over Lobstra's territory. He was supposed to start last week."

"Guess he changed his mind. Did he stay here?"

Darla shook her head. "Nope. I even went by his waterfall cave a few days ago, and he was fully cleared out. Even took his pots and pans and stuff."

"Wait. Jarko cooks?" Darla nodded. "Ugh. So hard to meet a tall monster who also cooks."

"Tyrone is tall."

"And he couldn't cook microwave popcorn if you gave him popcorn and a microwave."

"It's strange," Darla said. "If he's not here, and he hasn't taken over Lobstra's territory, then where is he?"

"Does it matter?" Gretl said, putting her arm around Darla. "You have me. You have our family. And you have...most of your mother. Until the right monster comes along and proves that he or she or they or it truly wants to be with you, wait." She looked at Tyrone, who was busy trying to pry Manti's jaws open to retrieve a petrified Stumpkin from within. "Because trust me. When your monster finds you, it's worth the wait."

. . .

Darla stayed until the end of the Catastrophism, figuring it would make up for leaving the Monster Mash early. She drank responsibly, made pleasant small talk, and even remained polite when the Cardinal asked when he might be able to perform a Catastrophism for Darla's own child, at which point she merely smiled and patted his feathers and refrained from slicing his beak off with her scourge.

When the party ended, she gave long, tight hugs to Gretl, Tyrone, and even baby Manti, who had worn herself out to the point where party guests no longer had to worry about their protruding limbs being munched on by the not so wee child.

She took a long, unhurried walk along Maker's Marsh, thinking how much her life had changed over the past year and, strangely, how little it did in the end. She was still living alone with Dolores. Still hunting. Still seeing Gretl when she could and...that was about it. She felt a little silly having even taken that sabbatical, only to end up in pretty much the exact same place as she had before. But Darla supposed she was more comfortable now than she had been a year ago. Back then, something felt off. Something felt missing. And even though that feeling hadn't *quite* gone away, she understood that even if she lived out her days like this, she could be satisfied.

Maybe not fulfilled. But satisfied.

So, she would go home. Get some rest. Wake up the next day. And when she opened her eyes, she would still be, would *always* be, Darla Drake, Duchess of Death, Creature of Clear Creek.

And that would be enough. It would have to be.

When she was finished walking, she traversed home. She felt lighter than she had in a year. Tomorrow would be a new day.

And then she arrived at her cave and stopped dead in her tracks.

Standing in front of the door boulder was Jarko Murkvale.

"Jarko, what in the hell are you do—?"

Jarko stepped to the side. Behind him lay a large potato sack, about five feet long.

Darla pointed at the sack. "What is that?" She stepped closer. Nudged the bottom of the sack. Felt what she swore was... "No. No way. You didn't. You couldn't. Is that...?"

Jarko nodded. "I found the rest of your mother's body."

CHAPTER 30

"**Y**ou did what?"

"I found her body," Jarko said. He grabbed the potato sack and dragged it forward, leaving it in a heap in front of Darla. "Go ahead and look."

Darla stared at Jarko in disbelief. Then she walked over to the sack and took hold of the rope that bound its opening. She untied it, pulled the sack's opening apart, and looked inside. Immediately, she pulled her head back.

"That. Smells. Awful," she said.

"What's inside has been buried a long time."

"You really found her? I mean, the rest of her?"

"Stop asking questions. Just see for yourself."

Darla shook her head. Impossible. There was no way. She took a breath, then opened the bag wide, peered in and...

She saw the hem of her mother's red tunic. The very same red tunic she'd worn to hunt thousands and thousands of times, the tunic Darla had loved when she was a little monster and watched with pride as her mother went to hunt the campground of Clear Creek. The very same red tunic she wore the night her neck met the flat end of Franklin Shine's shovel and had not been seen again in many, many years.

She recognized the tunic. The arm wraps. The dark blue cloth wrapped around her legs. It was all still there. Dirty and smelly, but it was definitely Dolores's body. Or at least the approximately 84 percent of it that had been missing.

"How did you find her?" Darla asked, incredulous. "I've looked everywhere. I've turned Clear Creek into Swiss cheese trying to find her body. How the hell did you do it?"

"I found Franklin Shine."

Darla blinked. "I'm sorry. You did *what*?"

"I tracked down the person who severed your mother's head and buried her body. And I got him to tell me where he buried it."

"You're telling me that you found Franklin Shine," Darla said, completely bewildered and awed. "*The* Franklin Shine."

"I did."

"Where did you find him?"

"New York City."

"New York City," Darla said. "You're telling me you *went* to New York City?"

"I did. Manhattan, to be precise."

"I'm sorry. I must have someone else's finger in my ear. You said you went to New York City and found Franklin Shine, the guy who bisected my mom, and you got him to tell you where he buried her body? How did you find him? And how in the name of Pinhead's pancreas did you get to New York City?

"That's a long story for another time," Jarko said.

"I don't understand. *Why* would you do all of that?"

"Sometimes you do things without really thinking about why you do them. You just do them because you know you should. You've learned not to question your gut. And once you're doing them, you just know deep down that it's the right thing to do."

"I don't know what to say."

"Don't say anything. Dolores has been a stump for fifteen years. Stop wasting time talking to me. Give your mother her body back."

"Jarko, tha—"

"Go, Duchess."

Darla nodded. She hauled the boulder out of the way, threw her mother's body over her shoulder, and traversed into the cave. She looked behind her to see Jarko standing there at the cave entrance. She didn't know what to say.

"Do you want to come in?"

"No. This is a Drake family thing. You need to be with her. Just you."

She nodded. "Thank you."

Jarko made a flicking motion with his tentacle. Darla turned back around and traversed into the main antechamber.

"Mom!" Darla shouted. "Mom, are you up?"

"In here, hon!" Dolores yelled. "I'm watching Hallmark's movie of the week. It's called *Ranch Hand*. It's about this stockbroker girl whose brokerage firm goes bankrupt and she has to move back to the small town she grew up in where she meets this ruggedly handsome—"

"Ranch hand."

"How did you know? Have you seen this one before?"

"No. Lucky guess."

Darla dropped the sack outside her mother's room and

entered. Then she took the remote and turned off the TV.

"What are you doing?" Dolores cried. "I need to know if they're going to end up together."

"Mom," Darla said. The quiver in her voice made Dolores stop talking.

"What is it, Dar?" she said. "Did something happen?"

Darla shook her head. She felt a tear slide down her cheek. "I have it."

"You have what, dear?"

"You," Darla said, her voice cracking. "I have *you*."

"What do you mean, you have...oh. Oh my goodness. Oh my goodness. No. That's not possible."

"It is," Darla said. "And I do."

She picked up the sack and brought it into Dolores's room. Her mother's eyes went wide.

"What's inside that bag?"

Darla opened the bag and gently pulled the body out from inside. As Dolores watched, her lip began to quiver.

"Oh my. Oh my word. It's me. It's all of me."

"Every last piece. Well, only one piece, I guess. But it's all here. I'm not sure if you had a wallet on you that night, though, because if you did, it's gone."

Dolores looked at her daughter. "How did you find me?"

"I didn't. Jarko did."

"Jarko? I thought he left."

"So did I."

"How did he do this?"

"He found Franklin Shine."

"He found Franklin Shine? Where?"

"New York City."

"New York City? He went—a six-and-a-half-foot monster—

to New York City to find the boy who cut off my head?"

"Yup."

"Can I...have it?"

"It's yours. You can do whatever you want with it. I could prop it in the corner, put a funny hat on it, maybe—"

"Give it to me."

"You got it."

Darla laid the body on the ground, arms straight at its sides. She remembered every inch of her mother's body. She didn't think she'd ever see it again.

"Can you help me, Dar?"

Darla gently picked her mother's head up off the counter and laid it down on the ground atop Dolores's neck, so the flesh of her head was touching the flesh of her body.

"Now what?" Darla asked. "What's supposed to happen?"

"I don't know," Dolores replied. "This may come as a shock to you, but I've never tried to reattach my severed head before."

Nothing happened. Darla began to feel a worry creep up inside, like all three of her stomachs were turning inside out. What if it was too late? What if her body had been separated for too long? All monsters faced dismemberment at some point— some kid got lucky with a machete or a shovel—but you always reattached the limb immediately. Dolores's body had been in the ground for *years*. Maybe it was too late. Maybe Dolores would live out eternity as nothing more than a head. In which case, what would they do with her body? Just prop it up in the corner? Seat it at the table like some macabre houseguest? Rebury it?

"Wait," Dolores said. "I think I feel something."

At that moment, Darla saw the skin on her mother's neck begin to stipple. Then it started to stretch out like fleshy little fingers, reaching for Dolores's head. Once they touched her head, they pulled the head onto the body, and the skin began to knit itself together.

"It's working," Dolores said, joy in her voice.

"I think it is," Darla said. "What does it feel like?"

"Like I'm being tickled from the inside. Not entirely unpleasant, I might add. Reminds me of—"

"Ew. Stop. I don't want to hear it."

The flesh continued to mend together, the body and head reuniting. Finally, after about three minutes, there was no longer any separation between the skin of Dolores's head and body. It was all one, solid piece.

"Well?" Darla said. "What now?"

"I...I don't know," Dolores replied. "Let me see."

Dolores made a grunting sound. "Just seeing if I can still..."

"Are you...going number two?"

"No! I'm trying to, ah, there we go."

The pinky finger on Dolores's right hand wiggled. Then the rest of the fingers on that hand did the same. Then both hands.

"It's working," Darla said, her heart fluttering. "It's working."

Dolores bent her wrists, then her arms. She moved her legs side to side, as though making a snow angel. Then, after a few more grunts, Dolores Drake sat up and looked at her daughter.

"It's been a long time since I could move anything that wasn't lips or eyebrows," she said. "Just needed to remind myself how it all worked."

"Mom," Darla cried out. "You're *you*."

Darla ran over and threw her arms around her mother. And when she felt her mother's arms wrap around her, Darla lost all control and began to weep.

"I've always been me, hon," Dolores said. "Now there's just more of me."

"I missed having you so much," Darla said. "I mean, I missed having all of you."

"I missed being able to do this," Dolores said, squeezing Darla even tighter. Then they separated, and Dolores held Darla's face in her hands. "And being able to do this."

Dolores leaned forward and kissed Darla's forehead.

"I'm sorry," Darla said. "I'm sorry if I was mean or short or anything to you since the accident."

"Don't apologize," Dolores said. "I would have been an enormous crab too if I had to wait on my head hand and foot."

Darla laughed, and wrapped her arms back around her mother and held her there.

"You know what this means?" Darla asked.

"What?"

"From now on, you're responsible for figuring out dinner some nights."

"I've been waiting a long time for you to say that. I'm so sick of Pop-Tarts, Darla."

"Why didn't you say anything?"

"Bodyless heads can't be choosers," Dolores said.

"Welcome back, Mom. All of you. I guess you'll need an actual bed now."

"Let's worry about that later. Where's Jarko?"

"He stayed outside."

Dolores stood up and took Darla's hand. "Come on."

Dolores walked through the cave, each step smiling wider and wider, reconnecting with both her body and the ground itself. When they got to the entrance, Jarko was sitting on a log. He looked up when he saw Dolores walk outside, and smiled.

Dolores looked around, closed her eyes. She placed her palm against the rock and brushed its surface gently.

"I missed this," she said. "God, I missed this."

Then she went over to Jarko, reached down, and took his tentacle in her hands.

"There's no thank you I could possibly offer other than to say thank you," she said.

"And that's the only thank you I would ever want. You're very welcome."

"How on earth did you do it?"

"As I told your daughter," Jarko said, "that's a long story for another time."

Dolores nodded. Then she looked back at her daughter. And again at Jarko. Then she said, "I'm going to go for a walk. It's been a long, long time since I've been able to say that. I think the two of you have a lot to talk about."

As she went to walk off, Darla took her mother's hand. "Are you going to be okay? Do you remember where we live in case you get lost?"

Dolores laughed and placed her hand on Darla's cheek. "Oh, sweetie. You may be the Duchess of Death, but I'm the original DOD. I've hunted in Clear Creek longer than you've been alive. The question isn't whether *I'm* going to be okay. The question is whether everyone *else* in Clear Creek is going to be okay."

Then Dolores Drake walked off into the forest, leaving Darla and Jarko alone.

"Thanks," Darla said. "You have no idea what this does for my mother. And for me."

"I have something of an idea," he said. "The original Duchess of Death deserves better than to be an ornament on a table."

"You really went through all that trouble just for my mother?" Darla asked.

"No," Jarko said. "I went through all that trouble—and let me tell you, it was a *lot* of trouble—for your mother. And for you."

"For me? Why?"

"Your mother is part of your life. I wanted to make your life better."

"Don't do that," Darla said. "Don't say you wanted to make my life better. You came into it and made me feel something for you and then you decided to leave."

"And here I am."

"And you'll be gone again."

Jarko shook his head. "I rescinded my claim on Lobstra's territory. She's going to keep hunting until they can find another monster to take it over."

Darla looked up at him, her eyes glistening. "Why would you do that?"

Jarko lowered his head and said, "Why do you think I would do that?"

"I went to your cave behind the waterfall," she said. "You were gone. There was nothing there. Not even your cooking equipment."

"That stuff was old," Jarko said. "Plus, you have no idea what a pain it is to have to scrub years of muskrat out of that pot. I was going to forge a new one as soon as I got around to it."

"So, you never even went to Maine."

"No. Never set foot there. I was in New York. It took some time to find Franklin Shine. I always heard there was something like seven million people in New York City, but you have no idea just how many that is until you get there."

"What was it like?" Darla said.

"Enormous. Beautiful. Crowded. Disgusting."

"Disgusting?"

"Let's just say I met a monster in Manhattan who made me realize who I never, ever wanted to become."

"And you managed to get there and back without getting shot, stabbed, or set on fire," Darla said. "I'm impressed. I like this new stealthy Jarko."

"Yeah," Jarko said, scratching his head. "About that."

"About what?"

"The stealth thing. Let's just say I got my fifteen minutes of fame while I was in New York."

"You got your what now?"

"It doesn't matter. Just don't google my name and NickelSmart bank."

"Oh hell, Jarko, what did you do there?"

"It doesn't matter. What matters is this."

Jarko took a step forward. Darla didn't move.

"I came back for you, Darla," Jarko said.

Darla felt her blood thicken, her body temperature rise.

"You've never called me Darla before."

Jarko smiled. "Everyone else knows you as the Duchess of Death. The Creature of Clear Creek. I know Darla Drake. And I want to make sure you know it."

"What do you want, Jarko?"

"You, Darla Drake. I want you."

Darla felt lightheaded, like the blood coursing through her body had thickened and could no longer travel through her ultra-wide veins and up into her brain.

"A week ago, you didn't. You said you didn't want to

endanger me. You didn't want to open yourself up again."

"You made a choice to let me into your life," Jarko said. "Knowing everything. Knowing the dangers. I haven't always been the best listener. I'm trying to change that. So if you're willing to open your rib cage to me, I'd be an idiot not to try to take your heart. Figuratively, of course."

"Jarko..."

"When I was in New York," he said, "I met another monster. A legendary monster I once feared and respected. But now he has nobody and nothing and hate has consumed him and I don't want to end up like that. I want to end up with you."

"I...I don't know. I don't know what to say."

"Say whatever you want," Jarko said. "Because I finally learned how to listen."

She looked at him, his eyes yellower than she even remembered, gleaming brightly in his dark face, like two jewels embedded in granite.

"My heart has been stabbed," Darla said. "It has been shot. Speared. Harpooned. Smashed. Smushed. Spooned. And sawed. But nothing that has ever happened to my heart hurt as bad as when you told me you were choosing to leave."

"Sometimes the pain of the past prevents you from giving the future a chance," Jarko said. "I want that chance. With you. Either I open myself up now, or I spend the rest of my life alone."

"I don't know," Darla said. "I gave you up."

"So, take me back."

"I need time," she said. "I need space. I need to think."

"I understand."

"But right now I just...I need to go."

"Go? Go where?"

Darla didn't answer Jarko. Instead, she found herself traversing through the woods at a blinding pace. Traversing was often the only way she could clear her mind. Let her thoughts focus. Figure things out.

"Darla!"

The voice came from behind her. She looked back and saw Jarko drifting through the trees, swinging as fast as his tentacles could carry him.

"Darla, wait!"

"Leave me alone, Jarko," she shouted.

She traversed faster and faster, so fast she could barely keep up with the layout of the trees and the brush. She felt branches scrape against her legs, her arms, her face. Her bone crown smashed through leaves and twigs.

She could feel Jarko trying to keep pace, trying not to let her out of his sight. But all it made her do was traverse faster.

"Darla!" he shouted. "Wait!"

She didn't respond. She didn't need to. Her speed through the woods let him know she wasn't going to.

Then a branch appeared, large and thick, at sternum height, and Darla was moving too fast to duck below it. It crunched against her chest, and while it didn't knock her down, it did stagger her, and before she had a chance to regroup and regain her previous traversal speed, she felt a tentacle shoot down and wrap itself around her wrist.

Suddenly, Jarko was next to her.

"Darla," he said, "let me—"

Before he could finish his sentence, Darla ducked down and slid out from his grasp. Then in one motion she unhooked her scourge, wound it up, and wrapped it around his neck. Not tight enough to cut off his wind, but just tight enough to let him know that if she wanted to, she could.

"Darla," Jarko said, his voice scratchy. "You are a hard monster to catch."

Darla approached Jarko. Leaned her face close to his. Smiled and said, "Who says I didn't let you?"

She could hear Jarko's breathing. Hear his heart beating beneath his jacket, beneath his thick skin. She released the scourge and let the whip fall from his neck. She could see marks where the bronze studs had embedded in his skin. Within moments, they had healed.

"Why would you let me catch you?"

"I'll let you figure that out."

Then Darla raised the scourge again, but before she could bring it down, Jarko shot out a tentacle and wrapped it around her wrist. She switched the weapon to her other hand, brought it down, but again Jarko caught her other arm. Her arms were both above her head, caught in Jarko's tentacles.

He walked toward her. Slowly. Delicately. Darla could feel her heart pounding in her chest, all nine ventricles threatening to burst.

"I never want to have to catch you again," he said, "and I swear on my life I will never, ever leave you. I promise that I will—"

"Shut up, Jarko," Darla said. "For once in your life, just stop talking."

He brought his face down to hers, their arms still outstretched, and pressed his lips to hers. Then he released his grip from her wrists and wrapped his tentacles around her, once, twice, three times. She looped her scourge around his back and pulled him closer, kissing him back, smoke rising from her nostrils, creating a small cloud above them.

He slipped her tunic from her shoulders, Darla's body alternating shivers and warmth in a way she'd never felt before, a way she never knew was possible.

Then Jarko removed his lips from hers and looked her in the eye, his own pupils gleaming. In that moment, Darla knew he would do anything for her. And she would for him as well.

"I love you, Darla Drake," Jarko said.

"I love you too," she said.

He kissed her neck and Darla felt stars behind her eyes. Then she pushed him away, creating inches of space between then.

"Do you not want this?" he said.

"I do," Darla replied. "But if we're going to try to make this work, I need three promises from you."

"Name them."

"First: you never leave. Ever."

"I swear on the eternal lives of every monster and demon who came before me, and the graves of those whose frailties have been used against them, I will never leave you."

Darla nodded. "Good answer. Because if you do, I will slice you into very, very small pieces. And I'll make sure nobody ever finds them."

"I have no doubt you will."

"Second: Clear Creek is still my territory. You want to stay here, with me, and hunt the same grounds as I do, you must obey my rules."

"As you wish."

"Third, and by far the most important: you're going to do all the cooking."

Jarko laughed and kissed her again. Deep and powerful, and as strong as Darla was, she found herself melting into him, relinquishing all control.

"Duchess," Jarko said with a whisper, "I wouldn't let you cook even if you wanted to."

"I'll accept those terms," Darla said.

"I want to hunt by your side until the end of time."

And as their lips met again, and her tunic fell to the floor, along with Jarko's coat, Darla hoped the end of time never came.

CHAPTER 31

Darla's eyes fluttered open. Before she had a chance to adjust to the early morning light, she felt lips on hers. Rough yet tender, firm yet soft. She let them remain there for a few moments before opening her eyes to see the beautiful yellow gems hovering above her, embedded in the face of the man by her side. She reached up and pressed her hand against Jarko's cheeks, tracing her fingers down his bluish-black skin, her nails leaving slight marks that disappeared within seconds.

"Morning, Duchess," Jarko said.

"Morning, Jarko," she replied. "I like waking up like this a lot more than I like waking up to Dolores yelling at me to turn on *The Great British Baking Show*."

"And waking up next to you is a lot nicer than waking up to the odor of several-day-old muskrat stew. You smell better, too."

He leaned over and kissed her, wrapping his arms around her. And unlike the first time they met face to face, Darla didn't want him to ever let go.

Finally she said, "Last night was…"

"Nice," Jarko said. "Very, very nice."

"I was going to say smoking goddamn hot."

"Yes, it was. And I could tell just how hot it was for you."

"Oh really?" Darla said, propping herself onto an elbow. "And how exactly could you tell that?"

"At some point there was enough smoke coming out of your nose I was worried a human might see it and call the fire department. And then we'd have to find a new make-out spot."

"Thankfully I know all the good make-out spots in Clear Creek," she said. "So were you worried at all about what Mantula said? That he'd kill you in your sleep?"

Jarko shook his head. "I've dealt with a lot of monsters just like Mantula. They're big on bluster but when you put them in their place, they shrink. Not to mention he's got twenty-five percent fewer arms to fight with than he did a week ago."

"Fair point," she said. "Do you remember when I asked you if there were any other body parts besides your arms and neck that were extendable?"

"Oh, I remember," Jarko said with a sly smile. "And your nose smoked when I said yes. You tried to hide it. But you didn't do a very good job.

"So let me ask you a question," she said.

"Shoot."

"It's personal."

"Good. I hate impersonal questions."

"How far can it," Darla said, parsing her words, "extend?"

Jarko paused, then replied, "I guess you'll have to find out."

"Don't tease me before breakfast," she said and kissed him again, feeling his arms wrap around her waist in several snug loops.

"Hey, Duchess," Jarko said.

"Yeah?"

"You're smoking again."

Darla saw the wisps floating into the air and smiled. "Do you mind my smoke poofs?"

"I can't get enough of your smoke poofs."

"Good. Because they're a part of me." Darla got up and looked around the cave. "Hey, speaking of things that are a part of me, have you seen my scourge?"

Jarko laughed. "There," he said, pointing at a large muskrat holding her scourge between its teeth.

"Hey!" she shouted. "Drop that! I need to do terrible things to humans with it!"

She chased the muskrat around the cave until it dropped the scourge. She hooked it back to her belt.

"Not that I don't enjoy spending time in your literal man cave," Darla said, "but we might want to find a place where my weapons aren't in danger of being stolen by small rodents."

"I was just checking Zillow yesterday but couldn't find anywhere with indoor plumbing," Jarko said. "Speaking of small rodents, I'm hungry. Want to grab some breakfast? I could rustle up a few eels from Maker's Marsh. I make a killer living sashimi."

"I could never say no to living sashimi, but I want to check on my mom first. This is the first night she's spent alone in fifteen years. I want to make sure she didn't actually get beheaded again."

"If she did, I would find the rest of her again."

"Very chivalrous, but I can think of better things to do with you than dig holes all over Clear Creek," she said. "By the way, one day you're going to have to tell me all about your trip to New York and this other monster you met."

"I'll tell you all about it over breakfast. Now let's go make sure Dolores Drake hasn't gotten herself into any trouble."

They exited the waterfall, and Darla began her traversal through the woods. Jarko followed, drifting above her. At one point she felt a wet *slap* on her butt, turned around, and saw Jarko swinging above, a childish grin on his face.

"Sorry," he said. "It was just there. I had to."

"What should I do with you?" she said.

"I can think of a few things."

"Well, keep your extendables to yourself for now. I don't need my mom seeing your purple business."

When they arrived at the Drake cave, Darla went to move the boulder aside. Then she felt a hand—or tentacle—on her shoulder.

"Allow me, Duchess," Jarko said, hauling the boulder away from the entrance. Then he whispered, "I still like calling you Duchess. May I continue?"

"You may," she said. "But just so we're clear, the chivalry stuff is gonna get old quick. I'll allow this one, but if you pull my chair out for me, or hold an elevator door open, I might have to smite you."

"Have you ever even *been* in an elevator?"

"No, but that's beside the point. It could happen."

When they entered the cave, Darla heard a strange sound coming from the antechamber.

"What is that?" Jarko asked.

"I have no idea," Darla said, heading through the tunnels. "It sounds like...music?"

When they reached the antechamber, they heard it more

clearly. It was music. Of some sort. A type of music Darla had never heard before. And then she also saw something she hadn't seen in many, many years. From the doorway to Dolores's room, she could see her mother's shadow.

"What in Beelzebub's bonnet is she doing?" Jarko asked.

Her mother's shadow was moving fast, awkwardly, crazily, joyously.

"She's dancing," Darla said with a smile. She went over to her mother's doorway and stood there, watching, a grin from ear to ear.

Dolores wasn't just dancing. She was *getting down*. Moving all around her room, jumping and leaping, perching on the walls and springing off, twirling at speeds that would have made Jarko's muskrat stew come up.

"Enjoying yourself?" Darla asked.

"I haven't danced in years," Dolores said.

"Kind of hard to dance when you're just a head."

"*Exactly*. I have a lot of catching up to do."

"What are you listening to?" Darla asked.

"Now that I have legs, I was able to get the Wi-Fi password from a diner nearby, and now that I have fingers, I figured out how to use the remote control to watch something besides culinary failures and bearded boy romances," Dolores said, still bopping around. "I found a music channel. It's called Oldies. This group is called…wait…it's on the tip of my tongue…Ace of Base. Apparently, they were very popular during olden times."

"It sounds like a microwave being assaulted by a forklift," Darla said.

"I know. And I absolutely *love* it."

Jarko walked up next to Darla and said, "Get down with the boogie, Mrs. D."

"Oh, I'm *down*," Dolores said. "And I'm never getting back up!"

Jarko leaned toward Darla and whispered, "We really need to get our own cave."

"Oh. For sure," Darla said. "So do you regret coming back?"

Jarko went back into the antechamber and sat down at the long wooden table. He then shot out a tentacle, wrapped it around Darla's waist, and pulled her onto his lap. He kissed her, long and slow, and her body felt like it had been electrified, a current coursing through it even stronger than the day she actually had been electrified (she was young, a new hunter, and a couple of teens had managed to toss a downed power line into a pool of water Darla was standing in, and it was definitely not one of her finer moments, but every monster is allowed to be young and stupid sometimes).

"My only regret is making you think I was leaving," he said. "And that will never, ever happen again."

"Good. Because if it did, I would hunt you down."

"Is that a promise?" he said, smiling.

"It's a guarantee." She kissed him again.

"Hey!" came Dolores's loud, irritated voice from the other room. "You two really need to get your own cave."

Darla and Jarko sat on a log at Maker's Marsh. Their fingers were threaded through each other, and she felt his thumb gently rubbing her palm. Or was it his pinky? To be honest, all his fingers felt the same. It would take getting used to, but so would all of it. But it would be worth it. For the first time in years— maybe even ever—Darla Drake felt content.

"The first time I laid eyes on you," Jarko said, "up there on the roof of the office building, you took my breath away."

"The first time I laid eyes on you," Darla said, "I wanted

to cut off all your limbs and cover your mangled torso with hot sauce."

"That sounds...unpleasant."

"To be fair, I didn't know you yet."

"You still have a lot to learn, Duchess."

"Good thing I have the rest of our lives to do it."

He leaned over and kissed her. His lips were rough yet tender, and she embraced his touch, slid into him. They fit together perfectly, like it was meant to be.

"So, what do you want to do tonight?" Jarko asked.

"I have an idea or two," Darla said, sliding closer. "Just how far does your neck stretch?"

"I guess you'll have to find out," Jarko said.

She went in to kiss him again, but as she did, the night sky lit up red, snapping them out of their embrace.

"What the hell was that?" Jarko said, standing up and looking out over the trees. There was another burst of red, following by a loud *bang*. "Is that a gun?"

Darla shook her head. She could feel her blood beginning to boil, steam drifting from her nose.

"Flare guns," she said. "And they're being shot out on Romero Pond, at the camp."

"Who the hell is shooting flare guns on Romero Pond?" he said. "Aren't there kids out there?"

Darla looked at him. Jarko smiled.

"I guess I know what our plans are tonight," he said.

Darla nodded.

"Let's go."

She began her traversal through the woods, Jarko drifting above her. She kept looking back to make sure he was still there, and he always was, matching her speed.

"I'm with you, Duchess," he said, and for some reason those four words warmed Darla's black-blooded heart.

They stopped when they got to Romero Pond. Darla leapt up into a high tree to join Jarko so they could pinpoint the location of the flares.

"Out there," Jarko said. "I see two boats."

"That one," Darla said, pointing at one boat. "That's where the flares are coming from."

There was another loud *bang* and a flare shot out from one boat in the direction of the other. They heard screams as the flare embedded itself in the side of the boat, which was filled with young campers. Some of the kids had jumped overboard and were hiding behind the boat to get out of the path of the flare gun. The flare gun boat was manned by three older cruel-looking teens, probably all named Kyle. The were laughing their asses off as the young children in the other boat screamed. Darla felt her blood begin to boil.

"You ready?" she said.

"Ready to hunt with the great Darla Drake?" Jarko replied. "It would be an honor."

They kissed, then leapt down from the tree and headed towards the pond.

They had no idea they were being hunted until Darla Drake emerged from the waters of Romero Pond and leapt onto the deck of their small motorboat. They screamed and fell backward, water cascading over the bow, spraying all four of them. Water dripped from Darla's bone crown and ran down her face like tears.

"It's her!" one of the boys screamed.

"The Creature of Clear Creek!" another boy yelled.

The third boy remained silent. His eyes wide in disbelief. Darla recognized him immediately.

Lewis freaking Cawthorn.

The very counselor who'd nearly killed those kids with Randy Horvath and Kyle Browning last summer and had been fired from Camp Clear Creek. Darla hadn't expected him to be dumb enough to return. Yet here he was, terrorizing young children once again. This time, though, the campers had a monstrous protector.

A flare gun sat on the bottom of the boat. Darla picked it up, examined it, and tossed it overboard.

"I didn't even want to be here," one of the other counselors stammered. "Lewis told us if we didn't help him, Randy's parents would get us fired.

"I swear we didn't want anybody to get hurt!" the other counselor whined.

"They're both lying!" Lewis said with such unprovoked anger that Darla knew the other counselors were telling the truth.

"I've been waiting a long time for you, Lewis," Darla said.

"Get the hell out of here, you monster," Lewis spat. "There are three of us and one of you and you're just a girl. You don't scare me."

"Oh, Lewis," Darla said with a smile. "The night isn't over yet."

Suddenly, two tentacles shot out from the water and grabbed the other two counselors. Before they had a chance to scream, they were flung far out into Romero Pond, their bodies tumbling end over end until they landed with a splash far in the distance from the boat.

"What the hell was that?" Lewis said, spinning around,

looking to see where the attack had come from. But the waters were placid. Lewis began to shake, fear taking over his body. He unhooked an oar from its mooring, holding it like an oversized baseball bat.

"I'll kill you!" Lewis said. He swung the oar at Darla, but with lightning quickness she brought her scourge down and splintered the wood into pieces, spraying sharp projectiles all over the deck. Lewis stood there holding nothing but the shattered handle. He looked at it, realized it could still be used as a weapon, and lunged at Darla aiming the makeshift weapon at her heart.

Before he reached her, a tentacle ripped the broken oar from Lewis's grasp, flinging it far out into the inky darkness. Another wrapped around his waist, imprisoning him. Lewis struggled, but was no match for the monster who held him.

Then, out from the depths leapt Jarko Murkvale, landing on the bow next to Darla, the boat rocking back and forth in the otherwise calm waters. The children on the other boat gasped as they saw the monsters standing side-by-side, hovering over the man who just minutes ago was trying to scare them, capsize them, or far worse.

"Who the hell are you?" Lewis gasped, unable to move with the powerful tentacle pinning his arms to his sides.

"Darla Drake," she said, unhooking the scourge at her side, its brass studs reflecting the moonlight. "Duchess of Death."

Lewis's face turned white. He turned to the other monster.

"Jarko Murkvale," he said, bowing dramatically.

"Jarko Murkvale, Duke of Death," Darla corrected.

Jarko turned to look at her, a smile on his face

"Duke of Death?"

Darla smiled. "You like it?"

Jarko grinned. "I like it very much."

Then Darla turned back to Lewis. She spun her scourge, twirling it so fast it emitted an audible *whirring* noise. Lewis's eyes widened as he watched each rotation of the weapons' tails.

"Welcome back to Clear Creek, Lewis," Darla said.

Jarko added, "We hope you enjoy your stay."

Darla looked at Jarko and he looked back at her, and before their first dual hunt came to an end they embraced, their lips meeting as the boat rocked beneath them, a faint plume of smoke rising into the air.

The last thing Lewis Cawthorn saw, as Darla Drake's scourge and Jarko Murkvale's tentacles closed in on him, was the sight of two monsters making out, thinking that they really needed to just get a room.

END OF BOOK ONE

Jarko Takes Manhattan

A Dating & Dismemberment Story

CHAPTER 1

It should have been simple. Leave the Monster Mash. Go back to his cave, pack up his meager belongings, have a late-night snack (preferably something without too many bones, his stomach had been acting a little strange recently, perhaps not coincidentally around the time he met Darla, and he didn't want to force his stomach to digest anything with more ribs than he had).

But it wasn't simple. He'd gone to the Mash, perhaps against his better judgment. And she'd been there. Of course she'd been there. He *knew* she'd be there. He supposed he'd hoped that if they did see each other, that feeling that had sat in the pits of his stomach would be gone. That he could see Darla and they could exchange pleasantries and shake hands, go their separate ways, never to see each other again. But he could tell when he saw her that she wasn't going to do that. His conversation with those other monsters—he'd already forgotten their names—had meant nothing to him. Small talk.

But Darla didn't take it that way. At first, he was annoyed. How dare she overreact? But then he thought about it, and if he'd seen her talking with other monsters in a similar manner, he would have squeezed their necks until their eyeballs popped out.

And when he did see her going off with Mantula, a monster whose reputation was smellier than the pits under each of his legs, he couldn't stay still. Darla could take care of herself. He knew that. But he also didn't want her to *have* to always take care of herself.

When he got back to his cave, he looked around. It wasn't that long ago that he'd shot a tentacle through the waterfall and grabbed Darla, fully expecting to have it out, let her know that Clear Creek was *his*. My, how things changed so fast.

Once he began to feel things for Darla he hadn't felt in a long, long time, Jarko knew he couldn't stay.

Now, though, Jarko also knew he couldn't leave.

But if there was any chance of him staying, of repairing what had been broken, he had to let Darla know how far he was willing to go. Words meant nothing anymore. She needed to *see* how badly he wanted her. How badly he needed her. And if he was going to do that, there was only one way to prove himself.

Find the body of Dolores Drake.

But Clear Creek was enormous. Even with his tentacles digging twenty-four seven, he could spend years burrowing holes only to find nothing but smelly, discarded camp clothes. Not to mention that he'd make an enormous mess, and likely get recorded by some Spielberg or J.J. Abrams-wannabe counselor and end up online looking like a combination pinwheel and octopus. No, he needed to find out *where* Dolores Drake's body was. And only one person knew that.

Franklin Shine.

He had to find Franklin Shine.

But where in the hell *was* Franklin Shine?

CHAPTER 2

It was still dusk. Jarko estimated he had another hour or two before the sun came up, the counselors began to prep for the day, and he would lose his chance. He would have to move quick.

Jarko leapt through the waterfall and began to drift through the trees toward Camp Clear Creek. Darla told him that Franklin Shine had decapitated Dolores fifteen years ago. He would remember. You didn't forget something like that. Now Jarko just had to find him. And make him talk. The second part, Jarko was confident he could do. The first...that was a little trickier.

He arrived at the main office and drifted to the front door. He pressed himself up against the wall. Then, a rumble in his stomach roughly the volume of a herd of buffalo echoed through the campgrounds. His stomach letting him know in no uncertain terms that it wanted—needed—food. And a lot of it. With everything that had happened at the Mash with Darla and Mantula, he'd forgotten to eat. His stomach was happy to remind him.

"Shut *up*," he said to his stomach, as though the organ responded to direct commands. Jarko sighed. He'd hunted for a long time. Stealth was not his strong suit. But if he had any hopes of finding Franklin Shine without exposing himself to the world, he'd have to work a whole lot harder at it.

When the rumbling stopped, Jarko stood still, waiting to see if he'd woken anything besides woodland creatures. Thankfully, the camp remained asleep. He jigged the handle to the front door. Unsurprisingly, it was locked. He checked the exterior. All windows were shut and locked. He thought for a moment, then saw an air duct on the side of the wall. He shot out a tentacle, gripped the metal, and yanked it off swiftly.

He placed it on the ground softly, then gripped the sides of the duct with his hands and pulled himself right through. It was a tight squeeze, but Jarko was able to shimmy through the duct and land inside the main office.

It was dark. Quiet. Jarko walked through the office, unsure of what to look for. A sign outside one office read **Dennis Weebly, Head Counselor**. The door was unlocked. Jarko went inside. He could feel his heart rate increasing to four hundred seventy beats a minute, a smidge above normal. He took a breath. Stabilized.

Jarko slid open Weebly's desk drawers. The top had nothing but paper clips, stamps, granola bars, and a photo of someone who was either his girlfriend, mother, grandmother, or aunt. Jarko wasn't good at guessing relations.

The middle drawer had some sugar packets and a set of keys. Jarko took those. The bottom drawer held a bottle of Jim Beam. Mostly empty.

Jarko looked at Weebly's computer. He was relatively computer literate from his time on the MFU, but Weebly's computer was locked with a passcode. Jarko checked everywhere in the office but couldn't find the password. Weebly may have been drinking on the job. But he remembered his passwords.

He left Weebly's office. He found two locked doors. The first was a bathroom. It smelled worse than a five-day-old dead muskrat. The second was a filing room. Jarko's eyes opened wide.

He went through the files. Unfortunately, camp counselors were quite disorganized, so it took him the better part of an hour going through box after box until he found one labeled **Camper Files – 2008**.

That was fifteen years ago. The year Franklin Shine left Dolores half the woman she used to be.

Jarko tore open the box and pulled out all the camper files.

Leonard Fitzsimmons

Willie Simmons

Benjamin Goldfarb

Suresh Patel

Franklin Shine

He found it. Franklin Shine.

He opened the file. The file contained a photo of Shine, family details, payment information, and more. Shine had short brown hair and grayish-blue eyes. He did not look particularly cruel or particularly meek. He looked like...a kid. A normal thirteen-year-old kid who just happened to take a lucky swing with a shovel and bisect a legendary monster.

He looked at the section titled **Contact Information**. Shine's parents were Barbara and Nathan. They lived in Sheboygan, Wisconsin. There was a phone number listed. Given that in 2008

Shine was thirteen, there was no current contact information for Shine himself. He didn't have time to waste. The sun would be coming up soon.

He picked up a landline office phone and dialed the Sheboygan number. With every ring, Jarko's heart sank. Then he heard a click, and a woman's tired voice said, "Hello?"

"Um, yes, hi."

He should have thought this through *before* dialing.

"Hello? Who is this?"

She was going to hang up. He had to think fast.

"Mrs. Shine?"

"Yes, who *is* this? It's the middle of the night."

"My name is Mantu…Manny Untula. I'm calling about your son. Franklin."

Jarko heard a male voice say, "Who the hell is it, Barb?"

"Something about Frankie," she said.

"Oh hell, what did he do now?"

"*Shhh.* Yes, hi, sorry. Mr…Untula?"

"That's right. I'm calling because your son is in trouble, and I need to speak with him. Urgently."

"What kind of trouble?" Barbara said. She was awake now.

"I'm afraid that's something I need to speak with him about."

"I'm not sending him any more money," Nathan Shine said.

"Nate, shut *up*. Where are you calling from again, Mr…?"

"Untula. I'm calling from…the bank."

"The bank?"

"That's right."

"The bank is trying to get in touch with Frankie," Barbara said to Nathan. "I think they're going to fire him."

"I told him not to move to Manhattan," Nathan said.

"Bunch of greedy mercenaries who'll drop you like a rock the second they don't need you anymore. Wait, which bank did he say he's with?"

"I'm sorry, Mr. Untula. Which bank did you say you were with?"

"I'm with…Warbucks Bank."

"I haven't heard of that bank. I thought he was still with NickelSmart. And you said you work with my son?"

"What did he say?" Nathan Shine asked.

"He said he's with Warbucks Bank," Barbara whispered.

"Warbucks Bank," Nathan said. "Warbucks. Warbucks. Why does that sound familiar. Wait, that's the guy from *Annie*. It's a prank, Barb. It's one of Frank's idiot friends."

"No, Mrs. Shine, I—"

"Get a life, sir," Barbara said. "If you call again, I'll call the police."

Barbara hung up.

Idiot, Jarko thought. Years back, he and Frederica Fimmel, the Frost Witch, had watched a movie at a drive-in from a treetop. The movie had been *Annie*. This was not going well.

But…

He had a lead. NickelSmart Bank. Manhattan. New York City. Franklin was somewhere in New York City. And he worked for a bank. He'd hunted down prey with far less information. It was time for Jarko Murkvale to hit the Big Apple. There were just two small questions:

How did a monster get to Manhattan?

How did you find one guy in a city of six million?

CHAPTER 3

Jarko didn't have time to consider this, because he heard an air horn bleat through the campgrounds and shatter the silence. The camp wake-up call. He wasn't going to be alone for long.

Jarko slipped back through the air vent, reattached the grate, and hoisted himself atop the roof of the office. A minute later, several counselors stumbled out of their cabins, rubbing their eyes and yawning. The sun began to creep up over the horizon, bathing the treetops in a golden yellow.

"Let's go!" one counselor shouted. "Up and at 'em! Breakfast in ten minutes!"

Then Jarko heard a car engine. He looked in the direction of the sound and saw a produce truck pulling up to the back of the cafeteria. Two counselors met the driver, who unlocked the back and began to unload crates of vegetables, which the counselors carried into the caf. Jarko looked at the license plate. Indiana. Not New York. But it was a start.

The driver took a clipboard out from the truck and brought it to the counselors to sign. When they were all preoccupied, Jarko drifted through the trees over to the caf, and quickly slid underneath the truck's chassis. He looped his tentacles around the metal and held fast. There were barely six inches of room between his back and the ground—but it was enough.

Then he waited. And waited. What the hell was taking so long? Jarko had a high threshold for pain and discomfort, but it had been at least fifteen minutes since the counselors had signed the paperwork. Where was the driver?

Then Jarko heard a pair of footsteps. Voices.

"Is he still in the bathroom?" came one voice.

"Yup," said another voice with a healthy level of disgust. "Every time he drops off food, he desecrates the bathroom. Next delivery, I'm going to lock that thing so he can't destroy it."

"God, please do. No spray in the world will cover that up."

Finally, ten minutes later, Jarko heard a series of grunts and the driver climbed into the cab, started the truck, and headed down the dirt road and exited Camp Clear Creek.

Jarko couldn't be sure which direction they were headed, but that didn't matter quite as much at the moment. He just needed to get out onto the highway. After Frederica's death, he'd traveled thousands of miles this very way. If he could do that, he could make it to New York. He had to prove to Darla that he was more than words.

But instead of the highway, the truck drove for fifteen minutes and then pulled onto another dirt road. From inside the truck's cab, he heard the driver say, "Dropped off delivery at Clear Creek. Heading into Camp Sudden Valley. Once that's done, I'll head back. Over and out."

Jarko sighed. He had no choice but to wait. When the truck stopped and the driver got out, Jarko stretched. He likely smelled like a combination of exhaust and mud. He waited. And waited. And finally, after another half hour, the driver came back to the truck and started it up. Jarko cringed at the notion of this man going from camp to camp befouling bathrooms.

Finally, the truck merged onto the highway. Jarko could see the gray asphalt speeding past just inches below him. Based on the time of day and the position of the shadows on the road, Jarko could tell that the truck was heading northwest. Not in the direction of New York City.

He shimmied to the edge of the chassis and looked up. He could see an exit approaching with a sign for I-70 East. That was where he wanted to go.

A silver minivan merged into the right lane for the turnoff, two lanes away from the truck. Jarko shot out a tentacle and latched onto the bumper. He then pulled himself toward the minivan, bumping his back and butt along the highway, and hauled himself under the chassis. He looked up and saw the face of a young girl plastered to the window of a sedan. She was staring at him, her mouth agape. Jarko smiled at her and waved as the minivan pulled onto the exit ramp.

The minivan traveled along I-70. Jarko then hitched onto a Mercedes heading onto I-76, an SUV heading through New Jersey on 295, and then finally a Lexus heading north on I-95, eventually turning into the Lincoln Tunnel.

The air was thick with exhaust. Jarko was surrounded by barely lighted gloom. He had never been to New York City. Never had a reason to. Everything he knew about it came from monster lore and what he'd read on the MFU. He was something of a student of history, but reading about something and experiencing it were two wholly different things.

The car exited the Lincoln Tunnel and daylight flooded his eyes. He blinked, adjusting. He realized he had no idea where this car was going. And given that one place in Manhattan was as good as any, when the car came to a stop, Jarko released his grip from the chassis, dropped to the ground, and rolled to his right up alongside the sidewalk.

He looked up to see a man hovering over him, a hot dog in one hand and a bottle of mustard in another.

"Where the hell did you come from?" the man asked. Then he looked at Jarko's hands. "Is that...calamari?"

Jarko retracted his tentacles back into his jacket and stood up. He towered over the man, who suddenly retreated at the sight of Jarko.

"Puh-puh-puh-please," the man said. "Don't hurt me."

"I have no plans to," Jarko said. "Do you know a man named Franklin Shine?"

"No," the man said, shaking his head. He held out his hand. "Huh...hot dog?"

Jarko cocked his head. "Don't mind if I do."

He took the hot dog and swallowed it whole, bun and all. Not bad. Though he should have asked for the ketchup.

But this man's reaction would not be dissimilar to the reactions of most, if not every, New Yorker. Jarko was six foot seven, with skin the color of morning dusk. Not to mention that his arms did, in fact, look very much like calamari.

Jarko walked down the street. New York was awash in sights and sounds and filled with more people than Jarko had ever seen in his life. All sorts of shapes and sizes and colors. In fact, Jarko wouldn't blend in all that badly here. At the corner, atop a garbage can, he saw a lone red glove. It was a little dirty, but he picked it up, swiped it through a puddle, and slipped it on one tentacled hand. A little snug, but it would work. A few blocks later, he found another. This one green, and larger. That fixed one problem.

He went up to a woman staring at her phone.

"Excuse me, miss," Jarko said. "Do you know Franklin Shine?"

The woman's eyes widened, but rather than running in fear, her lips turned up into a slight smile. "I don't. You're a tall drink of water, aren't you?"

"I am, in fact, mostly water," Jarko replied. "As are you. About sixty percent water. I'm more like eighty. Larger organs."

The woman nodded. "Tell me more about your organs."

"If you don't know Franklin Shine, or NickelSmart bank, my organs and I have no need for you."

The woman pointed across the street. "There's a NickelSmart branch right over there," she said. "Hell, you can't go more than a few blocks without seeing one."

Jarko turned. The words NickelSmart were etched in green above the awning, the dot of the I in Nickel a bright red balloon.

"Thank you, ma'am," Jarko said.

"I'm thirty-six," the woman said, irritated. "I'm not a ma'am yet."

Jarko felt like this conversation could quickly turn into an argument, so he left the woman standing there and headed toward the NickelSmart branch.

Jarko gripped the door handle with his glove and pulled. It didn't open. Jarko pulled again, harder this time, and the door buckled outward, the glass shattering as it ripped from its hinges and fell to the sidewalk with an enormous crash.

"Bank robber!" shouted a teller from inside the branch.

Two security guards began to run toward Jarko, but hesitated when they saw his size. Still, he saw guns at their waists. This was a problem he did *not* need.

"Do you know a Franklin Shine?" Jarko shouted. Nobody answered. One of the guards pulled the gun from its holster. Jarko sighed. He wasn't going to get answers here, and he also didn't need the whole city searching for him.

He looked up. Saw a windowsill fifteen feet above him. He took the gloves off his hands, held them in his teeth, and shot his tentacles upward, gripping the windowsill and hoisting himself off the ground. He climbed up the side of the building until he was on the rooftop. The whole escape took less than ten seconds.

Atop the roof, he caught his breath. The city looked incredible from this vantage point. Towering behemoths of steel and concrete. He was a long, long way from Clear Creek.

Then Jarko heard sirens. He looked down. Three police cars had pulled up in front of the NickelSmart branch. Half a dozen cops got out and began to inspect the broken doors. A woman ran up to the cops and pointed at the very roof where Jarko was standing. She'd obviously seen him. A news van pulled up. A cameraman got out, and within moments was interviewing the woman as well as the cops. Jarko sighed. This rooftop was a hiding place no more.

Jarko vaulted from rooftop to rooftop until he was reasonably sure he was far enough away from the mess he'd inadvertently created. Darla had claimed he was chaotic and undisciplined, and right now he wasn't exactly proving her wrong.

Going into a NickelSmart bank branch was no longer an option.

Perhaps he didn't need to ask anyone in person. There was plenty of technology at his fingertips. Or, more specifically, other people's fingertips.

Jarko peered over the ledge of the rooftop. Dozens of people were walking along the sidewalk. He waited until he saw what he was looking for: a guy taking his phone out of his pocket. Before the guy knew what was happening, Jarko shot an arm down, took the phone right out of the man's hand, and brought it up to the rooftop. He tapped the blank screen. It read: **FACE ID.**

Jarko paused. He held the phone up to his face. Nothing happened. Stupid phones. Things were likely a whole lot easier back in Dolores Drake's day when you didn't have to worry about facial ID recognition and people capturing monsters on their cell phones.

He looked back down. The man was standing on the sidewalk, staring up at the sky, clearly wondering just what the hell had taken his phone. Jarko tapped the screen. Again, it read **FACE ID.**

This time, Jarko swooped the phone back down toward the ground, held it in front of the man's surprised face for a moment, then brought it back to the rooftop. It was unlocked. Jarko smiled. Darla would have been impressed.

He tapped the search engine before the phone locked again and entered **Franklin Shine NickelSmart**. The top search result was a professional profile. Jarko tapped it. *Bingo.*

It was clearly the same person from the camp files, just fifteen years older. Jarko recognized the eyes, the facial structure. Franklin Shine was an account executive at NickelSmart. He wore a smart suit in his photo, with neatly parted hair and a clean-shaven face. Lucky for Jarko, the profile also listed the address of the branch Shine worked at, as well as his phone number. Jarko opened the phone app and dialed.

After five rings, the call went right to voicemail.

"You have reached Franklin Shine at NickelSmart. I am away from my desk right now, but if you would like to leave a message, please do so after the tone. If you are an existing client, I will return your call as soon as possible. If you are interested in becoming a client, please leave your pertinent informa—"

Jarko hung up. Shine worked at 832 Madison Avenue. He didn't know where that was, so Jarko opened the Maps app and typed it in. Shine worked on Madison Avenue between 68th and 69th streets. The blue dot on the map that represented the phone's location was about twenty blocks southwest of that address. No way he'd be able to keep the phone unlocked during the journey, so Jarko dropped his arm back to street level, placed the phone back in the hand of the ever-more surprised man, and drifted off toward the NickelSmart branch where Franklin Shine worked.

One good thing about Manhattan: there was no shortage of things for Jarko to drift along. Rooftops and chimneys, telephone poles and cell phone towers and antennae. He felt like that popular spider monster. Not Mantula, the other one, the one who could shoot webs and talked nonstop about responsibility, who Jarko was pretty sure hadn't even gone through puberty yet. Woods were thick and dense, and you constantly had to avoid trees and branches and shrubs and deer. Here, Jarko could roam free.

But there was something about the vastness that made him miss Clear Creek. Made him miss Darla something fierce. What was the point in roaming free if you roamed free alone?

The streets of Manhattan progressed numerically. And

while the avenues seemed to have no logical layout, he drifted quick, made a few wrong turns, until Jarko arrived at 68th and Madison. From the rooftop he could see the bank entrance. This time, he wouldn't be stupid. He noticed a small slot on the side of the door. A woman approached, took a card from her purse, slid it in, a light turned green, and she entered. Jarko did not have one of those cards. And taking someone's wallet in front of a bank would not aid his stealth efforts.

He slipped his gloves back on and vaulted down to an alleyway adjacent to the street where the bank was located. When he stepped out into the daylight, he barely drew a glance. In fact, just a block away he saw a man wearing a diaper and wearing a cowboy hat while playing a guitar. People seemed far more interested in this half naked cowboy musician than they did in him.

He idled across the street until he saw another woman approach the bank. When she slid her card in and entered, Jarko caught the door before it could close and slipped into the bank.

The air smelled like lemon and cement. On one side of the bank, Jarko saw a row of employees behind glass partitions taking slips and handing money over to customers. On the other were employees behind desks, either on telephones or typing what must have been incredibly important information into their computers, based on how focused they seemed. He did not see Franklin Shine.

A man in a suit approached him. He looked Jarko up and down, hesitant.

"Can I help you, sir?" he said. His pin read **Leon Garvey, Manager**.

"I'm looking for someone who works here," Jarko said. "Franklin Shine."

"Ah," Garvey said with a nod, as if understanding something Jarko wasn't privy to. "Mr. Shine...did not come in today."

Garvey said it in such a way that Jarko got the feeling Shine's absence was not unexpected, but also not necessarily permitted.

"Are you a client of his?" Garvey asked.

"No. I'm a personal friend."

Garvey nodded. "If I can be blunt then, sir," he said, "get your friend some help."

Jarko cocked his head. "Help?"

"Mr. Shine is...troubled," Garvey said. "I like the boy. I do. But if he doesn't get his demons under control, they're going to consume him."

"Demons. You mean figuratively speaking."

"Of course," Garvey said with a laugh. "What, you thought I meant real demons?"

Jarko shrugged. "Didn't want to assume. Listen, where could I find Franklin?"

"Well, I don't think he's home. I tried his cell but nobody's picking up. I called his doorman, but he said Franklin went out this morning and hasn't come back yet."

"Do you have any idea where he might be, then?"

Garvey thought for a moment. "It's Friday, right?"

"Yup," Jarko said, as though he had any idea what day of the week it was.

"Then I'd be shocked if Franklin isn't at Jarvis tonight."

"Jarvis?"

Garvey cocked his head. "You sure you're friends with Franklin? Jarvis Club is in the Meatpacking District. Franklin goes pretty much every Friday night. I went with him and some of his friends a few times. But they get a little...rowdy for my tastes. To be fair, it's more his friends than him, but he doesn't have the best taste in friends. Present company excluded, of course."

"Jarvis," Jarko said. "Thanks."

He heard a buzzing sound emanate from Garvey's pants pocket. He took out his cell phone.

"Hello?" he said. "No, I hadn't heard. Attempted robbery? That's awful. Yes, send the picture right away."

Garvey held the phone up, and a moment later he received a text message. He opened the message, and a photo appeared. Jarko needed one tenth of a second to recognize that the photo was of himself, taken from a security camera, tearing the doors off the NickelSmart branch.

Jarko was gone before Garvey could say another word.

CHAPTER 4

Jarko borrowed another phone and found the location for Jarvis Club. It didn't open its doors until eight p.m. Jarko had some time to kill.

He drifted across Manhattan as the sun began to set, casting a beautiful pinkish-orange hue over the city. He felt the sun on his face, let his tentacled arms bask in the warmth. Maybe he wouldn't want to live in New York City. But it would be a hell of a place for a vacation every now and then.

At seven thirty, he drifted over to the Meatpacking District. A line had already begun to form outside Jarvis Club. Dozens and dozens of well-dressed people waiting to be allowed in to do…something. Pay too much for drinks? Barely have enough room to breathe? It didn't seem to Jarko like they'd thought all of this through.

The mass of people waiting to get into Jarvis was packed in too tightly, and the sun had gone down. Even with his night vision, Jarko couldn't tell if Franklin Shine was in the crowd.

He needed to get closer.

He drifted down to the street level and took a seat on a bench across from Jarvis. Soon, they began to let people in. He watched the faces. No Shine. No Shine. No Shine. It was possible Garvey had been wrong, and Shine was at a movie or with a girlfriend or boyfriend. He'd have to stake out Shine's apartment and just wait.

The line moved along. More people joined and slowly made their way to the front.

Then he saw him. Franklin Shine. He had just joined the line and seemed to be with a small group: four guys and two girls. The others were laughing and drinking something out of a paper bag. Shine looked morose. Troubled. Jarko wondered why.

Then, before he could think any more about Franklin Shine, Jarko felt something grip his leg. Hard. And before he knew what was happening, Jarko was pulled off the bench, into the street, and then through a sewer grate into the darkness.

• • •

Jarko landed in a shallow pool of water with a *thump*. He leapt up, focused, looking to see who or what had dragged him down here. He didn't have to look far.

"Who are you, and what are you doing here?" the creature said.

Jarko's eyes adjusted, and he saw the monster.

He was small compared to Jarko, maybe five foot eight, but broad in every way possible. Folds of skin cascaded down his face like pancake mixture, and his head was bald except for a few strands of poorly combed-over grayish-black hair. His eyes were small and piglike, and he hunched over like he might dig into the ground or pounce at any moment. Smudges of mud dripped down his face in dark rivulets, but he didn't seem to notice. He simply stared at Jarko, his large, fleshy hands opening and closing like a crab's pincers, his breathing labored from the exertion of bringing Jarko down to his level.

"I know you," Jarko said. "You're The Mayor."

"Present and accounted for," The Mayor said with a dramatic bow. He spoke with a mild lisp, his voice low and guttural, and smiled with every word as though he amused himself and only himself. "And you must be Jarko Murkvale."

"How do you know who I am?"

The Mayor unleashed a belly laugh that rippled the waters. "You really are quite obtuse, my friend. You've become quite the celebrity around here today."

"What do you mean?"

"That stunt you pulled at the bank this morning. It's been running on every local news station nonstop. People wondering what kind of man could just pull a couple of bank doors right off their hinges. Little did they know they're not looking for a man."

"I don't care," Jarko said.

"Well, I do," The Mayor snapped. "Because there's only room enough for one monster in this city. And you're looking at him."

Jarko laughed. "Look at you," he said. "You're as scary as a bowl of pudding."

"Ah, you're wrong, young monster," The Mayor said. "The camera, it loves me. The people, they both fear and respect me."

"They fear your smell more than your strength," Jarko said.

"I am a terrifying beast for all to reckon with, and—" The Mayor halted mid-sentence to hawk up a glob of greenish phlegm. "As I was saying."

"What the hell happened to you?" Jarko said. "You *were* The Mayor. You used to run this city. You *were* feared. You *were* respected. Hell, I respected you. But now you're like a little homuncular goblin. I've eaten muskrats scarier than you."

"I am a hell beast from which no man can escape."

"I'm pretty sure I could outrun you on one leg."

"Did you come to my city to scoff at me?" The Mayor said.

"No."

"Then why are you here? I know about you. You were hunting at Clear Creek. But I checked my MFU and it says you've put in to replace Lobstra up in Maine."

"That's not happening."

"I don't care if you're hunting children or fishermen. But you don't belong here."

"I'm not planning to be here very long," Jarko said.

The Mayor squinted, as though sizing Jarko up. "Then why *are* you here, Murkvale?"

"I came to prove myself to someone," he said. "Someone I care about."

The Mayor released a hearty laugh, followed by an even heartier glob of phlegm.

"Someone you *care* about?" The Mayor said, his jowls rippling as he laughed. "How perfectly sad and laughable."

"Careful," Jarko said. "I don't care who you used to be. Overstep your bounds and I will take you apart."

"Oh, don't be so sensitive," The Mayor said. "Do you know the only way you can be a *true* monster?"

"Enlighten me."

"Hate," The Mayor said. "You must *hate*. Everything and everyone. Altruism is a prison, my friend. Empathy is poison, and love is a shackle with no key. Only by ridding yourself of all of it can you be truly terrifying."

"You're not terrifying," Jarko said. "You're pitiful."

"Then you need to open your eyes, Murkvale."

"My eyes are wide open. And I see a monster that I will never, ever become. Now if you'll excuse me, I have business to attend to."

"Leave my city now!" The Mayor cried. "Or I will end you."

"I will leave when I'm ready."

The Mayor ran toward Jarko, huffing and puffing, arms churning like stumpy pistons. Jarko merely stepped out of the way, and The Mayor tripped and fell face first into the muck. The monster got to his knees and said, "You cheated."

"Hate might work for you," Jarko said, "but not for me."

Then Jarko gripped the walls and pulled himself out of the corridor and back onto the street, leaving the disgruntled monster formerly known as The Mayor shouting in the gloom.

CHAPTER 5

When Jarko got back to the street, the line was still thick with people, but Jarko could no longer see Franklin Shine among them. He cursed under his breath. There was no way he could get into the club without making an enormous mess of things, and no way he'd be able to confront Shine without ending up on a hundred different cell phones. And he didn't need a phalanx of amateur social media content creators following his every move.

There was no doubt Franklin Shine was inside the club. Jarko just had to wait.

He drifted up to a rooftop across from Jarvis Club. He wondered what Darla was doing at that moment. If she was even bothering to think about him, or if the events at the Monster Mash had truly ended things for good.

All he knew was that he did not want to end up like The Mayor. A grim, angry, shell of a monster wallowing in his own filth, with nobody and nothing to care about. He had to do this.

For Darla. For himself.

Night had descended upon Manhattan. The sky was a deep blue, and Jarko blended in. He waited atop the rooftop, unwilling to take his eyes off the club door in fear of missing Franklin Shine. Midnight came and went and Jarko began to grow concerned that he had missed Franklin, that he'd ducked out a back exit, blending into the night.

Then, at 2:13 a.m., Jarko saw three people exit Jarvis Club. In the middle was Franklin Shine.

Jarko's eyes narrowed. He had his prey.

Shine walked slowly. The two friends on either side of him shouting and jumping like they'd just won the lottery. Shine did not seem to be participating in whatever joy the others were. He looked sad. Removed.

Jarko had to wait until they were a little farther away from the club. A block and a half later, he heard one of Shine's friends say, "Hold up, I need a pick me up."

The friend ducked into an alley, and Franklin and the other guy followed. Jarko watched as the friend took something from his pocket and put it to his nose. He then gave something to the other friend, who did the same. They offered it to Franklin. Franklin declined.

Jarko struck.

He drifted down to the mouth of the alley, his massive frame blocking the entrance. All three men stepped back, surprised.

Jarko pointed at Shine. "I only want him."

The other two looked at Franklin, whose eyes had gone wide as hubcaps.

Shine's two friends showed fear in their eyes, but that fear seemed to be dulled by whatever concoction they'd just ingested. They each stepped forward, eyeing Jarko as though he was a test of their mettle.

"Guys," Shine said from the safety of the alley.

"Get the fuck out of here," one of them said.

"Not until I get what I came for," Jarko said. "This can be clean. Or this can be messy. Your call."

Shine's friends looked at each other. Then they smiled and turned back to face Jarko.

"Messy it is."

They ran toward Jarko, fists raised, screaming like they were kamikaze pilots. Which, in a way, they were.

Jarko lashed out with one arm and slapped one guy's legs out from under him, sending him sprawling to the ground, where he landed on his side with an *oomph*. The other guy saw this and hesitated, realizing that their assailant a) wasn't quite someone who would be intimated by two d-bags high off their minds, and b) wasn't quite human.

"Don't try it," Jarko said.

The guy seemed to weigh this statement, saw his friend on the ground moaning, then turned back to Jarko, as though besting him could earn his friend's respect, or at least make him look like whatever movie or video game character was swimming through his hazy mind.

The other friend started toward Jarko, who promptly wrapped an arm around the guy's waist, picked him up, and deposited him head-first into a trash can. This, thankfully, seemed to prove that they were not going to win this fight, as they lay there groaning while Franklin Shine backed away.

"Who...who are you?" he asked.

"Wrong question, Frankie," Jarko said. "You meant to ask *what* am I?"

"What are you?"

"I'm the monster who's going to leave you in pieces all over this city," Jarko said, "unless you answer my question correctly."

"Your question?" Shine asked, his voice trembling.

"Where is the body of Dolores Drake?"

Shine's eyes widened. He looked so scared he could simply dissipate into thin air.

"I knew it," Shine said. "I knew she wasn't done with me."

"Done with you?" Jarko said.

Shine nodded. "I still see her. In my dreams. My nightmares. She's still coming for me, that studded whip in her hands. Telling me she's going to carve me and my girlfriend up for desecrating the camp with our...evil ways. We were just hooking up."

Jarko sighed. That's the way it used to be. He wasn't a fan of butchering teens for being horny. Hell, back when he was seventeen, Jarko would have humped anything with more than two legs.

"I got lucky with that shovel. She seemed...distracted. I don't know why. But she hesitated before she came in for the kill. If I'd swung the shovel at a different angle, I'd be dead right now. Maybe I'd be better off that way."

"Why do you say that?" Jarko asked.

"It's been fifteen years since I decapitated Dolores Drake," he said. "And I still wake up screaming. Some days, I can't think about anything but her face coming for me. That girl. The one I was hooking up with. We're still together. Fifteen years later. Well, we were. She broke up with me last week. Said I needed help. That she loved me, but I needed to fix myself before we started a life together. She was able to move on from that night. But I haven't. Maybe you should just...carve me up right now and put me out of my misery."

Jarko stepped forward. Shine stepped back, until he was flat against the wall. Jarko retracted his tentacles.

"I'm not going to hurt you," he said. "When this night is over, I want you to know one thing. Nobody is coming for you. Not myself. Not Dolores Drake. No one."

Shine blinked.

"You tell me where I can find Dolores Drake's body," he said, "and I swear to you on the grave of Frederica Fimmel you will not have to worry about Dolores, me, or anyone. The only person you need to fear is yourself. And that's all in your head."

"Who the hell is Frederica Fimmel?" Shine said.

"Someone whose name I don't use lightly," Jarko said.

Shine nodded. "It's on the baseball field," he said. "Right behind second base. The camp always did a crap job maintaining that field, dirt was always too loose. Wasn't too hard to dig deep."

Jarko laughed. Figured that hundreds of kids had spent the last decade and a half running literal circles around Dolores's body without anyone knowing.

"You're lying to me," Jarko said, "and I'll find you."

"I believe you," Shine said. "But I'm not lying."

"All right, then. Piece of advice," he said, looking at the two groaning, amoeba-brained morons. "Get new friends."

Shine smiled weakly. "I'd been thinking about that."

"Good." Jarko looked up at the night sky. The moon was full and clear. Beautiful. "Actually, kid, I lied."

Shine's eyes widened again.

"Not about that. I have one more question for you."

"What is it?"

"How the hell do I get to I-95 from here?"

Exclusive Bonus Chapter

Darla entered the cave to find her mother pacing back and forth, facing the ground, her hair askew, the hem of her tunic caked in dust and mud. She stopped to observe Dolores, who continued to circle the antechamber as though she'd lost a contact lens in the rocks.

Finally, after ten minutes, Darla said, "If I knew that reattaching your head would mean that you also went insane, I wouldn't have let Jarko do it."

Dolores stopped in her tracks and faced her daughter.

"I'm bored," Dolores said.

Darla laughed. "You spent years as a severed head doing nothing but reading the same books over and over and watching bad TV. Back then you couldn't pace around the room if you wanted to. Now you can do anything and go anywhere, and here you are circling your cave like a broken Roomba."

"You know, a Roomba wouldn't be a bad idea," Dolores said. "The dust in here is hell on my allergies. I suppose I didn't really notice before."

"I kept your room and the dresser where I kept your head clean," Darla said. "Plus, your lungs can't be inflamed when you don't even know where your lungs are."

"Easy for you to say. I'm not used to all this…freedom."

"You *are* free," Darla said. "Go outside. Roam the woods. Find a crusty counselor to maim. Entertain yourself."

Dolores thought for a moment. "It has been a long time since I've had a good maiming."

"See?" Darla said, putting her hand on the weapon hanging from her belt. "You can use my scourge. It'll cheer you up."

"Technically that's my scourge," Dolores said. "I just let you borrow it while I was…indisposed. I could ask for it back."

"You wouldn't dare."

"No. I wouldn't. But if I'm going to start hunting again, I'll need something to do it with. New Dolores, new weapon."

"That's the spirit, mom," Darla said. "You know what they say. Idle hands are the devil's plaything."

"I met the monster who first said that, and he only said it because he collected hands and was trying to convince everyone to lop theirs off to give to him to add to his shelf."

Darla laughed. "It's been a while since you made me laugh while our faces were at the same level."

Dolores smiled and looked at her daughter, a softness on her wrinkled face.

"Darla?" she said. The way she said her name, with a mixture of love and sadness, made Darla's nine-chambered heart feel like it was folding in on itself. Darla walked over to her mother and took her hand.

"What is it, Mom?"

"I'm…I'm embarrassed to say it…"

"You never have to be embarrassed around me."

Dolores nodded, took Darla's hand between hers and held it to her weathered cheek. Darla wrapped her arms around her mother. She held her tight, still getting used to even being able to wrap her arms around her at all, feeling her arms, her back, the muscles that, even though they'd atrophied, were still capable of delightfully heinous things.

Dolores put her head on Darla's shoulder, a sensation that would have weirded Darla out not too long ago, and whispered into her ear.

"Darla, I'm so lonely."

Darla gently removed herself from her mother's embrace and looked into Dolores's watery eyes.

"Oh, Mom, I..."

She didn't know what to say. Dolores's father, Darwinus Drake, had left them so long ago, and in the years since, even after Dolores had literally lost her head, she had never expressed loneliness. Sure, the first few times Darla went out to hunt by herself, Dolores had been anxious when she returned. Fearing that what had happened to her could also happen to her daughter. What if some lucky counselor discovered Darla's frailty? And Dolores had been unable to protect her daughter?

There had been fear and anxiety, but never loneliness. Over the years Dolores had expressed pain and regret and anger. This was the first time in her life that Darla had ever heard her mother express longing.

"I never heard you say that before," Dolores said.

"I never felt that way before."

"You were alone plenty of times," Darla replied. "All those nights when I was out hunting. You were here by yourself."

"Being alone isn't the same as being lonely," Dolores said.

"There is often a comfort in being alone. A stillness. You never get to know yourself quite as well as when you're alone."

"It's funny," Darla said. "I had plenty of time alone. I don't think I really knew myself until I met someone who could draw it out of me."

"Darla, you're old enough now where I can be honest with you."

"Of course you can."

Dolores nodded, took a deep breath. "The last few years your father was still here, I had never felt so lonely in my entire life. And I've lived a long time. I felt more lonely when your father was here, but *not* here, if that makes sense, than before we met. Sometimes you can feel lonelier in a relationship than you ever do when you're alone. And your father made me feel very, very alone."

"Oh, Mom. I didn't know."

"Of course you didn't," Dolores said. "One day, if you ever have a monster of your own, you'll learn that there will be hard times. And you'll do everything you can to shield your child from them. But I wonder if that's the right decision. Because while you're protecting them, you're also lying to them."

Darla nodded. "I had no idea how bad things were until dad left."

"And I knew how bad they were long before I ever told you."

"Did you feel lonely before?" Darla asked. "Before you were, you know, reassembled."

"Actually I didn't," Dolores said, wiping away a tear. "I think because when I was missing the rest of me, there didn't seem to be any possibilities beyond what I was or where I was."

"You mean sitting there like a decorative piece of fruit."

"I'm sure it's hilarious now," Dolores said. "I thought

the rest of my life was going to consist of waiting for you and passing the time, and nothing more. I never expected to get my body back. I never expected to have options to be anything more than a glorified paperweight."

"An angry glorified paperweight."

"Hey, one lucky counselor gets a hold of a shovel and you could end up just like I did."

"And if that ever happened," came a deep, booming voice from the cave entrance, "I would find her body and reassemble her and then turn that 'lucky' counselor's bones into human popsicle sticks then glue them together for my own personal Camp Clear Creek arts and crafts project."

Jarko Murkvale strode into the antechamber. Darla felt eight of the nine chambers of her heart flutter—the ninth continued functioning to prevent her from fainting. Jarko went over to Darla, wrapped a thick tentacled arm around her waist, and pulled her close. When they first met, Darla wanted to lop that arm off with her scourge and throw it into the middle of the lake. Now, she wanted nothing more than to be held in its (occasionally slimy) embrace forever.

He leaned down and kissed her, gently at first, then firmer, with a passion that spoke of a man who hadn't seen his woman in months, let alone just that morning.

"I never thought I'd say this to my own daughter," Dolores said, "but will you two *please* go back to your own cave?"

"Sorry Ms. Drake," Jarko said, with a smile that told Darla he wasn't all that sorry. "Your daughter just does that to me sometimes. I didn't mean to gross you out."

"It didn't gross me out," Dolores said. "It just made me think about the last time I was kissed like that."

"Was it Dad?" Darla said.

Dolores laughed. "No. Before he went from sand shark to gone shark, Darwinus was many things, but a romantic was not one of them. No, it was a young monster named Darren Fite, but he was known to the world as the Dragonfly."

"The Dragonfly," Jarko said, eyes perking up. "He's still around. I believe he hunts down in Texas these days."

"Oh I wouldn't know," Dolores said. "I lost track of the Dragonfly after a wild few months. But those few months...that monster could breathe fire, and when he did, his wings beat like a hummingbird's. I remember he would empty that hot sauce into my mouth and beat his wings so fast we'd both lift into the air and—"

"Mom!" Darla said. "If you don't stop talking right now I'm going to have to traverse over to the Tohotown quarry and dunk my head into the quarry water until my brain and ears dissolve so the memory of you talking about a fly monster drooling into your mouth is erased from my memory forever."

"Part of me wishes I knew how Darren was these days," Dolores said with a sigh. "I miss being a feral monster."

"That's it, quarry water time," Darla said.

"Would you like to find out how he is?" Jarko asked Dolores.

"Find out?" Dolores said, flustered. "I don't even know where he is exactly or who he's hunting these days. I couldn't. I mean...could you actually find out?"

Jarko pulled his MFU from a coat pocket and turned it on. He took a seat on a rock and beckoned Dolores. She took a seat next to him while Darla perched over them, curious.

Jarko tapped the Home button. It brought up two options:

Find a Monster
Find a Territory

He tapped **Find a Monster**. A search bar appeared. Using the tip of a tentacle, Jarko tapped in **Darren Fite – Dragonfly**.

A small skull with three ocular cavities and large fangs appeared and began to rotate above a small bar that read **Loading**.

"Did you break it?" Dolores asked, concerned.

"No, it's just loading."

"It's taking so long."

"It's *loading*," Jarko said.

"I don't understand the purpose of technology if it doesn't work right away."

"It is load—Darla, help me out here?"

"Mom," Darla said, "if Jarko says it's working, it's working."

Dolores sighed and tapped her foot impatiently against the cave floor. Finally the loading bar filled up and an image appeared on the screen. When she saw it, Dolores screamed and dropped to the ground.

"Can he see me?" Dolores said, peering up from the cave floor.

Jarko laughed so hard he nearly fell off his rock. "No, Ms. Drake, it's just his profile picture."

Dolores got to her knee. She looked at the screen with adoration.

"Oh my goodness," she said. "I mean, he's older. Less hair up top. More hair everywhere else. But that is Darren Fite for sure. My old Dragonfly." She began to comb her hair with her long fingers.

"Old is the right word," Darla said. "He has more wrinkles than Lady Sharpeii."

"But he's still so handsome," Dolores said, leaning closer to the screen. "Those little beady eyes could see right through me. And those hands—er, feelers—I'm shivering just thinking about them."

"What does it say about Dragonfly?" Dolores asked.

"Let's see," Jarko said, tapping the screen. "Darren Fite. One hundred and fourteen years old. Current hunting grounds: Austin, Texas. In 2014 he was the subject of a documentary called *Keep Austin Weird...and Dead* where local hipsters tried to catch Darren. The filmmakers apparently didn't survive, but their footage did."

"That's my Dragonfly," Dolores said, wistfully. "He only revealed himself to people he wanted to see the real him."

"He's still active," Jarko said. "Responsible for nineteen hunts this past year alone. My man the Dragonfly is still going strong."

"Can I see...is he..." Dolores said.

"Is he what?" Jarko asked.

"Is he...I can't believe I'm even saying this...is he single?"

Jarko burst out laughing. Darla glared at him.

"Is there a way you can check?" Darla said.

"There is," Jarko replied. "Obviously you never did online monster dating."

"Number one," Darla said, "I didn't even know there was such a thing. Number two, I would rather be immolated by boiling sriracha before making an online dating profile."

"Don't knock it," Jarko said. "Most single monsters have done the online dating thing at some point."

"Is that right?" Darla asked, pointedly. "Did you?"

Jarko's face turned one shade paler than normal. "I...might have."

"Really?" Darla said, placing her hands on her hips. Jarko eyed her scourge, just a fingernail away.

"I was single for a long time. And meeting monsters in person is a lot harder than you think."

"We were single and we met in person."

"True. And I had plenty of bad relationships before. And do you have any idea how hard it is to break up with a monster who doesn't want to be broken up with and can't be killed? Do you know how many sharp implements I've had to remove from my abdominal cavity?"

"Keep talking about all the monsters you dated before you met me," Darla said, "and I can assure you that you'll add one more to the total."

"If I can interrupt you for a moment," Dolores said. "Back to the Dragonfly. How do I know if he's taken?"

"Every monster's profile on the MFU has a section about their relationship status," Jarko said. "Not everyone lists theirs. But some do. Let me see."

Jarko tapped the MFU screen.

"Well?" Dolores said.

"Hmm."

"Hmm what?"

"His relationship status says 'It's Complicated'."

"What the hell does that mean?"

"It means it's complicated."

"So is he single?" Dolores asked.

"I don't know. It's complicated can mean a million things."

"But if he was married or in a relationship, wouldn't he just say that?"

"Most likely."

"So he's at least *open* to the possibility of meeting someone."

"You're asking me to read his mind," Jarko said. "I have many talents. Mind-reading is unfortunately not one of them."

"So how can I find out?"

"I can stab him," Jarko said.

"Stab him?" Dolores said. "Why on earth would you do that?"

"Not actually *stab* him, stab him," Jarko said. "It's like online poking. But for monsters."

"Online dating is very confusing," Dolores said.

"You have no idea," said Jarko. "There. I stabbed him for you."

"When will he respond to the...stabbing?"

"No idea. He might not even respond."

"And so, what, I just wait for him to stab me back?"

"You could see who, or what, else is out there while you wait," Jarko said.

Dolores's eyes narrowed. "You mean there are other single monsters on that device thing."

"There are."

"Jarko," Darla warned. "Do *not* go pimping my mother off to some strange creature whose feelings could have been... feeling up anybody."

"There's no harm in looking," Dolores said to her daughter. "I let you make your own decisions for years, and as we both know, you certainly made some questionable ones."

"Fine," Darla replied. "See what's out there."

Jarko filtered out all monster profiles by relationship status, then removed any creature whose profile read 'Married', 'It's Complicated', or 'Decapitated'. Four hundred and sixty-three matches popped up.

"There are *that many* single monsters out there?" Dolores said, as if she'd just been given the keys to a candy store and told to go to town.

"Probably more," Jarko said.

"*More*?" Dolores said.

"Mom, close your mouth, you're drooling."

"Sweetie, I have been single since before you could download books on one of those electronic contraptions. I haven't been kissed since before the last piece of your bone crown came in. Humor an old lady, would you?"

"You're not old," Jarko said. "You're just well-seasoned."

"I will assume you mean in that I'm experienced and not prepared like a steak," Dolores said. "Now, can I borrow that?" She pointed at the MFU.

"Why?"

"There are over four hundred single monsters out there," Dolores said. "They're not going to stab themselves. Well, I suppose some might be masochists."

"Just try to only stab monsters your age," Darla said. "I don't need a stepdad younger than I am."

Dolores kept scrolling. "Why does every single monster have a photo of them posing with a fish?"

Just then, Darla felt a rumble beneath her feet. At first she thought it may be because she hadn't eaten in nearly three days, but then she saw the pools of water on the cave floor shimmer, the dust around their feet shifting.

"What is that?" she asked.

"It's not an earthquake," Jarko said. "The MFU picks up tectonic plate shifts. This is way too small for that. And it's concentrated."

"What does that mean?" Darlas asked.

"It means whatever it is," Jarko said, "it's happening right beneath this cave."

"Mom, has this happened before?"

"A few times," Dolores said.

"A few times? How many times is a few?"

"I don't know. Three. Five. Ten. I'm not sure."

"And how long has it been going on?" asked Jarko.

"A few days. Maybe a week at most."

"That's very odd," Jarko said. "I'm not sure what it could be."

A thought popped into Darla's mind, but she quickly ignored it. There was no way it was possible. And yet she didn't want to upset her mother by even acknowledging that remote possibility. But still...she had a memory of those rumbles. Remembered feeling them when she was a small monster. She hadn't felt those tremors in years, but they felt familiar. Too familiar.

"We should go," Jarko said to Darla. "I have dinner planned."

"Is there any way to filter the single monsters by ones who don't have detachable limbs? I just feel like that could be very triggering."

"You can. But I'd like to have that back now," Jarko said, pointing at the MFU.

"You try to take this from me and Darla will have to dig up pieces of *your* body. And I promise you, yours won't be as easy as mine to find."

Jarko looked at Darla. "She's kidding, right?"

"I don't think so."

"All right then. Have fun, Ms. Drake. Don't get into any trouble."

"I've been waiting a long, *long* time to get into trouble," Dolores said, eyes glued to the screen.

"She'll be fine," Darla whispered to Jarko. She turned back to her mother. "Mom, if those tremors continue, you need to let me know."

Dolores ignored her, a crazed smile on her face as she swiped. "This one has a forked tongue. That could be delightful."

"I feel like I opened Pandora's Box letting her use that thing," Jarko said.

"And let out all the pent-up horniness, never to be put back."

"You have a way with words, Duchess."

They exited the cave into the cool night of Clear Creek. The stars above them twinkled in the dark blue sky. Jarko wrapped an arm around Darla, and she felt a warmth spread through her body. She knew it was a longshot, but she hoped her mother met someone real. Or some*thing* real. She deserved happiness. For too long Dolores had sacrificed her own joy for her husband. Making herself feel small to sate his ego. Now, it was Dolores's turn to feel adored.

"You ok?" Jarko said.

"Yeah. Just worried about my mom. I don't want her to get hurt."

"She'll be fine," he said. "You Drake women are tough."

"Maybe. But maybe we don't always want to have to be."

"Come here."

Jarko lifted Darla off the ground with ease, tilting her body into the air so her lips met his while her feet dangled in the air. Darla felt her heart soar as she tasted his lips, losing herself in his embrace.

Finally he put her down and looked into her eyes.

"I love you, Duchess."

"I love you too."

"Your mom will be fine."

"I know she will," Darla said. "I mean, what's the worst that could happen?"

Darla, Jarko, and Dolores return
(No promises as to which parts of them)

Read on for an exclusive excerpt of book 2
in the Mating & Monsters series:

Weddings & Witchcraft!

Chapter 1

The worst idea of Trevor Schaub's life would also be the last idea of Trevor Schaub's life.

Trevor Shaub was a truck driver. Emphasis on the 'was'. Prior to this, he'd worked for a brief spell as an electrician, until a faulty wiring job caused a model home to burn to the ground. Now he hauled goods for billion dollar companies all across the country, and made a decent enough wage to cover his alimony, childcare, and the rent on his one-bedroom apartment. What that wage did not, do, however, was cover Trevor's ever expanding taste for drugs of all shapes, sizes, and potencies. So when Trevor found himself unable to pay back the dealers who had, so generously, fronted Trevor on the promise that he would pay them back double what they were owed, Trevor had to find an alternative way to raise cash.

Trevor, far from the sharpest tool in the shed, had the brilliant idea of tipping off the dealers to his truck routes. The dealers would "hijack" Trevor's truck, take the smart TVs or smart homes or smart refrigerators or smart whatevers, sell them, and and take what Trevor owed them out of the proceeds. The plan was foolproof. At least in the mind of a fool.

So when Trevor pulled his truck over on I-95, a camera at a nearby gas station caught Trevor not only waiting patiently for his hijackers, but wandering into the woods to relieve himself, then ambling over to that very gas station where yet another camera caught him stealing a bag of Funyans and a Red Bull. He then ate his bounty, apparently unbothered by the fact that he had not washed his hands after said woods relief.

Given that Trevor's thievery was as subtle as an angry cow picking out wedding china, the gas station attendant quickly called the police. The cops, led by Officer Dale Kowalski, came right as Trevor's truck was being unloaded. They cuffed Trevor, also unaware that his hands were still covered in his own filth.

Given that Trevor had no prior arrests, he managed to get out on bail. And one night before sentencing Trevor, still not the fastest fish in the school, Googled the cop who arrested him. The officer had a Facebook profile, and Trevor was able to discover that Officer Kowalski had a young son, Nick, who had just left the previous week to spend the summer at a camp called Clear Creek.

And Clear Creek was just a few miles from Trevor's home.

Trevor had heard things about Camp Clear Creek. That some less-than-desirable people kept disappearing from the camp and its surrounding grounds. That dangerous creatures stalked the woods, waiting to water the grounds with the insides of troublemakers. But Trevor wasn't a bad guy, just unlucky. And the rumors were just that: rumors.

So Trevor, having less common sense than an inebriated

warthog, decided to get some payback on the family of Officer Dale Kowalski.

So Trevor staked out Clear Creek for several days, showing more dedication than he had at any point in his professional career, and learned that Nick Kowalski's camp troupe, the Brave Beavers (how that name made it through a focus group was anybody's guess) had swim every day from nine to ten a.m. It gave Trevor a perfect opportunity for payback.

So one night Trevor, after drinking enough beer to impair the entire Roman army, went out to the camp dock on Clear Creek Lake to rig an electrical wire onto the metal ladder leading down to the water. Everyone who attempted to climb out up would get fried.

Once he finished his DIY electrical trap, Trevor stood on the dock: proud and defiant and dumb. Even if he went to prison, Trevor should be able to look right into the face of Officer Dale Kowalski as he was led away, knowing that he ruined the man's life. Just as the cop had ruined his.

And so Trevor turned around to head home, when he heard a noise in the water behind him. He turned, expecting to see some electrified fish floating by the ladder. But he saw nothing.

Trevor chalked it up to the wind and turned back around. This time, though, he heard a different sound. A wet *thunk*. It made Trevor's blood run cold.

There it was again. *Thunk. Thunk. Thunk.*

Finally, Trevor turned around again. And this time, he screamed.

Halfway up the ladder was...a creature. That was the first word that came to mind. It was tall and broad and had dark hair and severe yellow eyes and wore a long black jacket that dripped with water. The creature looked *almost* human...except for the massive tentacles curled around the ladder. Trevor could see wisps of smoke curling from the creature's arms, and for a moment, he took a small amount of pride in knowing his electrical hookup had, in fact worked.

It was the last time he would ever feel good about anything. And just a few moments from the last time he would ever feel anything, period.

Trevor ran towards the beachfront, figuring if he could get home he could get to his car and if he got to his car he could get to the 9mm in his glove compartment and if he got to the gun he could shoot that monstrosity right between its eyes.

But Trevor never made it that far. As he neared the end of the dock, he felt a stinging sensation as something wrapped itself around his legs. Trevor fell to the ground hard, the air leaving his lungs in a *whoosh*. He rolled over onto his back, panting, expecting to see the tentacled creature standing over him. But the creature was still submerged in the water. Staring at Trevor with those gleaming yellow eyes.

He looked up. This time, with no air in his chest, there was no scream.

A woman stood over him. Well, she was as much a woman as the octo-dude was a man. She wore a light green tunic with laced up boots and looked like some badass Viking lady transported into the twenty-first century. All except her hair. She had a normal head, normal face, her bright orange eyes like small gemstones in her attractive face. But sprouting out from her scalp in different directions were what appeared to be tree branches. But they were too pale and smooth to be tree branches. Then it dawned on Trevor.

They were bones. She had bones sticking out of her head. It

almost looked like…a crown of bone. Trevor's face went white.

"You…you're not real. You're just a myth."

The female creature smiled, as one might with a naïve child. Then she spoke.

"You're going to find out tonight just how real I am," she said. "My name is Darla Drake."

"No. That's impossible. You're…you're Darla Drake, Duchess of Death."

"Has a nice ring to it, doesn't it?" Darla said. "And I'm, how would I put it, something of the unofficial tour guide to Camp Clear Creek."

Trevor heard a heavy thump. Boots. He saw the man-creature walking towards them. He was far larger than Trevor had guessed, with most of his body being hidden by the dark waters. His boot heel alone was large enough to turn Trevor's face into paste.

"Who the hell are *you*?" Trevor asked.

The man-creature sighed, almost in annoyance, and said, "My name is Jarko Murkvale. Duke of Death."

"I've never heard of you."

Trevor wasn't sure, but he could have sworn he heard Darla Drake stifle a laugh.

"I don't care whether or not you've heard of me," Jarko said, learning over Trevor, blotting out the moon with his enormous torso. "But after tonight, you'll be a warning to anyone else who tries to hunt in our territory. Especially children."

"Hey, semi-random question," Darla asked. "Is your name Kyle?"

"Nuh…no. It's Trevor. Trevor Schaub."

"Dammit," Darla said, stomping the ground with one laced-up sandal.

"Whuh...why?"

"The Duchess and I had a bet going," Jarko said. "Darla bet that your name was Kyle. I bet the field."

"Ninety-nine times out of a hundred their name is Kyle," Darla said. "Jarko took the field but the odds were still in my favor."

"But the field wins," Jarko said. "So that means I win."

"I guess you'll have to claim your prize later," Darla said, gazing at Jarko with, what Trevor believed to be in his limited sexual experience, bedroom eyes.

"Oh, I intend to, Duchess," Jarko replied, a grin on his face. Trevor was confused. Were the monsters...flirting?

"Can I go then?" Trevor asked. "You're obviously looking for a Kyle."

"No," Jarko said. "We were looking for you."

"You were hunting innocent children," Darla said. "Trevor, you silly little rabbit, you should know that *we* are the only people who hunt here."

Darla unbuckled a weapon from her belt. It looked like a cat-o'-nine-tails, but at the end of each strand was a sharp barb that looked like it could cut through wood as if it was warm butter.

"This is my scourge," Darla said. "My mother passed it down to me. And now I'm going to pass it down to you. In a manner of speaking."

"Please," Trevor said. "Let me go. I swear I won't tell anyone. Nobody will know I ever saw you."

Jarko laughed, his voice deep and sinister and seemingly entertained by Trevor's begging. "You seem to have missed the point entirely," he said. "We want *everyone* to know that you saw us."

The last thing that went through Trevor Schaub's mind, before Jarko's boot and Darla's scourge, was that he should have taken the job at the post office.

. . .

The moment they set foot inside their cave, Darla felt Jarko's arm coil around her waist. He drew her to him until their lips were barely an inch apart. She remembered their first face to face meeting, when she wanted nothing more than to cleave his limbs from his body. Now, she wanted nothing more than to have those limbs wrapped around her until her last day. Which, given that it was nearly impossible to kill a monster for good, was a whole hell of a long time.

And she was ok with that.

"Time to claim my prize," Jarko said.

"Stupid Kyles," Darla said, closing her eyes and leaning into him.

Jarko kissed Darla, deep and hard. She felt her heart begin to beat faster, faster, faster. Smoke trailed out of her nostrils as she wrapped her arms around Jarko's muscular neck.

"I could fight back," she said.

"I don't think you want to."

"No," Darla replied. "I don't. So, you're not annoyed at Kyle?"

"His name wasn't Kyle. It was Trevor."

"They're all Kyles, even if they're not."

"Why would I be annoyed at him?"

"He knew who I was but not…well, you."

Jarko kissed her again. "I don't get jealous."

"I think the whole reason we're here right now is because I wanted Clear Creek as my own and you were, in fact, jealous."

"Totally different situation."

"You say tomato, I say Kyle."

"That doesn't make any sense."

"Neither do we, but here we are."

"Yes," Jarko said, gripping Darla tighter. "Here we are."

Darla pushed Jarko backward with tremendous force until they both slammed against the cave wall. Small rocks and dirt tumbled down onto them as they kissed.

"Careful Duchess," Jarko said. "You might break the cave."

"So we'll find another."

Jarko picked Darla up and carried her to the bed, which was a duvet cover filled with rocks and pine needles resting on a pile of headstones. Jarko laid Darla down. She pulled him onto her hard enough to leave a dent in the mattress.

"Watch the bone crown," she said, wisps of smoke drifting up to the ceiling. "Don't need to accidentally gouge your eye out while we do it."

"It'd be worth it," Jarko said. He watched as Darla unbuttoned his coat, then tossed it to the floor. She looked at him, tracing her hands up and down his torso. Then she looked up at him.

"I never needed anyone before," Darla said. "It's not easy for me to admit that."

"I promise to earn your need every single day from now on."

"That's a heavy promise."

"It is."

"You sure you can carry that kind of promise?"

"I have strong shoulders."

"Some promises are heavier than boulders."

"I've carried a lot of boulders," Jarko said. "I know how

heavy this promise is."

She kissed him again and within moments they were naked in each other's arms. Darla had never felt as vulnerable with anyone as she did with Jarko. She'd had other monsters in her life before. She'd been intimate before Jarko. And as much as she would rather stick her brain in a blender than think about it, she knew he'd had other women before her.

But for some reason, it wasn't being stripped of her clothes that made her feel bare to him, it was being stripped of everything else. It wasn't just her body that Darla had revealed to him, but every fiber of her being. It made every embrace, every kiss, feel like fire, and when they connected physically, when they moved in perfect sync, nothing between them but a layer of sweat (and occasional swamp water), Darla's whole body felt as though she'd been dipped in molten lava.

They moved tender at first, then with greater force. She bit into his shoulder and he grimaced at first but didn't ask her to stop. At one point, Darla's bone crown must have torn open the duvet cover, because she saw pine needles stuck to Jarko's arms. She couldn't help but laugh as he moved inside of her, the laugh turning into a moan as he filled her in a way that, until this moment, she'd thought was impossible.

When they finished, a cloud of smoke hanging thick in the air, they lay on the ground in a tangled, sweaty heap. Darla's head on Jarko's torso, listening to his heartbeat, feeling his chest rise and fall with each breath, his tentacles wrapped around her body.

"I could stay like this forever," he said.

"Too bad there are a lot more Kyles out there in the world. A lot more hunting to do."

"I look forward to every single one." Then Jarko grew

quiet. The cave was silent except for the thrumming of their heartbeats. Then Jarko looked at her and said, "Darla?"

His face had grown intensely serious. For a moment, Darla felt scared. She hadn't felt like that since she found her mother's decapitated, angry head. And before that, since the day her father had left them. Intimacy brought fear. Once you loved someone, there was always a fear that they could leave you. That was the side effect of baring yourself to someone. The fear that, one day, it could all go away.

"What is it?"

"I meant what I said."

"About…"

"About forever."

"I'm glad," Darla replied. "I feel the same way."

"Then I need to ask you something."

Darla's brow furrowed. "If you're going to ask me if I still have any Trevor on my scourge, I cleaned it off in the pond before we got back."

"That's not what I was going to ask, but good to know we won't have random skull pieces laying around the cave."

"I don't know. A few skull pieces in a pattern on the wall just might make this place look a little more homey. Actually, I have a few more decorating ideas to run by you. Sorry, my mom has been watching a lot of HGTV and it's rubbing off."

Jarko didn't smile. "Darla?" he said.

"Yes, Jarko?"

"Darla Drake. Duchess of Death."

"You remembered my name. I was worried for a second considering you were just inside of me."

This made Jarko smile, but wistfully, like his mind was somewhere else.

"What is it?" she said.

Jarko got to one knee. The moment he did so, Darla's heart began to beat faster than it ever had before.

"Darla Drake. Duchess of Death. The monster I was meant for."

"Jarko…"

"Will you give me the hideously high honor of being my beastly bride?"

A plume of smoke belched forth from Darla's nostrils and blanketed the air like fog.

"Holy Cthulhu's butthole," Darla said. "Jarko, I…"

"I don't think you'd bring Cthulhu into it if it wasn't a yes."

Darla threw her arms around Jarko and kissed him for what felt like hours. When their lips finally parted, she whispered in his ear. "Yes."

"I didn't want to assume, but…" He gestured at the air, thick with smoke.

"Holy shit. We're going to get married."

"We're going to get married."

"I have to tell my mom. I have to tell Gretl."

"They'll be thrilled for you," he said.

"They'll be thrilled for *us*."

"For us," she agreed. "I love you, Jarko Murkvale, Duke of Death."

"I love you too, Duchess."

"Can I ask you one favor?"

"You can ask me a thousand favors until the end of days."

"Ok, this favor isn't *quite* that dramatic," Darla said. "I don't want this to be a big…*thing*. Nice and simple and quiet."

"Nice and simple and quiet it is. I can do simple and quiet."

"I've seen you demolish an entire housing complex with

nothing but an inflatable seahorse and a rubber band," Darla said. "I'll believe you can do simple and quiet when I see it."

"I want this wedding to be exactly what you want, Duchess."

"What *we* want."

"What we want."

Jarko kissed her again. Nice and simple and quiet. It sounded lovely. Perfect.

And yet deep down, Darla knew somehow that there was no way in the fiery depths of hell their wedding would actually happen that way.

ACKNOWLEDGMENTS

Most books are a labor of love. This book was no labor at all, but a work of pure, unadulterated joy. Darla, Jarko, Dolores, Gretl, and the rest of these characters came along at a time when I needed them most, and I hope they brought you, the reader, a fraction of the joy they've brought me.

Thank you to Nicole Goux for creating an absolutely stunning book jacket, and for taking Darla, Jarko, and Dolores out of my head and making them real. To Gillian Leonard for her invaluable copyediting prowess. To my agents, Amy Tannenbaum and Jessica Errera, for giving me their blessing to run wild with this book and for letting my monster freak flag fly. To the incredible, supportive, and hilarious BookTok community, for not just embracing my weirdness, but actively encouraging it and pushing me to expand the boundaries of my creativity. I wouldn't have had faith this book would find a readership if not for you. To my family for proving to me that, just as Darla discovers, life is far more fun when you have loved ones to share muskrat stew with.

To the incredible team at Entangled Publishing who saw the love people had for these characters and believed they could take them to new heights. From the bottom of my monstrously full heart I must thank Jessica Turner, Lizzy Mason, Justine Bylo, Liz Pelletier, Heather Riccio, Meredith Johnson, Bree Archer, Brittany Zimmerman, Ashley Doliber.

And to all the monsters who came before the ones depicted in this book: thank you for showing us that good and evil are really just a matter of perspective.

*Don't miss the exciting new books
Entangled has to offer.*

Follow us!

f @EntangledPublishing

⊙ @Entangled_Publishing

♪ @EntangledPub